Wakefield Press

Salt Upon the Water

Lyn Dickens is a writer, editor, and academic living on unceded Kaurna land. Her debut novel *Salt Upon the Water* was the winner of the 2024 Arts South Australia Wakefield Press Unpublished Manuscript Award. Of mixed Singaporean Peranakan Chinese and Anglo Celtic Australian heritage, Lyn is the Managing Editor and Co-Founder of *The Saltbush Review*. Lyn has been shortlisted and longlisted for a variety of awards including the Deborah Cass Prize, the Lucy Cavendish Prize and the Richell Prize, and she was the winner of a Write It Fellowship with Penguin Random House. Lyn's writing has been published in Australia, the UK, and the USA, appearing in journals such as *Kill Your Darlings*, *ArtsHub*, *Liminal*, and the *Conversation*. She has a doctorate in Sociology from the University of Sydney and she was a visiting researcher at the University of Cambridge. Lyn is a member of the JM Coetzee Centre for Creative Practice at the University of Adelaide, where she is currently completing a PhD in Creative Writing. After many years in Sydney, Cambridge, and London, Lyn now lives in Adelaide with her husband and two children.

Salt Upon the Water

LYN DICKENS

Wakefield
Press

Wakefield Press
16 Rose Street
Mile End
South Australia 5031
wakefieldpress.com.au

First published 2025
Reprinted 2026

Supported by a grant from the Government of South Australia.

Edited by Maddy Sexton, Wakefield Press
Cover designed by Hazel Lam
Designed and typeset by Debora Souza, Greenhill Publishing

ISBN 978 1 92338 820 8

A catalogue record for this book is available from the National Library of Australia

Wakefield Press thanks Coriole Vineyards for continued support

For Matt, Hamish,

and Josephine, and for Estelle

Kangaroo Island, October 1836

I arrive on the winds of a southern gale, the front of air ballooning the sails, the heave of the waves sending the hull keeling. The salt spray hits my face. At first, it's a fine mist with the fresh tang of the ocean meeting the shore, but it grows in weight and volume until waves are slapping me, pushing my feet along the rust-bitten deck. In the distance, I see it. The horizon line behind the white clouds, the rolling slope of land.

The whalers call out in joy. Around me, men move at speed, climbing the mainsail and hauling the rigging. It's new to most of us – verdant country beyond the ends of the earth. A Southern wonder. A place where a man may make his fortune and his name, a place of strange beasts and eerie bushland. Or so they tell me. I have heard other things about it, this terra incognita.

Bracing myself against the rigging as the wave to my left crests into whiteness, I inhale once. It curves and breaks, shuddering against the deck and sending jolts of water into my nose and throat. The first mate, Moses Widlow, steadies me with one hand as he passes, a grin cracking his face.

'Not bad, Miss.'

He is gone before I can speak. The saltwater holds my tongue.

I blink away the foam, taste saline bubbles and coastline silt, and somewhere beyond these, blood.

As the waves heave us forward, the shoreline draws closer. Behind the mist, the white rim of sand peeks back at us. There is the scent of something floral, and something like pine hovering above the marine aromas that have stalked me for the past three months. Will I find you here? On this crisp white shore in the shade of antipodean trees, staking out the land with your theodolite? I look for your tufted hair, your red coat, but I can see only the dark shapes of fallen tree trunks bleeding into the shore.

When I heard your name read out by a Company administrator four months ago, it had been years since last thinking of you. To hear your name is to see gardens in lamplight and taste West Indian sugar. It is the dregs of a party in Bath, a slash of claret leaking across the floor. It is betrayal.

The ship lurches and I stagger at the sudden movement. The deck is slick with ocean spray and blubber and old whale blood. It only takes a moment. My boots scuffle helplessly across the width of the deck, and I fly.

There is a shout behind me as I hit the water, slapping against the skin of the sea. The force knocks the air from my lungs. As the spray rises like shattered crystal, the waves draw me down into silence.

It is cold with the brittle chill of southern water. There is no translucent aquamarine or limpid warmth of the East Indies lagoons. I open my eyes to a raging, indifferent wall of green. Holding my breath, my chest contracts and the world glitters beyond my sight.

There were marigolds in the garden, a house of scarlet archways and pillars, the scent of dried patchouli and mangoes going to seed. Did you see it when you were in Calcutta? This home that has no form but in my memories. They knocked it down. It did not suit the new aesthetic, the obsession with neoclassical white.

As the pressure builds in my throat, I think of all the noble ways to die. I think of the Devon coastline, the mermaid sign over the village tavern that I was never supposed to visit. I think of Suvannamaccha, the half-fish princess of the Laccadive Sea. Looking up at the lattice of light coating the water's surface, I kick.

The water pushes me the rest of the way. As my face breaks into the cold air, the whalers cheer. I raise my hand, gulping air and sunlight, laughing.

They have lowered a buoy, but the tide carries me forward. Already the shoreline looms closer.

'I'll swim!' I call, dizzy with triumph.

'You mad woman!' someone shouts, but I twist onto my back, relishing the curve of the water around me and the sun on my face, the taste of salt and wind and unknown flowers in the air. I spread out my arms, palms flat, fingers wide, and for a moment I am a paper nautilus weaving her multicoloured way across the ocean's routes.

The land catches me sooner than I expect and my heels strike rocks. I turn, scrabbling along with the rushing tide. In the distance, I see again the dark shapes against the dazzling shore. They are not fallen tree trunks.

The seals lie limp on the sand. For the briefest moment I want to swim out again to the ocean or back to the ship – I have seen a festering seal bite on a sailor's leg – but there's no fighting the tide. When my knees meet the melting sand, I pause, crouching hip-deep in the water.

Nothing moves. Their bodies are round and glossy in the sun. Swirls of ochre adorn the shore, streaming from their skulls. Further in, I see the skins of others staked out above the sand to dry.

Beyond the murmur of the sea and shouts of the whalers behind me, the world is quiet. I look for life as I drag myself out of the water, its marine embrace begging me back. The beach is still. The corpses stretch along the shore, as far as I can see. Among the dunes, in the shadow of the low bushes, there is movement.

I step forward. 'Hello?'

A flock of birds slices through the sky, white wings flashing.

They tell me it's a big country, an uncharted land, but I imagine you somewhere close with your pen, your map, the sharp points of your compass.

Beside me, a dead seal turns its white belly onto the sand and gazes at me with blood-filled eyes.

My first weeks in this new world pass quickly. The sailors work and the shore bewilders us with its glaring sand and fractures of light. I walk into the settlement for news, grateful for the excuse to leave the scenes of butchery. The journey from Calcutta took almost three months. I slept and woke and ate in the shadows of baleen bones and sperm whale jaws and the giddy stench of a marine crematorium. Now, the sailors make quick work of the sea lions in the shallows. When the Scottish cook protests – seals hold the souls of strange women, he tells them – they call him a Highland savage. I say nothing and leave as the sea turns to crimson and rust.

I feel the eyes of the settlers on me as I walk through their cluster of tents. For the first time since leaving India, I'm wearing a dress. It's a scarlet piece past its best, but here, in this dazzling landscape, the colour takes flight like a flare against the beige canvas and grey faces. The men are greedy and the women are cautious.

Colonel Light is not here, they tell me.

'When will he return?'

Their faces are closed in the silence, except for one man, who smirks. I have forgotten this feeling. I wonder how I must look to them. Weird, unexpected, alien? No matter how strange my face, in England I could always be placed. I hated the country's cold social codes – the angle of my hat, whether I made conversation, how I held my fan – but it had some benefit. It gave me a place in the world.

'He's expected on Thursday,' says a small woman in a blue dress.

She is well spoken despite the burr of the Hampshire countryside; her hands are calloused and rough. When she senses my gaze, she hides her palms.

When I glance at the others' faces again, they drop their eyes. They may not know my place, but they know theirs in relation to it. I feel them staring as I walk back to the whaling ship, my red dress swaying around my ankles, my heart beating very fast.

South Australian Coast, October 1836

He sees her before she sees him. It's from a distance, but he recognises her. She's dressed in men's clothing among a group of whalers. The cuffs of her trousers are rolled at the ankle and her bare feet sink into the sand. She is laughing, hair loose and blowing to the side in a blaze of terra rossa. She grabs at it, but it escapes her fingers, again and again.

His mind crowds with questions, but they are overlaid with a single fact. She looks exactly as she did fourteen years ago, when they first met on a lamplit night at the Vauxhall Gardens. The realisation is piercing. William Light had been thirty-five, in full health, a veteran of more than forty military engagements. He had passed through them all unscathed. Now, his body erodes around him, a Roman Forum weathered and beaten by damp and rot. But she is unchanged.

Two urges pull at him. He wants, without conscious thought, to back away from the beach and the harbour, and to vanish into the sandy dunes and the reedy trees, not to let her gaze fall upon him. But he feels something else, too. The rasping cavern in his chest fills with buoyant air. So few of his friendships have endured from that time in his life when all things seemed possible. Now, he receives little news from England. There are those who have shunned him, those who have moved on to higher states of triumph, and those who have died.

Her hair flies out again and she does what she used to do, laughs with her face in both hands, and Light moves forward without further consideration, stepping out onto the beach. Clarissa Lucia FitzRoy looks over, and her laughter stops.

He can see now that she has changed. Her skin has a sheen of bronze that had not been present in London. Her hair is wilder. He had always thought of her as a brunette, but now, as her skin has darkened, her hair has lightened like a flare, a match flame streaking behind her.

It occurs to Light that she is not prepared to meet him here, miles from the settlement on Kangaroo Island, dressed in the garb of a sailor. Later, he will wonder why she is here at the end of the world at all. But for the moment, Light only feels a sense of trepidation, a remembering, and beyond all that, a secret hope.

Their last encounter was strained. He saw her by chance the morning before his departure for Spain, and he has carried this image of her through the years. Her white dress, in the fashion of the last decade, the pale-blue cloak covering her hair in the morning's frost. She had been so still, as still as the plaster Virgin Marys adorning the old house in Penang. But he wouldn't think of that now – its hibiscus gardens, the scent of frying sambal, the stickiness of pandan-flavoured sweets. The Catholic Madonnas, always watching. No, he wouldn't think of that now.

After that morning, she did not answer his letters or accept his offer to call. But still, Light had kept up with her news. It had been easy to come by. An ill-thought engagement to her brother's tutor. The engagement's abrupt end had brought her a certain notoriety when the tutor published a long novel satirising her family. And then her uncle had died, and suddenly formerly shy Clarissa Lucia FitzRoy was twenty-six and an heiress to a sum that transcended all blood and skin colour. There had been another engagement. This one highly proper. But it was not to be. She ended it; there had been no secret about that. But she had been (and here the fiancé's friends were suspiciously loose-lipped) indiscreet.

A different woman would have gone to ground, committed herself to quiet behaviour and waited for the scandal to pass. Instead, Clarissa had modelled for Henry William Pickersgill in a turban and a sheet. And then she joined the Abolitionists, wrote a scathing essay about the treatment of unmarried mothers, and got herself into all the papers.

Light had lost track of her after that. English news could be slow to reach Egypt, and his life at the time had its own disgraces. He knew only that, after five years of righteous infamy, she had somehow managed to get engaged again to some dull officer in the East India Company. James Ramsey. That was his name.

And now she is here, looking at him with an expression he can only describe as blank.

But the moment passes.

'William!' she says, and her face transforms into a wide smile tinged with harshness.

'Clarissa.'

As he walks toward her, the sand collapses under his boots, skewing his gait. She weaves her way through the group of sailors. He can see the fine coating of white sand adorning her ankles, the salt-chapped rawness of her lips. His bad leg buckles as the sand gives way beneath him, and she reaches out to steady him. He feels the warm surge of shame. Her hands are stronger than he remembers.

'I've been looking for you,' she says. He is aware of silence casting its muted net over the whalers. The wind beats at them again, and she takes hold of her hair. 'The settlers said you'd be back at the island on Thursday. I never expected to see you on this part of the coast.'

'I never expected to see you at all.' Time and war are the mistresses of coincidence. Strange encounters have happened in Light's life, but no person has seemed so out of context as this woman squinting against the light. 'I made it back to the island a few days early to pick up some supplies. I arrived here a few days ago.'

She smiles at him and his insides jolt. He opens his mouth to speak, but she turns and walks toward the sea. Light glances back at the silent sailors – they avert their gaze – so he follows her.

'Well – how are you?' What does one say after fourteen years? What does one say here, where everything is inverted and made strange?

She does not answer him, walking until the sand gives way beneath her and the water breaks into white shards around her ankles.

'What do you call this space?' she asks.

Light moves toward her, slowly. 'Sorry?'

She opens her arms. 'This world.' She looks at her feet as they are subsumed and exposed by the water. 'This piece of land that is half in the sea and half out of it, depending on the tide.'

He follows her gaze along the beach. 'Littoral,' he says.

She turns back to him now, her eyes questioning.

'It's the littoral zone. The space between high and low tide.'

She smiles, and it seems genuine. 'How interesting.' Bending down, she scoops up the gleaming water. 'Littoral. So, it has a name.'

'It's a unique environment. In warfare, in particular, soldiers need to prepare for specific challenges in these amphibious regions.'

She makes a small sound of acknowledgement. How is it, Light wonders, that she has followed him all the way to the South Australian coast, and still he is the one to feel he seeks something she withholds?

'Why are you here?'

'I sailed from Calcutta.'

'I see.' And he does. He sees where this is travelling. He sees again the small, damp room in Bow Bazaar, and a woman's searching eyes. Those eyes, dark and kohl-rimmed, look back at him now in a brighter, amber guise.

He sees the precarious, brown-skinned women with their frilled skirts and powdered faces haunting the streets of Eurasian Calcutta. He sees the well-spoken clerk, smartly dressed and paler-skinned than an Englishman, locked out of advancements because of his mother's bloodline. He sees the tired woman in Bow Bazaar and the misery that had plucked at her, and beyond that, the windows of his memory reveal a figure in a red sarong surrounded by palm fronds and the scent of ginger.

Although he closes his eyes, the sunlight pulses through his lids like an orange flame.

'Will?'

She hasn't shortened his name like that for a very long time. He hears the water slosh as she walks toward him.

'I know you were in Calcutta in 1806.'

He opens his eyes.

'I think you went to my old family home. I'm trying to find out about who I am.'

For the longest time he had searched for her through a haze of laudanum in Spain, in the tray of letters arriving in Suffolk at his old childhood home, which he would never own. And now she is here.

'Will, do you remember it?'

The reunion is not as he had hoped. Back inland, the sailors are relaxed, jostling each other as they go about their work. He can hear the strains of Nantucket, the Hebrides, the South Pacific Islands, and the Caribbean coast.

'Are you all right here?' he asks.

She laughs then. 'Of course.' She follows his eyes back to the whaling crew. 'They're a good crew. And I pay them well.'

'And you came all this way–'

'To inquire after my mother.'

'That's all?'

'I wouldn't call it *all*.'

'No.' A flock of black cockatoos take to the air, cackling. His leg aches and there is a strange rasp in his chest. The woman in front of him, in her sailor's garb and unbound hair, is a creature from another world, strangely complexioned and oddly gendered. Despite her youth, she seems straight from the past. The last time he saw her, Byron had still been alive and everything foreign and Oriental had been celebrated and en vogue. She does not understand how much has changed, and what she risks in her blatant difference.

He is aware of his surveying party working on the hillside

behind him and thinks again of fleeing the uncertain shoreline and rejoining his society, the network of men he has assembled and nurtured, drawn from all the reaches of the Empire. There is safety in their warm estimation.

'I must go. The men will wonder what's happened to me.' It's true. Most of them are wide-eyed and curious about the tall gum trees with their sinuous branches, the golden-blooming acacia, the ochre-painted natives with their ethereal music. But others are jumpy, on edge. Dangerous. 'I'll come back and see you. You'll be here, won't you?'

He expects her to speak, but she only looks back at him with her serious eyes. She has always had this power of silence. His errors or missteps never led to recriminations. They led to nothing at all. He waits. She turns away from him, walking further into the water where she knows he won't follow. The heat of embarrassment expands across his skin. For a brief moment, he is grateful that he's dark enough it never shows. He walks away, slowly, and her silence pursues him over the hillside.

~

He returns at nightfall to find the whalers' tents dotting the hills above the shoreline. Do they intend to stay? In the distance, around the curve of the beach, he can see the tip of the mainsail, the colours of the American flag. Some men will be on the whaler to take care of the ship, while the others camp on the shore to complete their work. Where will she be? He asked and she said nothing.

He felt foolish upon leaving. The whole encounter shook him. Fourteen years, and all his attempts at forgetfulness are snuffed out by a single meeting. Not even his work gave him back his equilibrium. His surveying team had watched, with generous bemusement, as he fumbled his calculations, and in the afternoon, ended their day prematurely. He had thought he'd never see her again. There was a reason he'd left England, spent a decade wandering the Continent and working in Egypt. He didn't have the stomach to come across her by chance at the Royal Academy or a London ballroom. Not after her long silence. He had taken her image with its manifold colours, placed it in a box and concealed it in a closed desk drawer. But now, on the shore of the last new world, she is here.

He pauses as he approaches the tents. A campfire burns in the distance, and silhouetted figures watch him in the night. Light feels the leadening weight of prevarication. He has not spoken of her to anyone. In the immediate aftermath, even in England, his friends knew better than to ask, and near death in Spain gave him a convenient distraction. So much of his time with her was concealed. But now he must bring it forth.

The men at the campfire stir as he approaches. He recognises some figures from the beach, hears again those melded accents. Liverpool docks, the West Indies, the Scottish Highlands, East Africa. Their voices fall silent as he speaks.

'I'm looking for the lady. Miss FitzRoy.'

Their faces, from what he can see in the firelight, are not hostile, but they gaze at him in frank appraisal. Irritation prickles over his skin. Who are these common sailors to question him like this? When their response comes, it arrives with the sound of the Caribbean, blunted with suspicion.

'Who's asking?'

Light does not respond. He steadies the flare of anger that

seeks to soar out of him. He's the Surveyor-General, but he cannot expect such men to know this. And besides, he realises, in their cautious assessment and suspicious tones, they care for her.

'It's all right, Mac.' Another voice, from deep in the darkness.

'But, Moses, I mean, Mr Widlow–'

'It's all right,' Moses Widlow says again.

Light strains his eyes to seek out the speaker, but he's only a tall shape in the gloom. Maireener shells gleam in the firelight, adorning the man's neck. A local custom, Light thinks. From Van Diemen's Land.

'You'll find her higher up the hillside, Colonel. In the marquee tent.' The figure pauses and shifts where he stands. 'She's expecting you.'

The man's final words hang in the night. Around the campfire, the whalers stir, turning back to their business, disgruntled and relieved. For a moment, Light wonders what they know of this, what they know of him and her. *I pay them well*, she'd told him. She had not hitched a passage. She had commandeered them.

He nods at the tall figure in the shadows and begins his ascent. She was always reckless, but this surprises him.

The night breeze tugs at his coat and hair as the tent draws closer. The less worldly settlers are still shocked by the chill in the evening air, but he has been in this climate before. In Egypt, the desert nights are always cold.

As he reaches the peak of the hill, he slows his pace. The tent is pale in the darkness, looming over the distant sailors' camp like an officer's marquee on a battlefield. He had a tent such as this once. It is not far from the sailors' camp, yet it feels remote. Isolated here, on a hillside cliff.

He pauses a few feet away from its entrance, hesitating. Unsure of what he will say to her. Their last conversation still follows him with limping, jagged steps. His third and final act of cowardice.

He reaches for his pocket, wishing briefly for a cigar. But he has long since abandoned the habit.

As Light walks toward the cliffside, he eases his steps along the uneven terrain. The weakness in his leg makes him careful, a steady reminder of the presence of failure. Yet here, in this new, uncharted country, he might make something of himself. Surveyor-General. Founder of a city. Almost as good as his father. He turns back from the ocean, watching the gentle buckle and sway of the tent's canvas in the wind. He might make something of himself here. The loose corner of the tent's door flaps in and out with the breeze. He might make this.

Despite the campsite and fires in the distance, he can hear no voices. But for the wind in the bushland and the rhythm of the waves, the world is silent, as though a glass globe has been placed over them and in this strange place there is only him and her.

He steps forward. He raises his hand as if to knock, then drops it. He straightens his cuff and collar, smooths the wind from his hair.

His voice is strong in the silence. 'Clarissa?'

~

I open the white flap of the tent and let him in. Outside, the waves crest and break against the rocks and the wind beats the canvas. I pull my Himalayan shawl around me, against his judgement, against the night.

He is watchful as he enters. There are crevices on his face that I do not know, a limp that is unfamiliar. It has been fourteen years, but his eyes are the same spheres of onyx. He smiles at me – the same small smile – and makes a bow. His hair is long and dark for his age and there is still, in the turned-up collar of his coat and the bronzing of his skin, the faint air of a weathered hero fallen on hard times. He passes close. I can almost taste the salt of the sea and the ash of West Indian cigars.

I step back, letting the night air fill the space between us. Already I feel a crackle in my limbs, like Galvani's spark. When he averts his eyes, I remember the shock of once realising that he was slightly shy.

'It's a cold night,' he says, prosaic as ever.

'Yes. Beautiful, though.'

We pause to look at the sky. It is clear and indigo-rich, like the ink of a startled squid.

'I don't know if I'll ever get used to those stars, or the moon waxing backward.'

'No, but I like the difference. The cross in particular.'

'It's a good navigational tool. If you line it up with Alpha and Beta Centauri it shows you the way south.'

'I know.'

'Of course,' he says. His tone is disappointed.

I pull my shawl more closely about myself. Fourteen years ago, I might have humoured him and feigned ignorance, but not now.

He glances at my grip on the wool surrounding me, and closes the flap of the tent, sealing out the wind. The world grows muted.

'About earlier–' he begins, but I turn quickly, loosening the shawl and draping it over a chair. As I pour two glasses of brandy, I sense his eyes on my hips, my waist, my hair. He drops his gaze as I hand him a glass.

We sit down. He moves with the body of a younger man,

although he favours his leg. Part of me wants to touch him, to lean forward and rediscover that terrain I had once known so well. But he has moved on to new territory. We both have. He is here, I'm sure he thinks, to chart an undiscovered country, to make order of the unknown, to take the dangers of the borderless and make it safe. Corralled.

'I think you know why I've asked to see you,' I say.

He looks back at me, eyes blank.

'My mother.'

He takes a sip of brandy. 'You know I missed you. In Spain and afterwards.' When he meets my gaze, his eyes are mournful. I have an image of a room in Bath, disordered sheets, a grey dawn creaking over the Roman stone.

'You can't have missed me so much.'

'I wrote to you,' he continues. 'Many times. When you did not reply–'

'You married.'

'In haste.'

In the silence, I can hear the sea curling into the shore. I have always wanted to live on the lip of the ocean.

'Did you receive them? My letters?'

Spidery writing fills my vision, the writing of a man with much to say and not enough paper. News of him shot and imprisoned in La Coruña. My heart beats simply now, but I recall a time of it clenching.

'Do you remember what you said to me before you went to Spain?'

He sits back and inhales. 'I have apologised,' he says. 'Many times, in those letters. I have regretted it. I have repented and God knows I have suffered since then.'

'That is as it should be.' The words leave my mouth before I can consider them, and I see a flash behind his eyes.

'Then you did receive my letters.'

I do not reply.

'All this time, I wondered. That maybe they went astray, or perhaps your cousin burned them.'

'If you thought such a thing, then why did you not try to see me? Why not explain yourself properly, instead of being such a coward?'

An anguished look crosses his face, but it is quickly supplanted by anger. 'I had a musket ball through my leg. It was months before I was mobile. I'd hoped you would come and see me if I wrote.'

My head shakes. 'You have no idea what you cost me.'

He shifts, his left hand gripping the armrest. It was always a habit he had when he was tense, or afraid. The silent clenching of his left fingers.

'I'm sorry.' He pauses. 'I did ask you to marry me.'

'After how you behaved. After you said I was unfit to mother your children.'

'That is not what I said. And I was wrong.'

'And it took near death in Spain for you to realise that?'

'It did, yes.'

I had dreamt it at the time. I had seen him, half delirious with pain, somewhere in La Coruña and thinking of me. But by then I had already turned my face to the wall.

Early autumn and the oak leaves ripen to gold. *I could never have Eurasian children*, he told me. *Not after what I've been through. I used to wonder why I was born at all.*

For weeks afterwards, I carried a quiet shame. I sought out

my face in mirrors and imagined excising my amber skin and almond eyes, that strange complexion that melded East and West. I pictured removing it, like a Dionysian mask, a foreign doll face, and casting it aside among the dying daisy beds. But what did it leave? I took off my face and saw only emptiness.

I had thought we were well suited. Me with my Hindu mother and my Hertfordshire father, and he with his more mysterious origins. A Suffolk father and a mother that was of Siam, Chinese, Malay and perhaps Portuguese heritage. I had thought our differences unified us, but I had not counted on how much he wanted to change his skin.

'It does not matter now,' I say, 'how wrong you were. I have asked you here to talk about my mother.'

He draws back into his chair, then leans forward and drinks more brandy. 'What do you want to say?' His voice is clipped.

'I want to know who she was.'

'You know,' he says.

'I know her face, and nothing more.'

'That was all I knew of my mother for many years. It should have been enough.'

'I know you met her when you were in India. You never told me about it. I am trying to find her.'

He sighs and runs his fingers through the top of his hair, leaving it tousled and untidy. He taps his bad leg. 'Your life will be more peaceable without this search.' I want to insert my anger, smooth as a hot knife, but I hold back. 'You're safer as you are,' he says.

A sound escapes me like a hiss as I stand. The night has stilled around us with a suffocating intensity. He watches me as I move to the entrance of the tent and lean my head by the cool opening. The air is scented with burning eucalyptus.

When I was a child, I wanted to live by the ocean. I remembered its briny taste and lazuli blue as the labyrinth thread that would guide me home. On the voyage to England, my Scottish governess told me stories of strange women in fur pelts who could transform between woman and seal. I thought of the freedom that would bring, to slink back into the ocean and chart my course home to the Bay of Bengal. That is what the selkie mothers did. They left their half-human children, took up their darkened sealskins and slipped away.

A selkie's child, they tell me, has webbed feet.

Behind me, he calls my name, but I do not turn. I have seen his maps and felt his cartographer's pen. He would have me peel back my skin and leave my natural space to live, skinless and bleeding, in his orderly house.

I leave the tent. He stands and moves behind me, but he is slow. The hard soil scrapes against the soles of my feet as I run down the hillside. Thoughts of exodus fill my mind, of chasing currents, sea-foam skin and island archipelagos. The sand embraces my toes. On the distant shore, embers glow. I've heard the people here burn off the land to let new life grow.

I walk knee-deep into the ocean, tossing aside my dress. For a moment it gleams red in the night, like fire. The gibbous moon casts shoals of light across the surface of the water. It froths around me, wet sand sinking beneath my heels with each ebb of the tide. Perhaps, in the deep, there are selkies. I try to picture them, but I see only seals with questioning eyes, rolling with the flotsam of the shore. *A selkie's child has webbed feet.*

I close my eyes and taste the sea. My skin is sleek with moisture. The sea foam clings like snakeskin, bubbling over me in iridescent mother-of-pearl. My legs coalesce into shining scales of silver.

My toes web. I inhale night and release my hair upon the surface of the claret-faced sea. Beneath me, my feet blossom into fins of agate. My legs shine, writhing and powerful, a gleaming shield over marine muscles and tendons beating in time to the water. I gaze into the night, then, breathing once, slip beneath the waves.

In the moonlight he sees only this: a serpent's tail, a translucent fin, a burning dress on the glistening shore.

Calcutta, June 1836

The sunlight pierces the monsoonal cloud as the last of the rain begins to dissipate. The downpour has left the streets coated in soft mud and riven with pools of mirrored glass. I wait under the shaking eaves of a teashop, drinking syrupy chai and watching the onslaught of water before me. Now the deluge has broken, and the afternoon heat brings the steam out of the puddles and the layered scents of gardenia and ripening earth into the air.

I have spent the morning walking and remembering. Or trying to remember. The memories I grasp at lacked cohesion. They come in fragmented forms, like the flower petals from the markets, dispersed and removed from their original stems. The images appear more frequently here than they ever did in England, but with no clearer narrative. Although I do remember this: the sound of thunder that seems to crack the world askew, the quick rolling clouds, the burst of rain. The still, languorous heat of the devouring sun that follows.

I leave the shelter of the teashop and pick my way through the sodden streets, choosing where to place each foot with the care of a mountain goat. The teashop owner rises from his seat to watch me go. I am used to the question-mark eyes that follow me.

At least the teashop owner was friendly. The openness of his face guided my choice of shelter.

As the sun returns, the city comes to life, rinsed clean by the rain. The shopfronts open and the streets begin to fill. I try to note each movement, each item, each sound and smell, and commit it to memory. The weave of a basket balanced on a man's head, the edged embroidery of a woman's tangerine sari, the shape of a street offering to a statue of Kali and all the textures of the smoking incense curling about the dark goddess. I spend my evenings recording these sensory experiences, but my words remain inadequate. How would one write it in Bengali? Or Sanskrit? It is an impassable gap, an absence in my experience of the world. When I reread my own words, I hear only the voices of eccentric Englishwomen, returned from the 'mysterious' East with their husbands, drinking at London parties and describing all the exotic colours and pungent spices and strange morals of a faraway world, wrapping their own licence in the trappings of adventure.

I skirt the edge of the market, avoiding the pool of stagnant water and the golden dogs napping in the afternoon sun, their tails twitching with dreams. I can see a path through the shopfronts and the throng of people. Strangers all. On my arrival several weeks ago, every face had been a potential friend, a distant leaf on the branches of my hybrid family tree. I wince to think of it now. My presumption, my arrogance. But still. Even now, I catch myself seeking my mother in the mascaraed eyes of the local women, in their familiar arms wrapped in cotton saris.

I cross the street and move into the quiet shadow of the lane. The path leaves the shopfronts and the calls of the traders and travels through the walled gardens of a residential district. Grand houses tower over their walled perimeters. Through the gates there are scarlet walls and Venetian shutters, gardens of jasmine and saffron marigolds. Do I remember all this?

A dog barks as I pass; a gardener looks up in surprise. This is the wealthy Bengali enclave of the city. Am I an intruder? Reaching out, trailing my fingertips against a wall. My hand seems to say I belong.

I pause at the end of the lane. A vine spills its tendrils and its purple trumpet flowers over the metal gate. I touch the rim of one of the petals. The name is somewhere in the recesses of my mind. It is just as tall as I remember. It had always been hardy – it had grown voraciously. And it has survived, soft but resilient. A Bengal clock vine.

Movement. I look down to see a puppy with an alert tail snuffling at the hem of my skirts. I lean over and stroke its soft ears.

'Can I help you, ma'am?'

The voice is polished English with a slight inflection. The man stands just within the open gates. He is tall – taller than most Europeans – with a straight back and a controlled bearing. A vivid blue turban winds its way neatly about his head. The question mark flares briefly, before being suppressed, as he checks my left hand, where the diamond blinks on my third finger. Then he gazes around me, as though seeking my escort, or protector. 'Are you lost, ma'am?'

'Thank you. No.'

I straighten my back. Behind the man, the paved drive stretches down toward the house, framed by green hedges. The house has changed. It sits in straight lines and sharp edges, a white monstrosity. But the garden is as I remember it. The scent of wet earth and tuberoses. I can hear the strains of my mother speaking in words that are indistinct.

'Tell me,' I ask the guard, who drops his questioning gaze when I look at him, 'who lives here now?'

He blinks. 'No one, ma'am. The owner is a merchant from Jorasanko. He rebuilt the house some years ago. The property is for sale.' He assesses the fabric of my dress and the tint of my skin. 'If you are interested, ma'am, perhaps you could come back with your husband.'

I smile. 'Perhaps. We are looking for a home here.' It is not entirely a lie. 'What of the previous house, and the former owners?'

'It was an old-fashioned place. There were tenants for some time, but they didn't care for the house. This is a great improvement.' He looks back approvingly at the neoclassical structure.

'And before that? Before there were tenants?'

The man's face darkens. 'There was an Englishman here, I believe. A Colonel FitzRoy.'

I didn't want to say it. My father's name. Specificities. Things that could loop round and ensnare me.

The man moves his head in acknowledgement. 'He passed away, ma'am. A long time ago.'

'Yes. You see, I'm looking for his wife. I understand she lived here for a while after he died, but then ... then she moved away.'

The man swings his gaze above my head. 'I don't know, ma'am.'

I study his expression. He is not a gossip.

'It's quite important,' I say, after a pause.

'I don't know anything about that,' the man replies. 'I heard she brought much shame to her family. More so once her husband died. It's not something I want to know about.'

'What do you mean, more so after her husband died? I thought the scandal was her marriage to an Englishman?'

'She didn't marry the next one, ma'am.'

'The next one?'

But the man's face closes. 'If you would like to view the house with your husband–'

'You see, I know Colonel FitzRoy's family and they are anxious to speak with her.'

The man blinks at the interruption, then recognition blossoms in the depths of his eyes. I watch as it congeals slowly into fear. And hostility.

I step back. The man pats his leg and the puppy bounds toward him, leaving my side.

'Please tell your husband to call, ma'am. Goodbye.'

Something shrinks within me. These moments of silence, when the world reshapes itself around me, twist the ground beneath my feet, loosening my fragile anchor. The man retreats into the walled garden, the puppy following. I walk away quickly, my head bowed, the shaded lane now glum and forbidding, the leaves of the banyan trees swaying in the breeze, whispering behind me.

South Australian Coast, October 1836

He waits on the shore for my return, his shape casting dark lines on the sand. The water swirls over me, grasping my hair and swooping over my head in a tunnel of foam. Beneath the waves, I can see the pronged tail of an electric stingray searching for prey. Further, into the ocean, the seals are watchful and questioning, feeding in the shallows. Waiting. Above the water, there is only darkness fractured by moonlight. And him.

~

He removes her dress from the edge of the tide. The red fabric had seemed to hover over the water like the spectre of his mother's tales of Ma Cho Po, until he grasped it and felt its sodden materiality. Its weight brought him back to his senses. He took off his boots in preparation for a rescue, but Clarissa waved him back. Her sleek shape bobs with the surging water, her dark head shining like a seal in the moonlight. Where did she learn to swim like that? If he were bolder, he would join her. But he still wears his clothes like a uniform. He sees the arc of the woman's body in the water, the way the waves break into diamonds on the tide, and imagines their buoyancy, the sea's grip suspending him between earth and sky. He envisions joining her, the touch of her salted skin, slick with moisture, the droplets of the ocean catching on her lashes and the top of her lip. He takes two steps into the water but falters. With his bad leg, he would never make it.

Never make it.

How had it come to this? Once more, he remembers the candy stripe of the hot air balloon, the milky sky of an English spring, wondering if he would ever see its like again. The coal fire coughed and dimmed as it descended, tilting the gondola so that its occupants screamed. That was when he saw her. Her laughing face, her red net dress, her hair escaping the confines of its pins. An untethered woman, floating out of the sky.

Later, when they were introduced, he saw other things about her. The alien contours of her face that made her so familiar. The Wedgwood brooch of the Abolitionists pinned in her hair. *Am I not a woman and a sister?* As the pamphlets said. The sheen of her dress that hinted at an income he did not possess. She was not pure English, but not wholly foreign, either. Where that strangeness had made him thoughtful as a boy and questioning as a man – with those questions always phrased so uncertainly – it seemed to make her luminous. She was not, like him, an awkward composite of disparate parts held together with a gloss veneer. She was something whole and new. In the growing darkness of the evening, she was pure illumination.

Of course, he would record this encounter in more straightforward tones. *Clarissa FitzRoy. English father, Oriental mother. Apparently legitimate. Heiress.* He learned these details after their meeting. Some of it he pieced together in the moment. Her face alone told half her story. There were men who flattered her and said she could pass for Italian. But his eye was attuned to seeking out difference. She bore the stamp of the East on Anglicised skin.

She was not the only one like him that he had seen. His eye would pick them out in London and coastal towns. There were the minstrels from Africa, and Madame Georgina, native of Calcutta, here in the Vauxhall Rotunda. There were the descendants of lascars and Irish women working the docks, there were the Creole heiresses from West Indian plantations seeking husbands whiter than white. They were not for him. He needed the money, it was true, but what game of chance would he be playing with his children's future? Besides, those women would not have him. No lady wanted a future plantation owner to look (almost) like a slave.

In this way, she was different. In her world, there would be no slaves picking cotton or harvesting sugar cane, no fear of the sun and the stain left by its rays. There would be no light, and no darkness, either.

Perhaps she had always been a little bit mad.

~

The water falls from my skin, shedding in silver scales. My toes separate and curl, digging into wet sand. Amphibious. But I walk forward, disappointingly human, wobbling against the roll of waves.

I can see him against the shoreline, holding my dress. I need answers.

He keeps his eyes on my face as I walk toward him, his expression steady and unchanging. For the first time, he looks his age. The water hangs in the fabric of my slip. It sticks to my legs like a seal pelt. Close enough to touch him now, I stop and hold out my hand for my dress. Confusion flickers across his face, before his gaze wavers and drops.

~

We walk back to the tent without speaking. The wind is sharp and dry. Each time it tugs the moisture from my skin I feel myself imprisoned once again in human form, subject to its categorical truths and Linnaean structures. We don't touch, but I feel his warmth next to me. I hold my dress bundled under my arm, and he has placed his coat over my shoulders. Above the cadence of the sea, I can hear him breathing. It follows its own pattern, devoid of rhythm. It shakes like a breeze clawing through a torn sail. I try to return his coat, but he will not take it.

We reach the entrance of the tent. Times have changed since that week in Bath, fourteen years ago. The other colonisers have mercantile wives, they go to church, they balance their books, they have a limited education. They are not devotees of Rousseau, they do not breathe in abstractions such as liberty, they do not worship Shelley or value the Renaissance man. They do not take mistresses to the ends of the earth, nor stand in night-time conversation with strange, half-Eastern ladies. They are not, in their own right, a shade or two away from white.

Within the shelter of the tent, I remove his overcoat and turn to hand it back, and again his eyes move quickly away from my body and onto the ground.

I'm tired of these games and restrictions. Perhaps it was a mistake to come here.

He takes the coat but does not move.

'Perhaps we can talk tomorrow,' I say. 'I'm not letting this go.'

'We sail up the coast in a day or two. There's much to do before the Governor arrives. I need to search for good freshwater and survey–'

'I see.'

'But we should talk. How long do you plan to stay?'

I can't tell if everything is slipping away. On that day at the cathedral of Leiston Abbey, the future mapped itself out with inevitable self-assurance, but none of it came to pass. 'A short while. The whaling ship has work here.'

'You don't intend to remain here with them, surely? Wouldn't you rather stay with the settlers?'

I smile. 'Not really.'

There is calculation behind the light reflecting on his eyes. 'I don't understand,' he says. 'Is that appropriate?'

I laugh. 'It's been fourteen years, Will. I don't need to concern myself with propriety anymore.'

He doesn't speak. I am damp and cold, and covered in sand and grit. I step back and start to close the flap of the tent. 'Well, goodnight.'

He places his hand over mine. 'Wait.'

His palms are rougher than I remember. I imagine him running with his surveyor's chain, adjusting the brass of his theodolite. Carving up the land for new consumption. There are fires burning through the gum trees on the hillside. There are people here, already.

'Why?'

His face has a narrow look. On my left hand, my ring grows watchful. The man who gave it to me – James – is somewhere in India. Far away, but thinking of me.

'I need you to understand.'

'Understand what?'

'Why it's better this way, without digging up the past.'

'Whose past? My mother's, or yours?'

He blinks once in the face of my question. He is still waiting at the entrance of the tent. 'May I come in?'

I consider his face in the darkness. 'Allow me a moment.'

~

Light puts his coat back on and waits. It must be late. His watch sits heavy in his pocket, but he doesn't consult it. He gazes again at the alien stars, tracing the shape of the cross, the flare of Sirius, the Eta Argus. How timeless this world is. He has felt it, away from the *Rapid*, in the beat of the red earth beneath his feet and the swaying of the lithe gum trees. This place is independent of the twelve-hour clock and the Gregorian calendar. In the weeks after his first arrival, he was beset by a feeling of trespass. The dense bush was watchful and breathless. The rocks were alive. The birds were aggressive and shrieking. He was not welcome.

But he brushed away the feeling. He was good at that. There was a place for romance and sensibility, but this wilderness was not it. And besides, if he felt regret during those early days, when he saw the seals skinned and bleeding on the sun-bleached shores, or the great eucalyptus trees felled for no purpose, or the Aboriginal man with the angry caverns of smallpox scarring his skin, he reminded himself that he would make it better. The contamination by the external world had already happened, independent of him. If he had not come here, the destruction would still take place. This was not a pristine land, or some original Eden he was defiling. The great colonial project had already begun, and he was here to make sure it succeeded. In his role, he could minimise the damage. He could build something that would fulfil its own ideals, that would include the Australian natives and make the best use of the land. That would make everyone benefit.

Had it been that way for his father? In England and Calcutta stories circulated of Francis Light's linguistic abilities, his sensitivity, his respect for the people among whom he had built his life. In his own memory, Light sees his father dressed in a baju sikap or a kain, his hair cut short and bereft of the last century's wigs. He hears his father's voice speak in Portuguese, Malay, the occasional phrase of Hokkien or Arabic. There was so little English in their household. But there, his memories cease. At six years old, he had been sent to England, and would never again see his father. On Light's only return to Penang, he had envied the local islanders for their devotion to his father and his founding ways. But most of all, he envied their proximity. Their familiarity.

He turns back to the tent. Familiarity, the familiar, family. That is the problem here. A thin white line of canvas separates him from her. He has memorised her face. She who was once so familiar to him, who has remade herself as a stranger. His body is crumbling and heavy, but there is still, beyond the grating in his chest, something like hope.

She pulls back the flap of the tent, her hair loose and mostly dried, burnished in the candlelight, gowned in sea green.

When he steps forward, she holds up a palm.

'I'm sorry,' she says. 'I can't do this now. Not tonight.'

'We have so much to talk about.'

Her eyes move over him. For one brief moment, her fingers touch the collar of his shirt.

'Goodnight, Will.'

'Wait–'

She closes the flap of the tent against him, the white canvas sealing him out to drift in the night.

His breath catches in a ragged whir behind his sternum. He thinks of sealskins on the white sand. He thinks of drowning, but he is beached.

Vauxhall Gardens, London, May 1822

Light watches the gondola sway under its sail of scarlet and white. Beneath it, the horizon line is shot through with silver; above it, patchy clouds froth. It is not a still night. He is envious then, of that exposure. To feel the wind and clouds as great waves on the ocean. To master the strangeness of that experience.

The globe rises, secured with one strong tether. He has made a balloon before, many times. From rice paper and bamboo, with his mother and the Chinese settlers on the shores of Penang, after lighting incense for the sea goddess Ma Cho Po. And then, more recently, with strips of silk and a flaming wick, the light vanishing into the ether over Suffolk's coast.

But how would one make a balloon to carry a man? Could he do it? He could do it. The thrilled cries of the passengers drift over to him. What it must be like, to explore that great expanse of air. He has navigated the waves and charted the land, but this last frontier is still foreign to him.

He had looked into it, of course. As soon as the Napiers invited him here, on this night, when the balloon would be launched for the season. But the cost and the waiting list were prohibitive.

Even after the year he had been through, he could not justify it. And so, he is here, on the perimeter of excitement, observing.

The balloon sways as the rope pulls taut, anchoring it to the earth. The passengers shift. He sees, for a fraction of a moment, a flash of red fabric in the gondola, a woman leaning over the side of the basket, gazing down. Precarious.

Beside him there is laughter, and he feels himself pulled back to the ground. Light peels his eyes away from the balloon, from the woman suspended between earth and sky. The Napiers are popular. Snatches of conversation drift over to him.

'*More nightingales and fewer strumpets,*' cries a male voice.

'Not in front of the lady,' protests another.

A red-headed woman stands in their circle, her brows knitted together. Beside her, a tall man with a familiar face taps his cane on the ground in jerky, impatient movements, staring up at the sky.

'Light.' Napier clasps his shoulder. 'May I present Mrs Harcourt, wife of Roger Harcourt, the Whig MP. And I believe you know Walter Fraser?'

The tall man's face brightens. 'Of course! Light! We met at George Jones's portrait studio.'

Light blinks. 'Yes. Yes, that's right.' Vague memories of an eager voice in the small studio return to him. 'You're a poet, aren't you?'

'After a fashion.' Fraser turns the grip of his cane in his hands. His fingers look weaker than Light expects. He has an image of the tall man stooped over a too-small writing desk in a narrow room. What was the man's work again? A tutor?

'And soon to be novelist,' Napier interjects.

'Is that so?'

Fraser's words come quickly. 'Too early to say. I'm working on something.'

Light nods. 'Good for you.' He has little time for novels. *Waverley* hadn't been too bad, but he dislikes the frivolity of fiction. The truth is always more interesting. And besides, there had been something about Fraser. Something that he hadn't quite liked.

Movement in the sky pulls Light's eyes upwards. A shudder shakes through the crowd, and Mrs Harcourt covers her mouth.

The balloon dances at the end of its tether, its movements trembling and jerking. Light is reminded of a pitiable sight – a wounded tiger in India, straining at the end of a leash.

'Why did Mr Harcourt ever let her go up there?' The woman glances at Light. 'My cousin is on that balloon.'

Light feels rising air within his chest, a lift of covetousness and delight. He opens his mouth to speak but checks himself at the woman's face.

'Such a foolish girl.' Fraser drives his cane into the soft green earth. 'I'm sorry for speaking out of turn, madam, but I really thought she'd be less impulsive by now.'

'So did I,' Mrs Harcourt replies. 'I wish my husband wouldn't encourage her.'

'Your husband is not here at present?' Light asks.

Mrs Harcourt shakes her head. 'He had to take my cousin Mr Oliver home. The young man was quite unwell.'

Light looks up at the balloon's reverberations. 'The movements are subsiding. I do not think you need to be concerned. I expect it was just a strong breeze.'

'They should call the whole thing off.' Fraser's stick continues to thump the earth.

'Perhaps we should ask them?' Mrs Harcourt says.

Napier catches Light's gaze and lifts his eyes.

'Yes,' says Fraser. 'Yes, I think we should.'

Mrs Harcourt nods. 'I'll ask them to bring it down. And we can all go to supper together. Please excuse us,' she says to Light and Napier, 'but I must find my cousin. She's already an orphan and our uncle will never forgive me if anything happens to her.'

Light bows as they leave.

'I never took Fraser for such a boor,' Napier says.

'What is his relationship to the lady?' Lights asks.

'He's the tutor. The former tutor, I suppose. To the young invalid, and his sister. The damsel in the balloon.'

Light laughs. 'I hope they don't bring it down. I hope she can keep flying.'

'As do I.' Napier is silent for a moment. 'Do you know much about them? Their family?'

Light watches the balloon sway against the darkening sky. 'I don't think so. Why? Should I?'

Napier rubs his chin. 'I thought you might have heard of them. Their situation, you see, it's similar–'

Around them, Light becomes aware of the crowds beginning to move.

'The fireworks are starting!' Excitement ripples through their party. Napier's brother grips his arm. 'Come along, Charles, Light. There's a better view by the pavilion.'

Napier moves to join his brother. 'Are you coming, old man?'

Light's gaze is drawn once more to the movement of the balloon. Its height is beginning to subside.

'I just want to watch the landing,' he says. 'I'll catch up with you.'

The bright match flare of the flame, the quick tug of the basket, the weightlessness upon my feet. Around me there are gasps and cries, but I lean forward, gripping the side of the gondola as we are borne upwards into the air. The gardens diminish, their mysteries and labyrinths laid bare for all to see. For a moment, I see my cousin's upturned face among the spectators. Then the world spins away and there are no cousins, no pleasure-seekers, no relatives. Just the uncertainty of shifting air, a bracing wind on a spring night, the meandering shape of the Thames coiling through an ancient city, and lights in the windows of St Paul's Cathedral.

I'm flying.

The silk globe draws us skywards. *A watch-light by the patriot's lonely tomb; A ray of courage to the oppressed and poor.* That is how Shelley describes it. Ballooning. And liberty.

The platform beneath me jolts and shudders, and a woman cries out. The gondola sways to the sound of staggering feet. I grip the basket, willing us higher.

'Nothing to fear,' the balloonist calls. 'That's just our anchor settling.' He turns to the woman next to him. 'We are tethered to the gardens, madam.'

Anchor. When was the last time I felt that pull? Docking in Portsmouth sixteen years ago. Reaching land. My brother crying out, determined to stay with the lascars on the ship. Four black horses and my grandfather's coach.

Beneath me, the Thames pushes through the detritus of London, greeting the estuary and snaking toward the Channel. I follow it into the cold and briny Atlantic, through to Holland and Calais, then further, to the Mediterranean.

Above, the first stars stare back at me. The evening wind plucks at my hair and drums against the gondola. The platform slides beneath us, dropping once, then rising, meeting our feet and leaving them in two quick percussions.

'Some minor turbulence.' The balloonist's voice is weak in the wind. 'Do not be concerned.'

My skirts pull at me, the world swaying closer before being torn away.

'Ladies and gentlemen, do prepare for our descent.'

Around me there are murmurs of relief. I reach out, as though I could grip the wind.

How is it that I can fly, that I can be here, among the clouds, and still not be free?

~

The basket thuds against the earth, bouncing once and dragging across the grass. Screams split the spectators as the crowd parts in front of the arriving balloon. Figures rush past. The balloon draws closer, looming over him, its bright sphere blocking out the gibbous moon and early stars. Light waits, watching the diminishing shape of the inflated globe, the juddering basket. Such modern wonder.

The balloon is almost upon him. He waits until the final moment. The balloonist waves his arms, shouting. A woman screams. As the basket bears down on him, he steps nimbly aside. It's close. So close he can see the lined texture of the gondola's weave, the threaded ropes, the stitches harnessing the scarlet-and-white silk. The passengers rock and cry out, gripping the sides of the gondola, white-faced. He sees again a flash of red, a dark-haired woman leaning forward, laughing, one arm out to catch the vanishing air.

As the gondola settles, the balloon deflating, passengers scramble from the basket. The spectators keep their distance. Light can see, tucked in their midst, the shapes of Walter Fraser and Mrs Harcourt. Alone, Light walks forward. He would touch the striped silk of the envelope and examine its rope and stitching. There are not so many mysteries to its construction. He could build one of these. And what then? He is at a loose end. How far could a balloon take him?

The iced peaks of the Swiss Alps, the canals of Venice. The Black Sea.

He reaches out, his fingers brushing the edges of the silk.

Weight thuds into his chest, small hands gripping his shoulder. He smells jasmine, magnolia, the keen, sharp scent of Vauxhall punch.

'I'm so sorry.' A voice drifts up to him from the region of his chest.

Without thinking he steadies the woman in front of him, his hand on the fabric around her waist. His fingers hesitate on the fineness of the silk, the texture of the crystals stitched into it. As she wobbles against him, he sees burnished brown hair, a red net dress. The woman from the balloon.

'I did try to get your attention,' the woman says. 'It's very difficult to climb out of a balloon dressed like this.'

He cannot get a clear sight of her face. He moves to step back, to maintain his distance. But she cries out in pain. Her hair is tangled in the buttons of his coat.

She works her fingers around the loop of her hair and the pale-blue ornament that has pinioned her to him. A Wedgewood brooch. The mascot of the female abolitionists. So. She affects to be political.

'Could you not have left via the gate? Like the others?'

'Not easily, no. Not without being seen.'

He watches the deft movement of her fingers, her hair coming apart across his chest. He has not yet, in all this time, caught a clear sight of her face, but he begins to suspect her identity. He looks around. She is entirely alone. He realises then who she must be. The only solitary woman to disembark from the balloon. Mrs Harcourt's cousin. A lady. Not a person he would expect to be clambering around alone in the night at Vauxhall. He releases her waist.

Flashes of light fall across the gardens, casting the trees in shades of red and pink and blue. Fireworks spin into the sky, cracking into glittering missiles. He thinks, as he always does, of cannon fire on the Peninsula, the red night and thunder of the guns. But he does not flinch like other men. All those years fighting Napoleon, and he was never wounded.

She frees her hair and steps away, turning from him. He feels the absence of her hands against his chest.

The fireworks flare again. Bright silver gold. She is lit up in flashes before him.

It is her skin that he notices. The texture, shade and sheen of it. He thinks, for one visionary moment, that if he were to reach out and touch her, and place his bare palm on her exposed shoulder, that their skins would cleave together, would dissolve into one another. Like water on water.

When she turns, he sees her face as in a mirror, his own features rearranged and given back to him. He understands now, all those Grecian legends. What it means to look upon a woman's face and turn to stone.

He senses he shouldn't be here. That he should walk on. But he could never resist it. Even as a child in the pepper gardens in Penang, leaning over the pond, reaching out with his palm. Touching the skin of the water.

'Are you all right, madam?' He hears his own voice as from a distance. Behind him, the sound of cheering layers over the fading fireworks.

She smiles. 'I'm avoiding someone. Two people, more precisely.'

He feels his face tugging into its own curves. 'Mrs Harcourt's cousin, I presume.'

'Yes. And you are?'

'Major William Light. I met your cousin earlier, with Mr Fraser.'

'So, you met my dull captors for the evening.'

'I believe they are searching for you.'

'I believe you are right. It's why I'm here.'

Light looks back toward the crowd, where a tall silhouette and a glimpse of a woman in purple loom. 'Madam,' he tells the woman, 'I don't think you should wander off alone. Not in the dark at Vauxhall. Your cousin is just–'

She shakes her head. Something about her is familiar. He sees her wrists and thinks of a backstreet in Calcutta, sunlight peering in through latticed windows. The sound of ox carts and children playing. Scented writing paper. Her skin changes colour in the gloaming.

'I saw you.' Her voice cuts through his thoughts. 'The man watching the balloon. I saw your face. You were the only one not to run. The only one who wanted to reach out and touch it.' She steps back, further into the darkness. 'You could have been crushed. Don't lecture me on caution, when you need it as much as I do.'

'Need what?' Without realising, he has followed her, moving forward, away from the crowd and into the trees.

She raises a hand to the sky, then smooths her tangled hair. 'Freedom. Risk.'

He laughs, seeing again the open vista, the gleaming horizon line, the skies crossing the Channel, flying to the Mediterranean, and further, the domes of Constantinople. To be in that basket, to be in the sky. To fly. With her.

She walks into the shadows, the hem of her dress rippling behind her. When he follows, she holds out her hand to the night. His palms long to meet her. To touch the skin of the water.

South Australian Coast, October 1836

I lean against the veined rock, its stone face slick with sea spray and spring rain. The mid-afternoon sky is marbled, shot through with clouds and a dark mist rolling over the hinterland. It has poured at intervals all day, the wind whipping the rainfall into diagonals before peeling back the clouds and letting the bright sun through. The mottled light casts its brightness and shade upon the beachside, where the whalers work on the shore and their ship lies at anchor.

Behind me, over the cliff face and the rolling stretch of green, the *Cygnet* is moored with its brood of unruly settlers. The ship arrived overnight, an unwelcome incursion into this valley, this world I have created of the shoreline, the whalers, William and me. I had thought to leave the South Australian Company and its rigours on the island, but now the *Cygnet* sits between this beach of rock and sand and Will's ship, the *Rapid*, at anchor, just moments away.

'Don't wander too far, Miss.'

The first mate from the whaling ship approaches, scrambling over the bronze boulders, squinting against the onslaught of rain and sun.

I shake my head. 'I'm not. I wanted to see the caves. And find my way out of the rain.'

'You have a tent. Or your cabin on the ship.' Moses Widlow moves quickly, his feet gripping the rocks as he ascends. In the shelter of the cave, he pushes the water from his eyes and looks around. 'But it's a good spot here.'

'It is.'

'Still. Don't wander too far.'

'As I recall, I was the one to rescue you from wandering too far in Singapore.'

Moses makes a sound like a laugh and sits at the fore of the cave, positioning himself to watch the whalers work below.

I think of his tall shape moving through the merchants on the Bugis canal, the way that even men known as pirates parted before him. He had no anxiety for me there, or anywhere else in the Indies. 'Please don't tell me that even you have a sailor's terror of being speared by the natives?'

His back stiffens. In the changing light, it's difficult to interpret his expression. He glances at me, the tattoos on his arms even inkier in the rain, blue-black against the richness of his skin. Around his neck, only partly hidden by his collar, his shell necklace glows iridescent in the rain-filled light. First one colour, then another.

'You don't need to worry about that.' He reaches into his satchel and removes a piece of scrimshaw and a knife.

I have never seen his hands idle, even on shore leave. Trading carvings for fruit in Singapore. Spear-fishing in Langkawi. Repairing a woman's roof in Borneo.

Moses brushes old shavings from his carving. 'But this is not an easy country. The terrain is unfamiliar to you. And it's the Straitsmen I worry about.'

The sealers. Convicts and deserters. Men who knew the lash in Van Diemen's Land and turned it on others. I have heard the stories.

On Kangaroo Island, the native women wear seal fur. I've seen them standing on the beach, working on the warm flesh of the dying seals or diving in the shallows, searching for shellfish. The whalers tried to keep the story from me, but I know. I've seen the women waist deep in the frothing water, looking out over the Southern Ocean, toward home. They were taken from their families, against their will, from Van Diemen's Land and the South Australian coast. The Straitsmen and sealers deserted their posts, abducted these women and set up kingdom on Kangaroo Island. There were women, I hear, so eager to escape they tried to swim. Some made it. *Were they selkies?* Others died. A woman who tried to take her half-European baby drowned and was found washed up along the coast. Were we really such a cumbrance to our mothers?

I look up at Moses, thinking of my grandfather's guns lining the walls of his estate in Hertfordshire. 'Those men wouldn't touch me.'

Holding my gaze, he shakes his head, as if to admonish himself, and turns back to the scrimshaw. I can see a form emerging in the carving. A tail, flat like a whale or a dolphin. Or a seal.

'Will you sell that one, too, when it's finished?'

The rain swirls before us, pattering against the rocks and disappearing into the spray.

'It's for my daughter,' Moses says, after a pause.

I blink, remembering the remote lagoons of Lombok and Moses's practised hands guiding me through the water, teaching me to swim. No, not just to swim. For I learned that in England.

One of my grandfather's unique ideas on education: logic, the arts, and physical activity. But Moses taught me to ride the water, to merge with it, make it my friend. All during the voyage from Calcutta, he was my guide in wild places – the sailing ports of Malaya, the volcanoes of Java, the day we tracked a Sumatran tiger. And he never told me he has a child.

'Is she back where you come from?' I ask. 'In New Zealand?'

He does not reply, instead leaning forward and sculpting the shape of the bone with precise movements. I can see the emergence of grooves along the flippers. The tail must belong to a seal.

'Do you know what some of them did here, these Straitsmen?' he says.

'I've heard some stories. I saw the women, on Kangaroo Island.'

'Karta. The Island of the Dead.'

'Yes.'

He continues to carve. 'They would raid the coastline. Here, and on Van Diemen's Land. Looking for women to take.'

I don't reply, sensing where this is heading, a warning of male brutality, as if I didn't already know. I think of my mother's disappearance, her face without a name.

Moses continues to speak. 'In one case, they found a Kaurna woman with a child by a river not far from where we sit. They took the woman and abandoned the child – left it alone, right by the water. That child was lucky. Do you know why I say that?'

I shake my head. Something has shifted between us. A gulf has appeared that was not there before. Wondering if I am being patronised, I watch Moses's face. It is contemplative, focused only on the intricacy of his carving.

'When the woman gave birth to another baby on Karta after a year, they took it to the sea and drowned it.'

I feel my muscles twitching, the skin creeping across my back. I think of Will's words, my uncle's anger. Walter Fraser's control. Gulls arcing through the white sky of Canterbury. 'How do you know this?'

Moses's knife continues to scrape. 'The woman changed hands. Many times. Eventually, she was bought by a whaling crew member. A sailor, from America.' He pauses, looking up. 'I heard she was bartered for a bag of flour. But at least when they had a child, he did not murder it. And that child grew up to be my wife.'

'I didn't know.' My words drift slowly through the cave, the grey waves moving below us, at the shore.

Moses inclines his head. 'There are other stories, too. Stories from Van Diemen's Land, on the Tasman Peninsula not far from Port Arthur.'

The name of the penal colony swirls in travellers' lore. An inescapable fortress, a convict's final nightmare. I am silent. I have no wish to venture there, to be part of the echo of the lash, the shark-infested waters, the gloom that drives sane men to seek the hangman's noose. I have no wish to think upon its older, deeper cruelties. The wave of death leashed upon the land, its people murdered on Furneaux Island. Decimated.

Moses continues. 'A young woman was diving for shellfish. When the sealers came to take her, her husband tried to stop them. They cut off his limbs and left him to die in the tide. When she gave birth to a son, they did not drown him, but they lashed her every time she tried to escape. And she tried. Many times. Eventually, she drowned trying to make the crossing back to the mainland.'

'I have heard such stories,' I say.

There is an assessing expression on Moses's face, as his hand moves to touch the shells at his neck. 'Her son was my father. This necklace was hers.' He drops his hand back to the carving. 'It's customary, where she came from, for the women to make these. For generation after generation to wade into the waters where the mutton birds fly and harvest the shells from the kelp. But she is not here to teach my daughter these practices.'

I watch his face. His eyes rest on the scrimshaw. On the voyage from Calcutta, he told me of his mother's people and the Māori significance of his tattoos, of his life on the sea. He said nothing of this heritage from Van Diemen's Land.

He turns back to me. 'The men don't know. No one does. Only the Captain. He was shipmates with my father.'

'I don't understand. What don't they know?'

'That my father was from Van Diemen's Land.'

'Why not? There is no shame in it. The only shame is in what was done to him, done to his mother.'

He laughs. 'Those men don't know shame.' He rests the scrimshaw in his hands. I can see, somehow, beyond the seal, the emerging shape of a woman. His fingers are tight on the hilt of the knife. 'There is a bounty on my people in Van Diemen's Land. Five pounds for a man, two pounds for a child. Living or dead.'

I close my eyes against the image of children's corpses laid out for money.

'When we go there for trade or for whaling, the Captain tells them I'm Māori. That I will eat them if they get too close. And they believe him. He does not tell them that I am also Aboriginal and that my people are from the island. I do not look much like my father. But that doesn't mean I don't feel it when I'm there. What they are doing to my country.'

I think of India then. Calcutta riven into white town, and black.

The thousands of indentured labourers, shuttled onto ships bound for sugar plantations across the seas. A fertile, verdant country gripped by famine.

'Your wife and daughter live here when you are away?'

Moses nods.

'Does that not trouble you?'

'Of course it does. But this is her country. And where else would she go? One day, I'll get a captaincy, and maybe she will sail with me. She and Judith. But until then, she won't leave her home. At least now, we have money. I'm the first mate, and my wife is clever. She learned what she could from the sealers, and she sells those skills for herself now. And that's power in this world, isn't it? Your world. Money.'

'My world. It is hardly that.'

'Maybe not. But it's how you got here. How you travel the world in safety like you do. Money.'

I look away from him. He sounds, for one uncanny moment, like my uncle, lying on his final sickbed, signing papers and hectoring his lawyer on the need for a separate estate. That all my inheritance would be for my sole use, and the heirs of my body. Even then, he feared it would not be enough to protect me. Money, and English law.

'Why have you told me all of this if not even your crewmates know?'

At first, he doesn't respond. Around us, the roaring sound of the rain hits water, and beyond that is the crash of the waves. 'We've been friends in our way, haven't we? You and I,' he says eventually.

I smile. 'Yes.'

'You are not like the others. Not like the usual English lady.'

'No.'

'And you are seeking something. Always searching.'

I look down at my hands.

'Part of yourself,' he says.

I nod. 'Perhaps.'

He turns the scrimshaw carving in his hands. 'You need to know what happens in this place, if you intend to stay. You need to know its history. And don't be fooled about the prospects–'

'I do not intend to stay here.' My words trip over themselves. The thought of an unnerving future, cast off here, at the end of the world, causes my chest to contract.

Moses's gaze is level as his brows draw together. 'Are you going to see the Colonel again?'

Will's presence is a ghost flickering in the darkness of the cave. There is much I have not told Moses. As much, it seems, as he has not told me. But he has gleaned the essence of the matter. I am gripped, then, by a need to unburden myself. A need to talk of my knotted past, of the uncertainty in my future, to someone other than Will. I open my mouth to speak as a shout rises from the beach.

The rain has intensified, turning the white sand slick and dark, the inky clouds blotting out the sun. Lightning flickers over the ocean, casting its spindled crackle over the waves. A party of men carrying muskets walks toward the whalers on the shore.

Moses pockets the scrimshaw carving and sheathes his blade. 'Wait here.'

I am startled by his brusqueness. His face is set, and he frowns as he stands.

Down at the beach, pale hair and faces are streaked by rain. Clean-shaven. Not sealers, then. Settlers. I blink against the heavy sheet of rain. Are they men from the *Rapid*? Or others? Thinking of the *Cygnet*, lurking behind me, I leave the safety of the cave and follow Moses's quick steps over the rocks.

~

Light leans forward, adjusting the telescope of his theodolite. The cold brass grows warm in his hand. Ever since he learned of the great trigonometric survey of India, he has relished this feeling: the sense of the stiff mechanics unbending, the apparatus coming to life, one smooth extension of his vision. When he peers through the lens, the rain-covered new world stares back, its image inverted, as though amused by his displacement, the earth turned upside down. Around him, the canvas shelter buckles in the wind. The drumming of the rain increases. He steps back from the tripod and holds the canvas firm, looking out to the coast. Lightning fingers across the skyline, crackling on the surface of the waves.

'Jacobs,' he calls to his assistant over the sound of the rain. 'We can't work in the storm. Help me pack up.'

Jacobs grips the canvas, holding it tight against the wind. Light's hands move quickly, dismantling the theodolite and packing it in its cedar case. He tries not to think of the cost of this delay. Their journey from England was so swift and uneventful that Light has allowed himself some small measure of optimism, a brief belief that their delayed departure did not mean all was lost. The *Rapid* outstripped ships that left long before them, arriving with a small crew and a simple task. Survey the land. Judge the quality of the soil. Build a relationship with the natives. Plan a city.

Light collapses the tripod. In the distance, his surveying party is sheltering the equipment. He counts the men. Someone is missing.

'Where is Hewitt?'

Jacobs blinks at him. 'He's with Mr Stephens. From the *Cygnet*.'

'Whatever for?'

'Hewitt said there was some trouble with the whaling ship.'

He sees again her bare feet, the flag of her hair. Her face at the close of night. Her refusal.

'What sort of trouble?' Light speaks after a pause.

'Trouble around them being here, near the South Australian Company. He didn't tell me anything more. He said you would know.'

Light says nothing. So, Hewitt lies. He sheaves his logbook and journal and closes his pack. Jacobs needn't know of his confusion. He looks up, speaking above the wind.

'Stay here with the others. Have the gear put away. I'll head over to the *Cygnet* now.'

Light secures the straps of his pack and swings it onto his shoulders, adjusting his coat against the rain. Ever since the *Cygnet*'s arrival, he has felt something change in a number of his men. The carpenter and the blacksmith returned to the *Rapid* late in the morning, soaked through with liquor, following hours in the company of the *Cygnet*'s crew. And now Hewitt is on some mad caper to confront the Yankee whaler.

Five men accompany Light; the others remain with the surveying equipment. He looks out to the ocean, where he can see the *Cygnet* at anchor, her hull swaying in the roll of the waves.

He walks on, wanting to reach the whaling ship quickly. If he can head off the *Cygnet*'s party, all the better. And if he can't, well, he would not be late.

The mast and sail of the *Port au Prince* rise behind the cliff side. Below them, on the rain-beaten sand, Light can see them. The crowded figures of the *Cygnet*'s passengers, straining toward the whaling crew. And then there is Clarissa, face obscured in the faltering light, her hair lashed to her back, laden with water. His body rushes down the hillside.

~

The first mate is faster than I am. His feet are sure on the shifting surface of the land, swaying over the boulders and the pebbled shore. Despite my pursuit, his figure shrinks into the distance. My feet slip in their too-large boots as I clamber over the boulders. The waves froth in and slide out from under me, tossing me into the foam. I draw myself up, coughing, and stagger on.

Moses reaches the party on the shore, his hands moving as he gestures in the deepening gloom. I see the settlers flinch at his approach. He looms over them, but they are armed and tense, lean and pale in the changing light.

Their voices drift over to me as I approach, their more uniform accents mingled with the varied cadence of the whaling crew.

'He's the first mate.' The boatsteerer looks askance at the small man in the pale coat. 'If you have a message for the captain, you can give it to him.'

The man's thinning hair is slick across his mottled forehead in the rain. He looks up at Moses and clears his throat. 'My name is Mr Hays,' he says. 'And I am afraid – well, you see, Mr Stephens was quite clear. The letter is for the captain. We wish to speak with him directly.'

Moses holds out his hand. 'Captain Jackson has authorised me to deal with matters on shore. Let me see your letter and then we will determine if you need an audience with the captain.'

There is a ripple of confusion among the settlers. This is not how they expect the meeting to go. A blond man on Hays's right mutters and shakes his head. I can see the bright start of confusion on the settlers' faces. Some look too long, some look away. The blond man stares.

Hays hesitates, holding out the letter. 'You will see,' he says, 'it is addressed to the captain of the *Port au Prince*. Perhaps you can't read, but–'

Moses breaks the seal and opens the letter in one clean movement. Hays flinches at the sound of splitting wax.

'He's the first mate,' the boatsteerer says, again, the West Indian strains of his accent deepening with irritation. 'Of course he can read.'

'What does it say, Mr Widlow?' another whaler speaks, and I hear the docks of Liverpool.

Moses laughs, his eyes flicking up to the settlers. 'You find our business here as an American whaler injurious to your enterprise?'

Hays breathes in. 'It is not my personal feeling about the matter.'

Moses shakes his head. 'We received permission to hunt here from New South Wales. As we do every year.'

'Ah.' Something like relief flickers over Hays's small face, and his eyes narrow against the rain. 'But you see, this land is no longer under the jurisdiction of New South Wales. It is the property of the South Australian Company.'

For a moment, Moses does not reply. He watches the man with a closed expression. 'This is not your property.'

'Now, perhaps,' Hays strains to speak above the wind, 'we can resolve this matter quickly. You agree that your ship will move on?'

'We will move on when we finish our work.' Moses glances at me. 'All of it.'

The settlers murmur, and the blond man turns to his companion. The musket shudders on his shoulder. 'Are you going to let him speak to you like that?'

The boatsteerer steps forward, one hand on his belt. I watch as the settlers' eyes flick to the flintlock pistol at his waist. His voice deepens as he speaks. 'You heard what Mr Widlow said.'

The whaling crew press close, the carpenter reaching out and drawing me into their party. The crewmen gather around me. I bring them luck, they've told me. A profitable voyage bathed in blubber, spices, trade, from Calcutta to the southern edge of the world.

Hays raises his hands as the settlers around him move toward the whalers. 'Peaceably, gentlemen! We must deal with this peaceably.'

I feel a tug of sympathy then, for his pinioning between two factions. But I have seen those soft hands raised before, that thinning hair and harried brow. In every middle-ranked official in India who saw injustice and let it be done with only a bleated protest. Weakness. My stomach curls against him. I look at the boatsteerer, at the crewmen. Their feet scuff the sand, their bodies humming with unspent energy.

The small man gazes past me. His mouth opens against the softening rain, his face wide and bright. 'It's the colonel.' The relief is thick in his voice.

~

They turn to him as he approaches. Light studies the lift of Hays's face, the frown of the tall Polynesian whaler, Clarissa's form tucked among the whaling crew, staring back at him. Movement flickers at the edge of his vision and he sees Hewitt, the young man's musket trembling on his shoulder.

'What is the matter here?' He is struck, when he speaks, by the tiredness in his own voice.

Hays steps forward, his hands moving in small, quick motions. 'Colonel, please can you explain–'

Men call out in unison, their voices tumbling over themselves. The whalers sense a shift in power, leaning toward him to make their voices heard.

Words jump out at him. Letter. South Australian Company. The first mate. Ridiculous. Savages.

He glances once more at the tall whaler. He has seen him before. A silhouette by the fire. 'Mr Widlow.'

The first mate looks back at him, frowning.

'May I see that letter?'

Moses Widlow's fingers curl tighter over the paper. His eyes slide to Clarissa, then back to Light, before he hands the letter over.

Light scans the words. 'What is this, Mr Hays?'

'There is a dispute about fishery rights, Colonel. The commissioner sent me. It was intended to be an amiable meeting–'

Hewitt kicks at the sand. 'We did not think we'd have to talk to baboons.'

'Enough of that, Hewitt.' Light's voice is sharp. He watches Hewitt flinch, a red flush blooming over the young man's face, before he steps back among the other settlers.

Light will need to address this later. Find out where it is coming from. How quickly some men become undone by strangeness.

He turns to Moses. 'Now, Mr Widlow. I believe this matter would be best resolved if we spoke to your captain. Perhaps you could accompany us?'

Moses hesitates, watching the men of the *Cygnet*.

'Just Mr Hays and I,' Light says. 'The others will return to their ships.' He stares at the men, who drop their eyes, deflated.

The first mate nods. 'All right.'

Light watches as Moses's eyes turn to Clarissa.

'Remember what I told you,' the first mate says.

She doesn't reply, appearing small and wan in the grey light. Younger too. Less otherworldly. A drenched fairy, devoid of her enchantment.

Light pauses as he passes her. Behind him, he senses the eyes of every man on the beach upon them.

'Will you be all right here?'

She nods but does not smile.

Aware of the weight of unsaid words between them, he places his hand on her rain-soaked arm. He wants to offer her something, but his clothes are drenched through.

'I'll come to see you tonight,' he says, more quietly.

She studies his face. 'Yes.'

He smiles then, despite himself, and releases her arm. Together with Hays and Moses, he walks across the beach in the direction of the whaler.

Vauxhall Gardens, London, May 1822

They move through the densely wooded path, like the silhouettes of theatre puppets from the wayang kulit of his childhood in Penang: two wayward strangers shadow-playing a story not of their making.

Her hand sits in the crook of his arm, their skin touching. There is nothing remarkable about this. It is what he would do for his former guardian, Mrs Doughty, or his sister Sarah. And yet, as they walk, the night shrinks from its expansiveness, narrowing down in its intensity until the whole evening seems to reside in Clarissa's five fingers and the bend in his elbow.

He looks down at her. Before he can speak, she releases him, striding forward as the trees thin and separate. In the distance there are rustles, a laugh. Footsteps hurry away from them, and Light is pulled back to the moment and the precarious nature of his social decision.

The grotto opens before them. He calls to Clarissa, but she slips away from him, moving into the lamplit grove, trailing her fingers in the water fountain. She turns, laughing, flicking droplets of water toward his eyes, blinding him as he seeks out the lines and contours of her face.

Protesting, he moves toward her and catches her hand. 'Let me look at you in the light.'

Her laughter fades and her eyes turn watchful. She stands under the lamp by the statue of Amphitrite and lifts her jaw, staring back at him. Her skin shimmers. Like a sand belt, fine and dry in the moonlight, like a sand belt coated in ocean spray in the midday sun. He raises his fingers to the side of her face, tracing her jaw, the curve of her neck. When he reaches her, he places his hand down slowly. The pads of his fingertips on her shoulder, the palm of his hand on the flesh beneath her collarbone, his thumb resting against the mid-point of her clavicle. It is just as he imagined. Water on water.

They stand in silence, the strains of distant revelry muted by the trees, the fountain murmuring.

Her gaze moves over him. 'Have you seen many faces like mine?'

He shakes his head.

'Not even in the East Indies?'

He blinks. He knew it, of course. As it seems she knew it of him. But he expected something else. A slow circling of awareness, a tacit acknowledgement. Not this bluntness.

'How did you know?'

She raises both hands, her fingers sliding down his jaw, across the collar of his coat. 'I can see it in your face.' Dropping her hands, she steps back, out of his reach. 'And I have heard of you.' She returns to the water flowing out of the grotto.

He follows her. 'Heard of me?'

'War hero. Governor's son. East Indies prince.'

'Not everything is to be believed.'

She laughs. 'But your mother is Malayan. And you were born there, on Prince of Wales Island.'

'In a fashion. I was born in the province of Kedah, but I was raised in Suffolk, among my father's people.' He does not speak of his mother's layered ancestry. The Chinese grandfather and Siamese grandmother. The Malayan mother. The Portuguese ancestor. Granddaughter of the Sultan of Kedah. Descendant of Alexander the Great.

The woman before him is more astute and fearless than he expected. But what should he have expected, from a woman who falls from the sky, who walks in darkness in Vauxhall Gardens? He looks at her and lets her see him looking.

She drops her gaze, but does not walk away.

'And your parents?'

'Do you not know?'

He shakes his head. 'Should I?'

'It's all very mysterious. I'm surprised you haven't heard about it. Or me. Baronet's granddaughter. Half-Oriental heiress.'

His muscles twitch at the mention of money, thinking of his own shallow pockets, his past of disinheritance, his own loss. 'I haven't heard the story.'

She touches the edge of a low-hanging branch. 'Well. It's not important.'

Silence falls between them. He watches her fingers move over the leaves in the lamplight. A baronet's granddaughter. He'd have to tell her of his meagre prospects. 'What is your family's name? You've only told me Clarissa.'

Her laugh emerges slowly. Out of place. 'It's not important,' she says. 'Tell me more about you.'

'What would you like to know?'

'So many things. All the countries you've been to. The people you've seen. What it was like to fight Napoleon–'

'Hardly a question for a–'

'For a lady?'

'I was going to say for a romantic evening.'

'Is that what this is?'

He doesn't answer. Even without her mention of a title and a fortune, he knows from her movement, her speech, the fabric of her gown, that while they might attend the same events, dance together in a London ballroom, she is above him. She is not someone with whom he should walk alone through the trees of Vauxhall.

She speaks again. 'What is it like to fight in a war?'

'Bloody.'

'Be serious.'

He thinks of musket shot and dead horses. Bodies piled up beneath a waterfall, festering. 'It's not all parades and medals and ribbons. I expect you can imagine the basics. Gunfire and bayonets. I won't tell you the worst of it. But there are other things, too. The value of a piece of bread. The men were always starving. And even the most respected regiments went looting.'

'Even yours?'

'Even mine.'

'What did you take?'

He hesitates. 'A candle. And a clean white shirt.'

She laughs.

'I mean it.'

'Why?'

'Why those things? Or why not more?'

'Both, I suppose.'

He looks back to the water bubbling out of the grotto. 'I wasn't raised to steal things. But I took a candle for writing on sleepless nights. And a white shirt as I thought I'd never be clean again.'

He senses her move next to him, then her hand touches the cuff of his sleeve.

'What do you think now, about clean white shirts?'

'They stain easily. But I still wear them.'

They are strange questions from a lover. Although, he should not think of her as such. She does not ask him what he is thinking, when she will see him again, what he thinks of her, if he finds her beautiful. She does not ask him any of those things, as though she already knows his answers.

Her fingers tighten on his cuff. 'Can you hear that?'

There are rustles in the distance. The sound of footsteps. Voices drift over to them from the direction of the balloon landing.

'Come, it's my cousin.' Clarissa releases his arm.

The sycamore branches sway in the night as she turns from him, her red-clad form swallowed by the gloom.

Above me, the first stars peer through the sycamore boughs. Beneath me, the path is subsumed by murky darkness. I place my feet carefully on the earth. Haven't I dreamed of this? Getting lost in Vauxhall. All those years before my grandfather's death, when my peers went out into the world to be presented, and I stayed in Hertfordshire, away from all entertainment. Where they had balls and dinners and carriage rides in Regent's Park, I had Rousseau and logic. Brisk walks and shooting. I could load and clean a flintlock before I knew how to waltz. There were visits to the Royal Academy, the occasional poetry recital, but for the most part I lived only on snatches of descriptions and second-hand adventures. Vauxhall with its enchanted lights and water music, with its groves of stone goddesses, its performers from America, France, Algeria. All of London society condensed, as in a music box, and placed here, in Vauxhall Gardens.

My grandfather's death has freed me. Guilt tugs at the edges of my skirts. I can hear my uncle's voice: *He has protected you.* But what protection is there in imprisonment? The day after my grandfather's funeral I sat in my neighbour's radical library reading Wollstonecraft and Shelley, concealing it no longer. My brother owned such books and was merely censured. But there was always greater outrage when I was the one to read.

Cheers from a performance drift toward me in the night. Beneath the merriment, I hear the strains of John Parry's music and a woman's voice. I am missing Madame Georgina's performance. I move toward the sound, but it is all around me. No lanterns gleam along the Dark Walk. There is just the weaving path beneath my feet with no beginning, and no end. I stand for a moment. Is this how my grandfather wanted me to be? Disoriented?

I walk slowly, first one way, then another. I am lost, but I am also waiting.

His steps behind me are certain, as though he can see in the dark.

When he touches my elbow, I sense the callouses on his palms. The hands of a gentleman who does something useful with his time. They tell me he paints and writes. I think of those hands around a single taper lighting up the wreckage of war in Portugal. The brightness of a clean white shirt.

'We should move on,' he says. 'This is the most disreputable part of Vauxhall.'

I laugh. 'I'll do my best to protect your reputation.'

He runs a hand across his brow. 'Believe it or not, that is something I'm concerned about. I wouldn't have anyone thinking I'm a fortune hunter. Or a rake.'

Furrows line his forehead, and his lips thin. His back is straight. I try to cover my mouth, but I can't repress it. Laughter gushes out of me. He blinks, startled.

'The look on your face!' I spin further down the dark path. 'Come on, Major Light. I'm leading you astray.'

I see the struggle in his posture, but after a moment his shoulders relax, and his smile flashes white in the dark. 'Don't joke, Clarissa.'

I draw further away, walking backward, until his coat starts to blend with the shadows.

'Clarissa. Come back.' His tone is a blend of laughter and exasperation.

I turn to face the night. The promenade spreads out into the darkness, framed by wych elms. In the distance, the music has changed. *Rule Britannia.* I hear his feet on the path behind me.

'You'll have your way, then, it seems.' He walks in step with me. When I glance at his face, I can see from the creases at his eyes that he is smiling. 'Where would you have us go?'

'Honestly?'

'Is there another way to answer?'

'Oh, always.'

'Well, then, honestly, yes.'

'I'd go away from here.'

'Out of Vauxhall?'

'Out of England. When I was in that balloon, I kept thinking if only we could cut the tether loose and keep flying. To France, Italy. To India.' We have stopped walking. In the distance, the path turns. 'You have been there, haven't you? India?'

He nods. 'And France.'

'I have heard that story. That you were interned during the war and led the escape.'

'Something like that.'

'I envy you. Your life has been so ...'

'Colourful?'

'Free.' I point toward the path. 'Where does that lead?'

'It's the entrance to the hedge maze.'

'Shall we go in?' As I take a step, I feel his hand on the small of my back.

'Wait,' he says. 'There'll be others in there.'

I turn. I can only half see his face in the dark. The slivers of light reflected in his eyes, the narrowing of his expression.

I lean forward. For a moment it seems like he would flinch, or step away, but he remains still. I take his collar between my fingertips, his hand still on my back.

'I wish I had what you had.' The Duke of Wellington's man. Adventures in Spain. A dash across enemy lines. Heroism. Comrades. An identity.

'I don't think you do.'

I place my palm on his chest, curling into him in the dark. 'Why not?'

He doesn't answer. At first, his hand remains on my back. Then it slips to my waist and the other hand slides into the hair at the base of my neck as he leans forward.

I taste claret and saltwater. The dark path dissolves beneath my feet, warm light crackling and flaring in my memory. The white sails of a ship pulled taut in the wind. The heave and fall of the Indian Ocean. Salt spray and the cry of gulls. Freedom.

~

They part with promises. The flare of the lamplight blinds him as they leave the wooded path and make their way toward the supper boxes. Words trip from his mouth, speaking of certainties, charting a terrain of inevitability. She takes his declamations lightly, as though all is her due, as though his words were meaningful.

As they draw closer to the lights of the supper box, he sees the familiar height of Walter Fraser, the thin silhouette of a walking cane.

'Miss FitzRoy!' The tall man's voice is thick with relief, and something like complaint. 'Thank goodness we've found you.'

'Hello, Walter. I'm afraid I got lost. Major Light assisted me.'

Light stops walking. The name takes shape in his memory. 'FitzRoy,' he speaks aloud, without meaning to.

Walter Fraser gives him a hard stare, the warmth from their earlier conversation dissipated. 'Yes,' Fraser says. 'The late Sir Charles FitzRoy's granddaughter. The heiress. As I am sure you well know.'

Fraser's voice is laden with accusation, but Light ignores it. The name rolls around in his memory. He sees an address on an envelope. A neat hand.

Sir Charles FitzRoy. The FitzRoys and India. Calcutta.

A woman in an orange sari runs along a white verandah. He sees again the lattice window, the side streets of Bow Bazaar. He smells stagnant water, scented paper. Failure.

He barely hears them speaking.

Calcutta, August 1806

Light watches as they escort the woman from the garden, the thin silk of her orange sari draped across her face. Now, the house is quiet, the shutters closed, the servants corralled or sent back to their homes. The two children stand apart, silent, held in place by their ayah. The colonel's private secretary watches from the front of the house.

Light peers down at the letter of introduction in his hand. Colonel FitzRoy would be sympathetic, they told him. He had helped others who crossed the colour line negotiate the contoured terrain of inheritance law, and win. The stuff of the man's own marriage to a native woman had been legendary.

But now he is dead, his estate commandeered by his secretary, his widow arrested. The private secretary turns from the crowd on the drive, pulling at a thread at his cuff. FitzRoy may have been sympathetic to him, but Light is not so certain that Percy Whitworth will feel the same.

'Where are they taking her?' He speaks to the captain next to him. The man is not much older than himself, but he looks on the scene before him with eyes that are jaded and shot through with red.

Light notes the man's assessment of his face, his clothes. He passes the test.

'To the courthouse.'

'Isn't Mr Whitworth concerned? About her family, I mean.'

The captain scuffs his left shoe against the dirt. 'You mean her father in Koch Bihar, I suppose. Haven't you heard? Her father died, and her grandfather cut her loose.'

'Why?'

Light doesn't need the man's answer, but he waits for it anyway. The familiar words of disapproval, dishonour, and betrayal course out of the officer's mouth.

'But what about her mother's people?'

The captain frowns. 'Who are they?' He keeps speaking without waiting for Light's response. 'They say she killed him, you know.'

'What?'

'Apparently, he might have been smothered in his sleep. And she was having an affair.'

'With whom?'

A wail erupts from the garden. The youngest child runs toward the woman in a blur of fuchsia skirts, her arms stretched out. The ayah lunges toward her, grasping at the girl's dress, her arm, her hair. She misses, her fingers closing in on emptiness. The woman turns back, the thin tangerine cloth falling from her face. He sees the kohl-rimmed eyes, long and turned up slightly at the corners, the ink running in wetness across her face. The woman shakes off her escorts, scooping up the child in one quick movement, the dark expanse of her hair falling across the girl's body.

Light steps back. He has never liked goodbyes. The air grows full with the sound of weeping. He has seen the urgency on the woman's face before, in the eyes of his own mother. But that parting was different. His father still lived, and their home was intact. They were all, as it turned out, borrowing days, but as a child Light had not been there to witness this final disintegration.

He wants to leave, to pass through the iron gate and the shade of Bengal clock vine. He might return to his sister's new house and ask career advice from her kindly husband. She warned him not to come here, not to pursue the futile task of retrieving his inheritance. He was angry with her. *Some things are easier for women*, he said.

Male voices fill the garden. The sergeant speaks softly, 'Come on, madam, come on, miss.' Two privates hold back the Indian guard, not meeting each other's eyes. The woman speaks – *I'll take her with me* – but the sergeant glances at the captain and looks away, crimson burnishing his cheeks, shaking his head. He reaches forward, placing his hands around the child's waist and tugging gently. The child screams, her hands forming two fists and striking the sergeant on the jaw. The woman wails. Beyond the gates, a distant chorus courses through the city. The sound of crowds, of discontent.

The captain runs his hand across his sweat-stained brow. 'Good Lord. These people.' He gestures to the ayah. 'You. Get that child back. And you,' his finger lands on the flushed sergeant, 'take that woman away. Tout-suite, Sergeant, tout-suite.'

Light flinches at the mispronunciation. When the captain grins at him, Light wants to raise his hands in repudiation, to say *I am not like you at all. Not at all.* But instead, he only smiles weakly as the soldiers usher the woman to the gate and the ayah carries her shrieking daughter away.

A tall man in a bright white uniform strides over the grass from the house. He bows to Light, never losing his expression of careful assessment. 'I heard you had an appointment with the colonel, sir. Mr Whitworth will see you now.'

Light reads the letter of introduction in his hand. He folds it in deliberate movements, each crease a confirmation, a slow collapsing in on himself. 'No. Never mind. This was a mistake.'

South Australian Coast, October 1836

The rain clears as swiftly as it started, dark clouds fraying and splitting at the edges. When he leaves the *Port au Prince* the sunlight strikes him, disorientating in its intensity. The seawater, chilled and cobalt, drags at his trousers as he wades onto the shore, balancing his pack and equipment, straining to keep them dry.

He tries to find her as he walks, seeking her out on the shoreline. The crew of the *Cygnet* has gone, as he had ordered, and the whalers are dispersed, watching him from a distance. He searches for her hair, turned to pitch by the rain, for her body in a man's outfit, for those ungainly boots hiding her feet. But she is nowhere.

It pricks at him. This absence. He hadn't meant to speak to her as he did, in front of everyone, least of all in front of the crew from the *Cygnet*. But he needs to see her again. He needs an explanation, a resolution, something. She'd been elusive all day after rejecting him the night before. Surely she had not come all the way from England just to do that.

He ought not to think about it. His team from the *Rapid* are waiting for him. He removes his damp scarf and reties it, awakening the dry rasp behind his sternum. This fickle weather will be the end of him.

He ought not to think about that, either. He has no time for illness. No time for the budding weakness in his chest, for the same delays that meant he couldn't set sail for months in England. He had meant to arrive before the settlers. Meant to have been here and mapped and charted every inch of territory, discovered its features and terrain, the best harbours and rivers and plains. How could he survey the land, how could he design and plan a city, with scores of merchants, bourgeoisie and penniless intellectuals already chafing to stake the boundaries of their properties? How can he do this while mediating the petty disputes of the South Australian Company, eager to show its teeth, frightened of a few Yankee whalers? He has so little time.

He is grateful for the *Port au Prince*'s captain, a large man with Nantucket morals and Quaker sensibilities. There was no needless bravado from him. Even Mr Hays had been reassured. The whaler did not intend to stay. But when Light tried to glean more of the ship's detailed plans (how long, exactly, would they be in South Australia? and were they here just at Clarissa's bidding?), the captain looked at him with an unnerving gaze. *The lady's business is her own*, the man said. And Light had been no wiser to her plans or decisions, to the time he might still have with her.

He strides quickly, ascending the grassy hillside toward the camp of the *Rapid*. It is too late for further surveying. Time to work, perhaps, on his charts. There have been no maps of the region since Matthew Flinders. He will change that. He must. Just as he must find a source of fresh water if this burgeoning settlement is ever to survive. For he can feel it already. The heat of this place. A taste of the summers to come, like something out of Naples or Crete or Alexandria.

He pauses on the hillside. He can see the tents set up by the whaling ship. Hers is the largest among them, set higher and further along the rise, away from the others. The white canvas flap is drawn. Is she there? The wind rattles the tent walls; the structure quivers.

He starts to walk again. It won't be long before he returns to her. But for now, he must use the daylight.

Suffolk, June 1822

'Tell me, does anyone not love you?'

I look back from where I stand, my heels sinking into the soft earth of the hillside. Above me, the arched windows of Leiston Abbey open up into a cathedral of sky.

I laugh. It is difficult to say the words. That love is a currency. To be liked as a woman is to be part way to safety. To be loved is to survive. 'I wouldn't say that everyone loves me.'

Will stands among the ruins, his feet buried in the long grass. Just a few hundred years ago, the place was the centre of the presbytery. Now, the racing clouds are the structure's only vaults and livestock take shelter in the Lady Chapel.

It is not difficult to imagine: the waft of frankincense and myrrh, the waving candlelight on the gold chalice and the host. The butchery of the Dissolution. I have a sympathy for Catholicism that I nurture in private. My mother too had marked ritual with flame and scent and colour.

'You made an impression on Mrs Doughty and George. He looked positively jealous.'

I smile, remembering how the old lady's face lit up as I entered Will's childhood home. 'Does that please you?'

'A little. Is that terrible? We get along well enough these days, but I think he resented me when I was a child.'

'Because his mother adores you so much? Or because you're so much more talented and interesting?'

A smile flits across his face. 'Something like that. Yes.'

'Major Light, I do believe you are blushing.'

'There's no way you could possibly tell. Not with my complexion.'

The long grass sinks underfoot. The morning was inundated by a summer downpour, leaving the earth damp and soft. Now, sunlight frames the contours of the Abbey against the clouds, rendering the landscape shaded with light and dark, like something out of Constable's six-footers at the Royal Academy.

'Is that why you left? Because you weren't close to Mr Doughty?'

He inclines his head and drops his gaze, causing me to wonder if there was some deeper sadness.

'I wouldn't say that, exactly.' Will looks across the open fields and ancient woodlands, toward the sea. 'Old Mrs Doughty has been very good to me. After my father died, there was some money for my upbringing, but it didn't go very far. Even George allowed that I was always welcome here. It's probably the only place I've ever felt like I belonged.'

'Suffolk?'

'Theberton and the village. And yes, I suppose Suffolk. The coast. This is the only place where no one has ever questioned me. They knew I was Captain Light's son, born in the East Indies, but I was still from here, all the same.'

'It is beautiful. So much wilder than Hertfordshire. But if you love it so much, why did you leave?'

'I couldn't live on borrowed resources forever. Theberton feels like home, but the estate was never mine. And it never will be.'

A corner of his mouth turns up. 'I had to make something for myself and make something of myself.'

'So, the army.'

'Seemed the best way of doing that, yes.'

'And what of your home in Penang?'

His eyes seem to shutter. 'What of it?'

'Have you ever been back? Is it really so irretrievably gone?'

'When I was in India I ... well. Enough of that. There's nothing to be gained from looking backward.'

'I thought the past is how we make sense of who we really are.'

'You're very sweet.'

'Don't patronise me, William. I mean it. There must be something worth fighting for. What about your mother – have you seen her since you left the East?'

'I saw her once, yes. I saw my home once, too. My father had been dead for a decade and the place had entirely gone to seed. It had been sold off. My mother doesn't live there anymore. She remarried and moved away.'

His face shifts. I step forward and place my hand on his coat. He turns to me, bright and expectant.

'At least you've seen her,' I say. 'I would love to have that feeling. To have that freedom, to pack up and sail to Calcutta to find my mother.'

He takes my hand, not meeting my eyes. 'I think it might be a case of be careful what you wish for.'

South Australian Coast, October 1836

By the time Light reaches his tent, his shirt is dry. He hangs up his coat and stands for a moment with his eyes closed in the afternoon sun. The light is warm. He curls and uncurls his hands. He tells no one this, but he knows home for him will always be a warm country. But, of course, he has no home.

He returns to the interior of the tent. No home. How different that was to what his father wanted and worked for. All those years developing Pulau Penang into Prince of Wales Island, felling trees and clearing land to build George Town. He heard stories of his father's small landing party arriving on the island's gleaming shores. How quickly it progressed from a fishermen's outpost to a settlement with roads, rice paddies and spice plantations, his father's house and gardens, the stone fort overlooking the sea. And his father did it all properly. At least for a time. At least to the best of his knowledge. He was there with the permission of the Sultan of Kedah. He had a scrupulous mastery of Malay. He allowed the Malays and the Chinese and the settlers from Siam to manage their own communities. Like equals.

Light moves to the centre of the tent and considers the partial map on the table. He could do this from the ship, but it helps, at times, to be on land. Some things require stability. He is not so different to his father: always at sea, always seeking a port.

But in some ways, he is different. He sits and opens his logbook and journal. His father was the master of his own destiny. Francis Light sought out Penang and advocated for it. He balanced the demands of the British Government, the East India Company, the Sultan of Kedah, and was made governor and commander, while Light, his firstborn son, is only the master of maps.

Of course, that was only part of the story. His father's initiative, his father's settlement, the sultan's permission. In other stories, it was his mother. Granddaughter of the Sultan of Kedah. The red-gowned Catholic Nyonya from Junk Ceylon, who spoke Malay and Portuguese, and still left incense at the shrines to Ma Cho Po. She had gone to Francis as an emissary and negotiated their settlement of Penang. Where would Francis Light have been without this multilingual lady, who had her feet in all the Southeast Asian camps? Not that her abilities and connections saved her, in the end. Her daughters were sent to India. The Company claimed the island. Fairlie claimed the wealth. The jungle took the rest. And Light had done nothing about it.

He shakes his head. It wasn't the way it was supposed to go. He still feels that. A smarting ache, a gash upon his side that has been bandaged and stitched but still won't heal. One more node in his knotted cord of missed opportunities. How is it that he, a surveyor, has had such an inaccurate life?

'Sir?' A shadow falls across the entrance of the tent.

Light finds Jacobs standing, framed by sky. 'What is it, Jacobs?'

'It's Mr Stephens from the *Cygnet*, sir. He sends word that he'd like to meet with you about the governor.'

Frowning, Light's finger traces a point in his logbook. Something isn't right in his records. 'What about the governor?'

Jacobs shakes his head. 'I don't know, sir. Mr Stephens only said he's available this afternoon.' The young man fiddles with the flap of the tent.

Light exhales. What would he have to manage now? He nods at Jacobs. 'Very well. I'll see to it later today.'

He watches as the younger man leaves, disappearing into the glare. From what Light has heard, the governor's journey has been slow, and he is not expected to arrive for several months. Light weighs his feelings, wishing the governor were delayed indefinitely.

For Hindmarsh is governor. Hindmarsh, the man Light knew in Egypt. The bluff, friendly, duplicitous sailor who took advantage of Light's connections. Another of Light's missteps, his inaccuracies. Napier had been everyone's first choice, with his status and charisma, his idealism. Light would have been proud to serve under him. But Napier was not in need of opportunities. He had turned the offer down, and in doing so he'd recommended Light as his replacement. Light as governor.

He still remembers that hot, still evening in Egypt. Drinking whisky with Hindmarsh on his ship docked on the Nile, the silhouette of palm trees leaning over them, the ribbed shape of the river crocodiles rippling the surface of the water. Together they had reminisced about Napoleon – a time when life had purpose, when they were more gilded men in favour with the great names of the age. Light with the Duke of Wellington, Hindmarsh with Lord Nelson. And Hindmarsh had bemoaned his reduced circumstances, his lack of opportunities, the half-pay life of an officer, the dullness of working in service of the Egyptian Pasha.

Light, in a moment of magnanimity, wrote Hindmarsh a letter. An introduction to Napier, and numerous other friends. He'd felt lofty, in that moment. Pleased that he'd been able to be so gracious.

He learned the full story later. That Napier had turned down the governorship and mentioned his refusal to Hindmarsh, newly returned to England from Egypt. That Napier had written to the South Australian Company to recommend Light for the position. But that Hindmarsh, upon hearing of the vacancy, had beaten Napier to it, triumphantly offering up his own name and services, and wrangling an acceptance before Napier's letter even arrived.

An inaccurate life. What would the enterprising Francis Light have to say about that?

Light rubs his jaw. He still has time. Not much of it, that's true, but still some. He can make something of this place, and make it properly. He examines his entries from the morning. He has doubts about one measurement. One cathetus of the triangle covering the hinterland. He runs his finger over his unfinished map. Ambiguity won't do. Of this landscape and this fragile city of his mind, he must be certain. No room now for inaccuracy, uncertainty, for being weak in his position. He will build something modern, precise, a city of innovation. He will redo this measurement. And then he will see Mr Stephens.

Light picks up his case and pack. A harbour, good soil quality, fresh water. Dialogue with the natives. A city plan. These are the things he must focus on. He steps out of the tent and into the glare.

South Australian Coast, October 1836

I stand on the hillside. The restless weather of the day has given way to a still night.

I sense his approach before I see him. My eyes search for him in the darkness as his shadow moves up the hillside. I recognise his slight limp, his uncertainty. Is he so changed from before? I cannot tell. His body moves with more weakness and yet he inhabits the world with more authority. Men listen to him, here. His word means something.

In the distance behind him, campfires adorn the coast. They are fires from the whale ship, the *Cygnet*, the *Rapid*. The settlement encroaches. I think of Moses's words and anger. This is not their country. And yet I cannot help but feel the land is being riven and carved up around us. Under the harpooneer's gun and the sealer's club, the settlers' axe. The surveyor's map.

He calls out as he approaches. Further inland, away from the settlement, orange strips line the horizon. Where last night's flames cast tiger stripes into the sky, the glow now is muted, disgruntled.

'The fires are back.' I speak as he reaches out toward me.

He drops his arm and turns his gaze to the southeast. 'Yes. Nothing to worry about at that size, or at this distance.'

'I'm surprised by the flames. After all that rain.'

'I've noticed the land dries out quickly. But the people here know what they're doing.'

I look back at him. His profile is touched with a faint orange glow.

'I'm sure they do. Perhaps they want to burn us all out.'

His face is blank. 'Why would they want to do that?'

I think of the seals bleeding into the white shoreline, the hands of the whalers peeling back their pelts, calling to the Scottish cook with laughter. *No souls of women here.* I think of Moses's story.

Of course, Will. Why would they want to burn us out?

'You know what happened, don't you? To the Kaurna and the Ramindjeri, and on Van Diemen's Land. What the men on Kangaroo Island did.'

He flinches. 'Those men were criminals. Deserters and convicts and murderers. Nothing like the men and women who have migrated here.'

For a moment, I don't speak. I think of the riven streets of Calcutta, of the indentured workers docking in Singapore. Of the sugar and cotton I boycotted as a younger woman. 'Are you certain about that, Will?'

'Of course I am. Of course I am. I wouldn't be here ... I wouldn't be here with a band of brigands.'

'What about hypocrites?'

'Clarissa, there are Letters Patent. The Colonial Office refused permission to the venture until it was made clear that the rights of the Aboriginal natives would be respected. They wanted to avoid the very situations in Van Diemen's Land that you talk about.'

I don't speak.

'And it is just this sort of authority that will prevent the types of actions there have been on Kangaroo Island. There won't be any more coastal raids or virtual slavery. Not in a colony run as an ordered and progressive society. You must remember, this isn't a penal settlement. It's not like New South Wales or Van Diemen's Land. It's a place founded on ideals.'

'Do you honestly believe that?'

'Yes.' His voice is emphatic in the dark. 'I have to,' he says more quietly, looking at the walls of my tent staked into the ground. 'Why don't we go inside?' He touches my forearm. 'You feel cold, Clarissa.'

I nod. The earth still feels warm from the afternoon sun, but the air is chilled. I open the flap of the tent. 'Come in.'

The candle still burns within the lantern on the table. Will closes the flap of the tent behind him, and the world is sealed out.

He sits as I pour amber-coloured brandy into glasses. As he rises to help me, I wave him away. 'What about the East India Company?'

There is a silence. Then, 'What about it?'

'Did that behave with all the values of your fellow settlers?'

He shifts in his seat, tapping his fingers on his armrest. 'No. But those were different times. And it's an organisation rife with corruption.'

'My fiancé is in the East India Company.'

'So I've heard. The most recent one, anyway.'

I laugh. 'Are you sure that's a direction you wish to pursue?'

He says nothing. I think of an early promise, and that ugly term, breach of contract. It's been fourteen years. I let it go. For now.

'Besides,' I say. 'Didn't you want to join the East India Company, once?'

He makes a sound. I can hear the thin whistle of his breath in the quiet. 'You know I did. And you know why I couldn't.'

'Because no person who is not descended from European parents on both sides can serve in the army, except as a bandsman or a drummer. Presumably, they think Eurasians have better musical talent.'

'You'll find your future husband's superiors may not approve of his choice of bride. And you certainly won't get a pension from the Company should you ever need it.'

'I'm aware of all the qualities that make me undesirable, William. I simply don't accept that judgement.'

He glances up in a swift movement. 'You're not undesirable.'

'No. I'm rich.' I laugh, but my voice is high and cracked.

'Perhaps you see now,' he says, 'why India will not be your path to happiness.'

I think of the guard's eyes outside my old home in Calcutta, and the fatigued Company official who looked me over and boxed me up. *Half-caste.*

'This isn't about happiness.' The bare walls of the tent buckle in the breeze. I turn my face to the wind slithering through the canvas flap over the entrance.

'I was born in a house the colour of terracotta. They said I came into the world to the sound of bells. They said my brother broke into the room because he was so excited to meet me. Of course, I don't remember. Not really. I remember fragments. Scents. My mother's oud perfume, my father's linen shirts. The incense of offerings. The wolf smell of our dog. Old blood during the Durga Puja. And I can see images. A gecko darting over a cracked ceiling, flicking its tail. My mother's hair. But these things, they don't exist anymore. The house is gone. My parents are dead. The dog is dead. Even the gecko. They still mark the puja and ring the temple bells, but that is not for me. The first thing they did when I arrived in England was christen me.

'What I'm trying to say is ... I'm not looking to go back. I can't go back. The Calcutta I knew isn't there anymore, and the woman who visits the city now isn't the same as the child who was born there. I'm not seeking my happiness in India. I'm not trying to relive the past.'

'Then what are you looking for?'

'Do you really need to ask that question? I have a family I've never met. I know my father died in 1806, but I don't even have a date for my mother's death. Just after I left India, is what my grandfather told me. But when I made enquiries in Calcutta, she was still alive in 1810. Someone said she died in 1818. There are no records that I can find. Every time I tried to approach the Zamindar community, it was a locked door. *Come back with your husband*, they told me. *Send your cousin. Does the East India Company know you're here?*'

I take a sip of brandy. I would prefer water. My lips and tongue are dry from speaking. 'That's how I came to you. One of the families told the Company that I was asking for information. They sent me off to some aging Englishman in an office full of papers. He claimed he had no real record of my mother's story, just a fanciful tale about my parents' marriage written by a French tourist. And a letter from one Mr William Light, mentioning a visit in 1806 to the widow of Colonel FitzRoy.'

His eyes flick up at the mention of his name.

'The man then went on to say perhaps I would be best placed

to ask you for more information. Given that he had heard we were acquainted.'

He makes a sound. Derision? Disgust?

'And so I am here. You may wonder why my family didn't arrange for someone to show me around properly, but they never would have done that. My grandfather terrified them all into never talking about my Indian family. They would have given me some charming guide who did nothing but take me to tourist spots. So, I didn't tell them.'

'And your fiancé?'

'I don't want to ask him for help. Not about this, not yet. I want to know a little more about my own story first. He understands.'

'I see.'

'Do you?'

He doesn't speak.

I meet his eyes. 'Will you help me?'

'Nothing,' he says, 'in what you've told me makes me change my mind. The past is gone. You have so many opportunities. You have a future. I don't see how dredging this up is going to help you.'

That word. *Dredging*. I think of bloated bodies hauled out of the Thames or the canals of East London, old violence bleeding into the present, and I rub my temples.

'You see, William, that's what everyone says. My cousins, my great-aunt, my brother's friends. But I don't understand. It's not as though there was anything shameful about the marriage. She was a Brahmin and a Zamindar. Her mother was from the Koch Bihar court. I know this to be true. This was one fact my grandfather would allow us to know. Tell me if I'm wrong.'

'No. I believe you're right, although it's not unknown for those with Eastern heritage to exaggerate their antecedents.'

'But what is the shame of it? Just a few decades ago, an Englishman would have been proud to have such a wife.'

'We live in different times. A changing world. Things aren't as they were under the Regent. The new generation attend to their morals with puritanical zeal.'

I shake my head. 'It doesn't have to be that way.'

'There are those who believe it is both kinder and more appropriate for the British and the Asians to remain separate.'

'But that doesn't explain why they won't even let me find my mother's relations.'

'Have you ever thought that they don't wish to be found? It's not only the British who disapprove of these unions.' His words are quiet in the dark.

I look away. 'That's a horrible thing to say.'

'I meant what I said before. We live in different times now.'

The candle flame jumps. I think of the small woman in the blue dress, over in the settlement. I see her hard eyes, hear her uncertain voice.

'Where is your wife?' I ask. His eyes flick away from me as the candle flame flares and dims.

'Mary is in Italy, last I heard.'

'Yes, I heard that, too. With three children under your name.'

His eyebrows crease. 'They are not mine.'

'No. But they are named Light. Ironic, isn't it.'

I close my eyes as he asks me my point. I see a Paris dinner by candlelight. I see Rome. I see a small window, framed by white, looking over the bay at Whitstable.

Gulls circle, crying, white against the ghostly sky. Pain. The bells of Canterbury toll. Around me, the world flickers. The sound of the bell vibrates through the air, singing a song of payment, of sin.

After Bath fourteen years ago, we went to the Continent, leaving London by night like thieves or lovers who had not made up their minds. We took the ferry to Calais and as the inky waves moved in the darkness I thought, for the first time in many years, of that original voyage through the Indian Ocean. It seemed the turning points of my life were to be determined by this: a passage, a crossing, the space between two countries, the water moving beneath me, helping me pass. Pass through.

I was sick after half an hour, the wood of the deck falling free, switching my stomach with my ears until the rolling waves cast us back into the air, setting my body parts to rights again. He rubbed my back as I vomited, turned inside out, and I thought of all the things within me others wanted to expel. As I rested, I tried to read my book, but Mary Wollstonecraft's lines blurred before my eyes. Was love ever really free? Or was I making a choice on credit, and who, one day, would collect? When I slept that night, I dreamt of falling into the ocean, of seeking abundant treasure chests filled with plunder and gold. The price of freedom, out of reach.

I open my eyes to find him watching me, unsure how much time has passed. The wind has stilled, the silence thick. I shift in my seat and the fabric of my skirt rustles.

'Are you all right?' he says.

'I was thinking about Paris. And Italy.'

'I see.'

'You went to Italy on your honeymoon, didn't you? A sort of Grand Tour.'

'Yes.'

'Did your wife know you went there with me?'

'No.'

'Of course not.' My voice echoes in the dark. 'Nobody knew, in the end.'

'Your family did a very good job of hushing it up.'

'My family are good at secrets.'

'Mine were only good at fading away.'

Paris was greyer than I expected, the boulevards still haunted by the ghost of Napoleon, a whiff of the guillotine floating over the Seine. I imagined the city during the Terror, the feet on cobbled streets, men and women shoulder against shoulder, the flash of falling steel, like ice. When I went to Notre Dame to pray, the locals spoke to me in French, thinking I was from Martinique.

I'd wanted to visit Brittany, but we'd had no time, and perhaps we were both afraid. It was so close to England and those white cliffs (always white). To go so far north, and so close to the coast, was to lay bare what we had repressed. We had fled in the night. I was twenty. We were not married.

The Continent was kinder to lovers and rule-breakers. But I was no Mary Shelley.

'Perhaps it isn't your family who fades away,' I say. 'Perhaps it is you.'

He raises his eyebrows. 'What do you mean?'

'You seem very good at leaving. Your mother, your brother. Your wife. Others.' *Me.*

'I never left my family. I was sent away.'

'Never to return. Very dutiful of you.'

'I went back, once. You know this.'

'I know your brother was left begging for handouts from the East India Company.'

'Lanoon was–' He shakes his head, his face twisting. It is the most expressive I've seen him since I arrived. He runs his hands through his hair and slumps in his seat. Then he squares his shoulders, rigid.

I can hear what he would say. His brother was tarred with ill-luck and darker skin. He married a Javanese lady. He made his bed.

~

He imagines standing and peeling open the canvas flap behind him and moving to the safety of his cabin on the *Rapid*. Away from this woman's Medusa stare. He imagines leaving. He has perfected the art of departure. Ever since, as a six-year-old, he was put on a ship to England, he is more at home with the thrust of onward movement than the stasis of still earth beneath his feet. The first thing he sees in a building is a way out.

But he remains, immobile, his back fixed to the chair, petrified or enthralled, he can't tell which. The conversation has not progressed as he'd hoped. Her words loop around him, insidious and hostile, and he wants to stopper his ears like Odysseus. But Odysseus had Ithaca, his island kingdom stronger than a siren's call. Light's island is so far from his own, so far from any sort of home, that he has nothing but the faint roar of the sea to drown out her words.

She shifts in her chair, the sea-green gown swirling about her feet.

'Perhaps we should talk about this tomorrow.' Her voice is a bell in the dark. The wind outside carries the scent of burning. He feels the smoke curl in the air and rasp in his throat, rattling down the canal to his lungs and unfurling like two fists. Not even the saltwater air can allay it. The *rasp, rasp, rasp* makes him edgy and wired. Wide-eyed.

She has given him a way out, and yet he cannot bring himself to exit.

'You still won't let it be,' he says.

She shakes her head. 'You'll tell me, one way or another.'

Their eyes meet and for a moment he thinks she will join him in a shared amusement, but her face is stone.

'It's not your secret to keep.' She gazes at him until his eyes flick away, then leans forward. 'The sooner you tell me, the sooner this can all be done with.'

His mouth forms a half-smile. 'Perhaps that's what troubles me.'

'What do you mean?'

'I don't want to be done with this. To be done with you.'

He imagines reaching out and retrieving his words, pulling them from the air. But it's too late.

Bath, July 1822

She walks back, her red dress catching the light of a hundred candles. It is just past midnight. Her hair has come loose and shines in bronze ripples over her shoulders. On another woman it might look untidy, but on her, here in the Assembly Rooms, it is all as it should be.

He is not the only one to think so. All evening, she has drawn men's eyes. It is not so different in London, or Suffolk, or Hertfordshire. When they walk out together, he feels that secret pride of one who knows he is the envy of others. But here, in this city of Aquae Sulis and golden Roman stone, she takes on another life: the mirrors turn to watch her as she walks, the water bubbles in the fountains and on the streets. The juices in their drinking glasses, the wine in his mouth, the blood in his veins, all strain to greet her.

It is a city where anything is possible, a perpetual pleasure garden, the closest thing to Venice in England. What would happen if he took her there? Would the canals rise forth and flood into the basilica, casting mist over the lagoon, for the sake of touching her feet? As she moves toward him, the ballroom transforms into the arches and the Istrian stone of the Venetian

Gothic, while the floor beneath their feet begins to ripple, flowing into the mermaid streets of this floating city, half human and half Atlantis.

She smiles as she draws nearer. 'I'm thirsty.'

Lines of sweat bead across her hairline, and she beats the air with her fan. He holds out his claret, but she shakes her head. 'Water. I need water.'

He looks around but sees only wine and candle flame. She moves past him, her skirts touching his leg, her hand on his arm. 'Let's go outside. I believe there's a drinking fountain there.'

'Your cousin–'

'Oh, never mind her. She'll be here until dawn. As long as we're back by then.'

If he senses danger, he does not act. Wine caramelises in his veins. He follows her.

Night air coats his skin, cool with a hint of mist. The roar of the crowd fades behind them, sealed silent as the door closes on the Assembly Rooms. She moves down the steps, heels echoing in the still night as she strides onto the footpath and away from the waiting carriages. She pauses, a finger on her lips. 'Which way?'

'Which way where?'

'To find water.'

'I thought you knew.'

She laughs. 'I thought it would be easy to find in Bath.'

He laughs too. 'If we go back inside, I'm sure we can find you a glass of water.'

'I couldn't bear it. Not with the crowd and the heat.'

She starts walking, then turns back. 'The Pump Rooms have spa water.' She stumbles a little, walking backward, then grabs the hem of her skirts. He catches up with her and offers his arm.

'The Pump Rooms are closed at this hour.'

'Come on,' she says, taking his hand.

She walks quickly for a woman. He tries to guide her – he knows the most direct route – but she sets off diagonally, taking them toward the river.

The city is well lit despite the lateness of the hour and the Bath stone glows golden from the lamps. How the Roman ruins had been restored, the wondrous masonry polished and brought to new life. Here and there the night is punctuated by conversation and laughter, the rattle of a carriage, a strain of song. An endlessly celebratory city. A city he can't afford.

'Where did you say you were staying?' She looks up at him with expectation. They reach the river and the lights from Pulteney Bridge flicker over the dark surface of the water. He hadn't told her. He knows well enough where she resides. Over the bridge, on Sydney Place, four doors away from the former residence of Queen Charlotte.

'I'm in a hotel near Green Park.'

Her face is blank.

'In that direction.' He gestures broadly.

'Oh. I've never been there.'

'No. That doesn't surprise me. There isn't much cause to, really.'

She looks back to the bridge over the river. 'I wish I could go into the water.'

'I thought ... the Pump Rooms.'

But she is already making her way over the low stone wall and onto the grassy slope that rolls to the water's edge.

The water bubbles in the dark, giving me an unspoken urge to throw my shoes into it and watch the river subsume them. A strange offering. Instead, I place them side by side on the grass and fold my stockings within their soles. I hear Will pause on the slope. The soft sound of incredulous laughter.

'What are you doing?'

I gather my hem and make my way to the water's edge. Footsteps follow me.

'Be careful!'

The earth is soft underfoot, the crust of grass giving way to river mud. Green blades squeeze through the crevices of my toes. Oh, to walk on water. The night smells wet. It is not cold. Clouds obscure the stars, but the face of the moon breaks through the mist.

For centuries, Sulis Minerva lurked in these depths, an ancient mother goddess of wisdom and bounty, an enactor of curses and dispenser of justice. After the Romans fell and retreated, she lingered, haunting the Anglo-Saxon Christians with homes of giants, a whisper of gold splendour and wine halls over the hot springs.

What prayer do I have for this lady of water?

I move along the riverbank. Behind me, I sense him pause. The grass thins into sediment and mud. The water of the river is always moving, a giant serpent carving its way through Somerset. Just one step. One toe into its cold depths. What would it bring?

Earlier that evening, a man – a gentleman – danced a quadrille with me, and said I was a stunning mulatto. I ignored him until that point; my eyes, hot and sticky, had ever been seeking Will. I saw him across the room, his dark, curled head moving in laughter and conversation. There was a particular way the corners of his eyes creased that made me smile. He was with the Napiers and some others I did not know, and I had been trying to interpret their air of deference and admiration.

Now, my eyes snapped back at the man's words. Heat coursed through the ribbons of my veins, surging upwards across my neck. He smiled at me with an unblinking stare that even here – on this night, in this city – was not appropriate. The world condensed, its boundaries pressing on my skin, my chest.

I could not recall his name. I opened my mouth to speak, words forming in the hollow of my throat. Perhaps I had misheard.

He said it again. *Mulatto.* 'But perhaps I'm mistaken,' he continued. 'Perhaps you're an octoroon?'

Words flinched and died on my tongue. I stared at him, voiceless. My feet completed the dance without incident. They moved as marionettes in time to the music. They displayed no outrage, no offence, no whisper of the crack that ran through me, that deep, jagged line, half shame, half indignation, that always threatens to split, to split, to split wide open.

I fought to breathe. Moments ago, I had been a girl at a dance with a cousin and maybe a lover, joyful, ensconced in bodily integrity. Now the world around me spun apart. I saw myself in this man's eyes, my body re-formed and reflected to me, something strange and rare, grotesque, desirable only for its perversity. The music thrummed off key. Sweat crowded my brow and I closed my eyes.

The dance ended. When I opened my eyes, Will turned to look at me. His face lit up across the room. His skin bronzed and shaded, his teeth very white when he smiles.

I place my foot in the water, leaving the other anchored in the sod of the riverbank. The river bites, and then it consoles, the coldness warming as it touches my skin. I imagine removing my dress, here under the clouded night, the red net burning on the riverbank, my body falling into the water.

There is no silt in the riverbed, just stone, pebbled and worn smooth by the passage of the water. When I slip, he catches me, bracing himself on the sloping earth, steady and unyielding. We stand, suspended between the sky and the surface of the water. For a moment, I do not know if I want to return to the earth or dive further into the cold. But he rights himself, straightening and stepping further onto the grass, and I am pulled back to the land, facing him. We collide gently. He is warm against the night.

We could get married. He will say this later, speculative and in passing.

When it happens, he tastes like sugar and West Indian cigars. I place one hand on his stubbled cheek. The other is twisted against his chest, where his pulse beats against my wrist, the bloom of wine pumping through his veins.

Behind us, the river pauses its quest toward the Severn Estuary. The water winks in the moonlight, spray rising to meet us. Wetness falls upon my hair. Rain?

We sit on the grass, carefully negotiating its sloping bank, my skirts, the placement of our limbs. We kiss, his arm looping around my shoulders, his hand resting within my hair.

Even with my eyes closed, I know the moon is bright. I see the weave of the plane trees crossing the clouds.

Later, he takes my hand and leads me toward the street. I look back, just once, and see the shape of a water woman staring at me. Then the river re-forms, just a river, rushing onwards to the sea.

We walk in silence, our heels echoing on the ancient stone. The lanterns pierce the mist and light the Roman city with gold. There were others here, once. Infantrymen from Spain and Greece and Italy. Generals from Ethiopia, traders from Palestine. Maybe even someone like me. With my free hand, I reach out and touch a wall. Perhaps the past was a more enlightened place. I look at him from the corner of my eye. He catches my gaze and smiles. I want to speak to him of this, a dream of an old world where difference is not so strange. But he does not like such topics. He does not like to speak of what unites us and sets us apart, a memory of the Orient, a duality that has somehow birthed something fresh and new, like the mermaid women of the Scottish islands – or a mulatta. Again, the heat surges up into my neck and across my face, and I glance at him. I have seen the way he looks at me. Prideful. The status of our blood and skin has always hung between us, unspoken. I would not be fallen before him. I would not be this: *mulatta.*

South Australian Coast, October 1836

At the tent's threshold, I can see the barrel-shaped waves crashing into the shore, coating the boulders in shards of white water. The cliffs rise on either side of the bay. It's suffocating. I try to tell myself I am alone, that I have felt the calming solitude of the open ocean, the joy of anonymity in a coastal port, the isolation of my cabin on the whaler. But there is no such reassurance here. They told us this land was empty. They lied.

Behind me, Will's silhouette sits against the buckling canvas. I will not look back. I can picture the darkness of his profile, a thin outline, without depth, but I cannot place him. That night in Bath, we had been loose allies, at least. Where I quavered at the label pressed onto me, he moved through the city with pride. A dispossessed Eastern prince, on his way up in the world. Now, he has folded in on himself. He repeats banalities and survey statistics and enthuses about systematic colonisation. He lies.

'Will you tell me why you're really here?' he'd said. And we had argued insidiously, mimicking the tide, until he had no breath left.

I still have breath. I always have it now. There is no argument for which I lack energy. I used to be able to choose my moments wisely, but now I always carry it. A cracking anger that threatens to split me in two. Sometimes it seizes my tongue and paralyses my speech. At other times it shrieks out of me.

They said this land was empty and unspoiled. But flotsam already lines the shore. Old rigging, felled trees, splintered cargo boxes. The empty rum bottles that glint on the sand like fragments of the evil eye. The seal carcasses lining the edge of the ocean on Kangaroo Island, giving up their pelts to dark-skinned women who work on them with questioning faces. I would ask if it transforms them, if the skins are their key to freedom, a way to swim the Backstairs Passage and make their journey home. But I don't ask. Such a question seems sacrilegious.

No. There is nothing empty here. If anything, in daylight, it is all too much. The sun is bright and too defined. All is laid bare in an excess of clarity, and the fruits of the colony are already beginning to spoil.

I look back. His left hand lies clenched along his thigh as he turns to face me, his expression clouded in the dark.

I try again. 'Tell me about the time you met my mother.'

When he speaks, his voice is quiet. 'I honestly don't understand why you need to know.'

I say nothing, waiting.

'There was a room in Bow Bazaar, above a tailor's shop. That is where I met her.'

I nod. 'Yes.'

'I remember the latticework on the windows. The ceiling cornices were covered with mould. It was dark.'

'What was she like?'

He pauses, eyes flicking down to his feet, then back up again. 'It was a long time ago. And she's dead now anyway.' He watches for a response, but I am still.

'Then there is no harm in telling me.'

A smile escapes him. Is he caught?

'She wore glasses.'

'Glasses?'

'Yes. Little half-moon silver eyeglasses. For reading.'

'What did she read?' I straighten my back.

'She taught English and translated poetry. I gather it didn't pay very well.'

My memories of my mother have always been corporeal, the cool touch of her skin, the way the golden bells on her bracelet jingled as she came to check on me. I had never thought about her internal landscape. What pigments coloured the contours of her mind, and the reality reflected in it.

'Why didn't you tell me this before?' I ask.

'Look at you. We've spent the last hour arguing my voice into the dust, and I've never seen you so alert. This is what you wanted.'

'Yes. All I want is to know her.'

'But this isn't enough.'

'I don't know what you mean.'

'Are you satisfied with this knowledge?'

I shake my head.

'No. You want more. And there is more. And it's not all poetry and eyeglasses.'

Light rubs his temples, remembering the crack across the wall, the scent of dampness, and outside, the sound of children playing. Her clothes were European – well cut but faded. Her eyes deep and sorrowful. He remembers the woman's movements. Like a dancer, or a courtly lady. Even her poverty couldn't obscure that. She had placed her half-moon glasses onto the bridge of her nose, read his papers and shaken her head.

'Yes. I do want more.' Clarissa moves toward him. 'What was her name?'

He raises his eyebrows. He'd forgotten. Even this she does not know. But then, how would she? He remembers her grandfather's cold house, shuttered after his death. The impassiveness of the servants lining the hall, framing her timid paternal relations. Her quiet, sickly brother. They'd all worked so hard to keep the old man's silences. What was it they called her? *Poppet.*

'Didn't you ever find out?'

She shakes her head.

'Not even in India?'

'No. I've never sat in so many anonymous offices, or had people say so much but tell me so little.'

'That's what you said about that salon I took you to in London.'

'This was much, much worse. There's no poetry in a colonial office.'

His eyes flick up to her. He has heard that phrase before, in English accented with the strains of Bengali, her mother passing the papers back to him with ink-stained fingers. She opens her hands. *There's no use for it*, she says.

'Who told you that? No poetry in a colonial office.'

She shifts against the entrance of the tent. 'One of the Company men. The last one I saw.'

'The one who told you about me. '

'Yes.'

'Do you remember his name?'

She opens her hands. 'I'm not–'

'Was it William Fairlie?' He rises now, then drops his body back into the chair. 'But it can't have been. He's long dead. He must be.'

'It wasn't Fairlie. I don't remember his name, but he was young. I doubt he would have been there when you were in Calcutta.' She looks over at him. 'He was Percy Whitworth's successor. I tried to get an appointment with Mr Whitworth himself. Apparently, he knew my father, so he would have been there about your time.'

Light blinks, thinking of that man, thirty years ago, standing on the verandah and smiling. 'Yes. He was. Whitworth was there.'

Fairlie's friend, and Colonel FitzRoy's private secretary. Percy Whitworth had been there that day, before his sister's wedding. When he and Fairlie had that conversation.

Light stands and walks toward the entrance of the tent. She lets him pass. The scent of smoke wafts over to them, and he frowns.

'Whitworth refused to see you?' he says finally. Surely, she would have found that strange. She, Colonel FitzRoy's daughter.

He can tell she senses something. A crack in the darkness. Light turns to her.

'After a fashion.' Clarissa runs her thumb across the back of her hand. 'He didn't exactly refuse. He'd retired some years ago. He had been in Calcutta at the same time as I, but when I tried to visit, his servant said he'd been called away on urgent business. To Pune, apparently.' She walks out onto the cliff side. The earth looks rough under her feet. She should put on shoes.

'He was called away.' Light's voice is low but deliberate. 'So you saw his successor who told you I was the one to help you.'

'Yes.'

'Is that all he said?'

'I met with him twice. The first time, he tried to brush me off. He offered me a tour of the city and suggested I wait until James could join me. As though only he could ask the right questions or stomach the answers. The second time, I lost my temper.'

'And that's when he told you about me.'

'Yes.'

'I think you've been misled.'

She winds her hair about her hands in the wind.

'You know, I thought that was possible. They were trying to be rid of me.'

'It seems they succeeded.'

She shrugs – valiantly – and he remembers the first time he saw her make that gesture. A café in Venice on the edge of the canal. Another world of endless blue.

'How did you feel when you were there?'

'Where?' She has moved further out onto the hillside.

'India. Calcutta.'

She looks at him steadily. 'You want to know if I felt at home.'

For a moment, he can smell jasmine and lemongrass and freshly caught fish. 'I know you didn't feel at home.'

Clarissa raises her eyebrows. 'What makes you so certain?'

He sees too late where she has steered him. 'I didn't feel at home in India.'

'No, but why would you?'

He doesn't reply.

'And what of when you went back to Penang?'

The sound of gulls. The taste of astringent laksa. The hot, wet air coating his skin. 'What of it?'

'Did you feel at home then?'

He shakes his head, less in negation than denial. They do not speak of it. Where he came from.

'You see,' she steps back into the awning of the tent, 'as much as the East India Company was unwilling to talk about my mother, they were very happy to talk about yours. They showed me your letters to them from thirty years ago.'

'They shouldn't have done that.'

'Perhaps not. But they did. Why didn't you ever talk about her?'

Light looks around him. A thin sheet of canvas offers them haven from the night. Beyond its walls, strange insects call, and the staccato trilling of a solitary night bird fills the air.

He does not like where this is leading. The evening has not gone as he'd hoped. And what did he hope? To feel, again, Clarissa's skin in the dark, to be a welcome incursion, to hear her speak only words of forgiveness. To touch the water. But what right did he have, to hope for anything after all his failures? 'I think I should go. It's late.'

'Will, wait–'

He moves ahead of her, the heels of his boots sending pebbles ricocheting down the hillside. Beyond the cliff face is the American whaler, and beyond that still lies the *Rapid*. The terrain is uneven and the slope curls under his soles, causing the tendons in his left leg to tense as his foot shifts to stabilise his body. He can feel the twitching scar tissue rippling up the muscles of his thigh, his groin. The limp is intermittent. There is tightness in his hip accompanied by a twinge of pain. But he is still steady.

I can guess where he is going. Back to the ships, whence he came. I move into the tent, lacing my boots over my dusty feet, picking up a shawl lying across the chair and blowing out the candle as I go. When I return to the hillside, I can barely see him in the darkness. He moves quickly for an injured man. I look around at the creeping silver smile of the ocean, biting into the shore, the alien stars watching over us, and the sheer spread of bushland to my right. It is vast and overwhelming. It would swallow us up.

Light hears Clarissa's feet hurrying behind him. He has feared many things this evening but not, somehow, her desertion at this moment. When she appears, she is wrapped in tartan. It isn't possible to make out the colour, just the square strips, light in the darkness. Rubbing the far edge of the cloth between his fingers recalls similar fabric from when he lived in Ireland. He drops his hands, breathing in quicker than he intends, and something rattles in his throat.

'Clarissa, you shouldn't be out here.'

'You don't need to go. There's more that you haven't told me.'

He doesn't reply. What would it mean, to unburden it all to her now? Just a few days ago, he could have written her a letter informing her of everything. But just by virtue of being here, she has altered the equation. She has given him something to lose.

'Clarissa.' He steps forward and touches the curve of her cheekbone, the line of her neck, the edge of her clavicle.

She does not move away. 'Best not,' she says in a quiet voice.

He drops his hand and looks away from her face. The deep colours of her shawl glint back at him. 'Tartan.' His voice sounds flat in the dark. 'I didn't know your father was part Scottish.'

'He wasn't.' She pulls the shawl closer. 'This is from an old governess.'

'I think I remember you telling me this. What was her name?'

'Her name was Mrs Jensen. She'd married a man from the Faroe Islands. But her maiden name was Murray.'

'A proper Jacobite, then.'

'Probably. I never asked. But yes, now that I think of it that would make sense. She had a little cameo of Charles Stuart.'

He laughs.

'Does that amuse you?'

'The man only lived because he was smuggled out dressed as a woman, by a little girl.'

'A very brave girl, by the sounds of it.'

He hears her short laugh in the dark. Light could never abide her laughter at him. He begins to walk again. The moonlight draws strange shapes on the earth. But he knows this terrain.

'You don't ask me why I laugh.' Her feet speed up to match his pace, boots crunching over the same earth, a dissonant echo. When her skirts swish, the sound seems to bring the sea closer.

'I don't need to ask. You'll just find a way to quote Mary Wollstonecraft at me.'

'Is that so terrible?' Clarissa stumbles, once, and rights herself quickly, batting away his proffered hand. They read Wollstonecraft together, in Venice. 'You were never against her ideas before.'

'I don't need a lecture on the rights of women. Not these days.'

~

I feel, not for the first time, a jolt of strangeness. His face, so familiar, made alien. Who is this man? He is narrow-shouldered and diminished. In my baser instincts, I'm repelled.

Our pace slows. Behind us, the fire hisses. When I look back, the hill is crowned in light, reminding me of riverside pyres. Of a thousand temple candles, lit up to the goddess Durga.

He walks again, his burgundy coat becoming greyer in the night. I don't move. The air is sharp, with only a hint of the ocean. Inland, the bushes are twisted into ropes of supplication, their branches beaten down by years of salt wind.

'What are you doing?' he asks.

I don't reply. Men feel entitled when they're angry. My brother, my uncle, my grandfather. Two of my former fiancés. It came out worst of all in rejection, in being told no. Will has never been entitled. I have always liked that in him. But now I wonder if there is something else. Always this urge to walk on, empty-handed. That was how he became when his wife left him, I heard. Empty-handed.

'Why didn't you fight the financial provisions when your wife left you?'

'She didn't leave me. I left her.'

'Well, regardless–'

'There was nothing to fight. It was her money.'

'You were entitled to it.'

'That didn't mean taking it was right.'

'No. And that's why you don't want a lecture.'

He looks away. 'It's one of many reasons.' When he turns to me again, the lines of his face are carved by moonlight. 'You should go back to the tent, Clarissa.'

The air crackles. When we don't speak, I can hear a pulse, a hum, around us. If I close my eyes, I can still see them. The seal pups rolling on the white sand. The fronds of the golden sea dragon. The dehydrated pelts and the scent of rust and brine, that sticky marine smell that follows me, wherever I go.

'Doesn't it feel strange to you, to be here?'

He casts his eye across the coast. 'No.' His voice is even. 'The landscape's not so different from Spain, or Italy. The climate is temperate. The seasons are reversed, but that's more familiar than the tropics, really–'

'Is it? You grew up in Penang.'

He shakes his head. 'That was a very long time ago.'

Beside me, Light stares at the landscape around us, then touches my arm as I step forward.

'What is it?'

He shakes his head. 'This isn't the way.'

My eyes see only so far in the night, but even I can tell we are following the coastline. 'What do you mean?' The ships are due north, not visible, but close. Somewhere over the cliffs are three floating worlds built from timber and tar that will end our strange seclusion. After this evening, I will never have this opportunity again.

'Look.' Light gestures in front of my feet.

I shake my head in shock. The rock slopes away in front of us, vanishing into an inky chasm. 'But this is the way we came.'

~

Light has studied the stars and memorised them. He has rendered their foreignness safe and knowable, and can name the movements of Sirius, of Canopus. But tonight, their meaning is opaque. When he looks up, the sky is impassive, indigo glass smeared with the thick cream of the Milky Way. But there is no clarity or direction. The brightest stars are absent.

'This is the way.' Clarissa speaks again, looking between the ocean and the rift in front of them. The half-moon lights her face enough for him to see her determination. 'I know this place.' She gestures inland. 'That tree with the twisted trunk. Those white flowers. This is the way I came.'

All Light can see is darkness, riven by the deeper pit at the base of their feet. No twisted trunk. No blooming flowers.

But Clarissa steps forward with that confidence that he has always envied. He hears the rattle of loose stones, their echo as they slip down, into the deep.

'Wait,' he says, taking her elbow, but when she winces at his touch he releases his grip. 'Not that way.' To the left, he can see the path that his surveying team cut through the undergrowth leading down from the ridge and onto the beach. At the base of the hill, the luminous shoreline smiles up at him, slyly. 'This way,' Light says, ignoring the twinge in his left leg. He knows this land, doesn't he? He charted its elevation, its rocks, the consistency of its soil.

Behind him, Clarissa follows, calling out, 'But this is not the way. This is not the way at all.'

He grips the muscles of his upper thigh, willing them to hold, as he slows his pace. 'We'll follow the coast.'

The terrain grows stonier and the way is steep. The rocky base looms out at Light like a hand moving swiftly in the dark. He clings to tree branches as he descends, palms stinging. He calculates the distance. A few more steps. His right boot fits into a groove in the cliff face. Good. Step. His right foot again. The easy one. He grips a bush for good measure, the leaves stiff and unyielding. Flora is built to survive here. He will investigate its type in the morning. She moves behind him, as she always does, each rustle and creak a reminder of those footsteps that have dogged him ever since he left the port of George Town, crossing the Indian Ocean, the English Channel, pursuing him through the ruins and temples of Alexandria. Step. Good. He should be a gentleman. The thought creeps around the front region of his brain, but the rest resists. Whatever social niceties that have groomed him to turn and offer the lady his hand have been eroded by this strange night. Just a few more steps. Step.

It is his right leg, after all, that gives way. As the stiff edge of his boot slips on wet rock – they are closer to the sea than he realised – he reaches out to grasp another branch, but it is barely a shrub. Time pools for a misshapen instant. The smiling arc of the sea reaches out beneath him as he floats free in this interstitial moment. He hears her speak, and at the sound of her voice, the earth comes rushing up to meet him.

It hits his side first: shoulder, ribcage, abdomen. Air squeezes out from his lungs, contracting his chest, coarsening the rasp within it to a roar.

Sea-green silk rustles in front of him. How did she make it here so soon, in that dress and those shoes? The fabric of her skirts ripple like serpentine water. Where has he seen that before? His mother told him the people in Java thought sea green was a forbidden colour, only worn by the Queen of the Southern Sea, who reigned over the Indian Ocean. But that was superstitious nonsense, really.

Venice, July 1822

We arrive in Venice in the late afternoon, crossing the Adriatic blue of the lagoon under a white-gold sun. I tilt back my head, feeling the last of the day's heat on my skin. They say bad spirits can't cross running water. Waves balloon and dip beneath us. I look back to the mainland. Have we left our shadows behind? The shopfronts along the harbour darken as we draw away. Two streets back I discarded the last letter from my brother. A simple parroting of my uncle's words. No backbone, no grit. But still, his words disquiet me.

The boatmen steer in silence as the hazy marine air coats our bodies with moisture. But for the rare white cloud, it is impossible to tell if the sea is in the sky or the sky is in the ocean, mirrored and doubled.

I loosen my hair, and the breeze licks at the threads of sweat sticking to the nape of my neck. Behind me, Will sits in the shade. He has given up asking me to join him. *This is all so new*, I say, maintaining my post by the side of the boat. But it is more than that. It has been a lifetime since I have seen water like this, the pigments of a Renaissance fresco brought to life. Almost as blue as the sea in the Bay of Bengal. It is the colour of sunlight and forget-me-nots. The slippery scales of the unknown sea creature.

The floating city rises out of the water before us. *The gateway to the Orient*, someone calls. Will has been sketching, but now looks fixedly at his page, his pencil still.

There it is again, the charge I'd felt in Florence steals upon me. There, in the halls of the Uffizi, I saw the shadow in the hallway mirrors, flitting between the colonnades. A heaviness dogging our steps.

We rent a house on the Grand Canal from a small Venetian woman. Her black lace shawl marks her as a widow. Her words are sharp and rapidly articulated. My operatic Italian is no use. But Will is quick with languages. He has an ear for dialect. At one point, she looks at me and smiles. Her eyes are dark and smooth with a sickle of reflective light, like the shell of an ebony beetle. By the time she takes us to our rooms, the shadows have lengthened with the evening, and they dance in triumph along the walls of the staircase, as she walks before us holding a candelabra.

The night falls more swiftly here than in England. Again, I think of that world I left behind: the hot sun vanishing in narrow twilight, the rising perfume of gardenia, strengthening in the night. Here, the air is soft and marine, scented with the tang of slow-moving brine and the flesh of fish. Somewhere in the evening I smell jasmine. I open the shutters. Beneath us, a solitary lamp hovers above a gondola gliding through the canal.

We lie together on the brocade bedclothes watching the curtains swell. His body feels hot. It's a warm night, but the film of sweat across his brow is sickly. I've noticed it lately. These moments of silence, these night sweats. I want to shake him back to himself. To shake him alive.

'Did the lady say something about Marco Polo?' My voice seems to have its own life in the dark.

He turns toward me. 'She said he used to visit here. His house is nearby, and her late husband claimed he had some maps and sketches from Polo himself, hidden in their tapestry room.'

'I wonder how many rooms there are in the house.'

'Two dozen or so.'

'I wouldn't have thought that was possible.'

'These canal houses seem narrow but they're deep and tall. Two dozen rooms should hardly impress you. Your grandfather's house must have more than that.'

'That's true. But everything feels so different and alive and somewhat familiar. Don't you think?'

'I have been to Italy before, I suppose.'

I shake my head. 'No, not that.' The night seems to still into silent solidarity, as though the house is listening. 'I feel there is something in the air, on the breeze, in the water. A smell. A memory. It makes me think of India.' I cannot see his face clearly, but I hear him exhale. It's almost a sigh. 'Does it not bring it to mind for you, too?'

'India's a very different place.'

'Of course. I know that. But this is where Marco Polo came from. And you heard them call it the gateway to Asia. I can see it in the architecture.' And I can taste it in the water.

He sighs openly now. 'Clarissa.' His fingers curl through the loose strands of my hair. 'It's time to sleep.'

But sleep doesn't come. The house creaks and the shutters rattle. The moon emerges, a Maundy penny at the bottom of an abandoned wishing well, its light piercing the shutters and casting a rectangle of silver upon the carpeted floor. It's hot.

Removing my shift, I walk to the window. I remember this feeling. In the heat and humidity, I do not know where my skin ends and the air begins. I kneel at the edge of the carpet where the floor extends to the balcony, resting my back against the wall and angling my head to see the canal. I wanted to come here for Byron, for Shelley, for my own Grand Tour. Venice is the pinnacle of any Romantic flight. I had not expected this. The arched colonnades and Byzantine domes and silhouetted gondolas gliding like canoes upon the Hooghly.

I think of Marco Polo's maps, rattling the locks on their trunks, somewhere above me. Beneath me, on the surface of the canal, I see a ripple with no wave.

Where could those waters take me?

~

He sleeps badly and wakes with a dust-coated mouth, the room swelling golden around him. Where is he? He reaches out a hand. The sheets around him are damp with last night's sweat. He gropes red brocade, inhales salt water. Of course. Hope blooms expansive, bursting through the tightness of his chest. Clarissa. Venice. The room stabilises around him as he props himself up on his elbow.

He sees her foot first, extended along the Ottoman rug, where she lies, dressed only in her underskirt, her fingertip resting on the edge of the window. As her back swells and contracts with each breath, he realises she's asleep. He sits up, intending to call to her, but he pauses. The thin muslin of her skirt is wound tightly about her hips and knees. Her back gleams gold. In the rays of the early morning, her hair loses its earthiness and becomes pure flame. It would be a sin to disturb her.

Reclining against the pillows, he pours himself some water. In moments like these he allows himself a secret swell of triumph, like a zoologist who has finally possessed the plumage of some rare and desirable bird. He had felt it again the night before, his hands on the skin of her hip as she moved above him. He had never claimed something so expensive.

It had made their flight all the stranger. It was the current pulling at his knees at moments when he wasn't paying attention, threatening to drag him out to sea. Why did they run? Why wouldn't she just marry him?

It was all at her insistence, and he'd let her convince him, wanting to live up to the narrative she'd constructed – of him, a Byronic hero, and herself, an independent woman. And he'd thought in that moment, after the first night in Bath, that if this was all she would offer him, little as it was, then he would take it. But something had changed.

He stands, feeling the old house creak beneath his feet as a breeze travels through the room, billowing out the faded curtains. A cooler day lies ahead.

She stirs as he draws a sheet over her. In the clouded sunlight, her hair has lost its fire, dampening to an English brown. But her hair is the only English thing about her.

It is still early when he leaves their rooms and speaks to their landlady. She tells him to call her Nona, but he refrains. She remains Signora Zambon and she laughs at his formality. But when he tells her his mission – the Marco Polo map room – she becomes serious. She will not accompany him to the rooms, she tells him. They remind her of her husband, only recently dead, a noble man much maligned in life. Light does not ask for the story, although Signora Zambon pauses with expectation. In the face of his silence, she flicks a tiny hand and draws out a faded document from her bureau.

'See?' she says. 'The floor plan. This is the room with the maps.'

He unfolds the weathered paper, carefully. It feels soft and worn. The writing is minuscule, the date of the document uncertain. He raises his eyes to ask for more information, but his hostess is leaning out of the window, calling to a gondolier. Light is in her favour for fighting Napoleon, but he is wary of outstaying his welcome. Folding the floor plan, he steps out into the corridor.

The building dates from the thirteenth century and the plan feels almost as old. He can see the markings of a globe in a little room on the fourth floor, and the tiny scrawl of 'Marco Polo' in the corner. Light chooses what appears to be the most direct route and begins to make his ascent.

Sunlight, dust, the sound of sneezing. An ignominious start to world exploration. He pushes his way into the mahogany rooms scented with decaying adventure. An astrolabe spins.

He loses the morning to cartography, to tracing the borders of nations and following the shipping routes through mermaid-encrusted waters. The maps are not originals – he sees this straightaway. They are prints from some time, he guesses, shortly after the invention of the Gutenberg press. But his pleasure in exploration is undented. He is with the Polos as they journey to Baghdad and cross Samarkand on the Silk Route and explore the wonders of the splendid city. He is with them in Mongolia, in Xanadu with Kubla Khan, within the *stately pleasure-dome decreed.* He is with them in Quanzhou, as they leave by boat with the princess Kokochin. He is with them until they sail into the straits of Malacca and make harbour in Sumatra. And then all wonders cease. For he cannot, as much as he tries, maintain his solidarity with the intrepid European explorers, or his faded guise as one of their number. For he has seen it all, already, long before, on a breezy day in April over thirty years ago, when his mother birthed him in their garden house to the sound of Kedah rain.

He leaves the map; he leaves the book; he stands and turns within the room.

~

It is late in the morning and the sun is high by the time I ascend the staircase. Signora Zambon listened with laboured impatience to my slow Italian. She understood me perfectly, but her reply washed clean through the air, leaving me blank and staring. Finally, she spoke in the clearest French, in tones of last resort.

'You understand me now, yes?'

I smiled, grasping at the familiar words with gratitude. 'Yes, yes.'

'I hate to speak a filthy tyrant's language. But it is better than English.' She laughed and looked at me with a knowing expression, waiting. When I didn't reply, she prompted me, 'What is your language, dear?' and I lurched with a familiar feeling – my own body, seen through the eyes of a stranger, made alien to itself.

It was the first time I had felt this since leaving England. My arrival in Paris had granted me a new provenance – French, potentially with strands of Creole, but such heritage is not uncommon there. From then on, I had passed as Italian, but here, in this floating stepping stone to Asia, my guise had fallen from me.

'English,' I told her.

Her shining black eyes questioning, she touched my cheek. 'You do not have an English face.'

Something shifted in the room and stalked across my expression. She dropped her hand.

'It is a very pretty face.' Her voice was kind. 'Now your husband–' I flinched a little at the word. 'He is upstairs. In the map room. He took the floor plan, but it's very easy to find.'

She guided me into the corridor. The walls were rinsed gold, the late-morning sun bouncing from the brocaded wallpaper, highlighting the faded carpet and the cracks along the cornices. 'There,' she said. 'This way.'

The higher I ascend, the clearer the house's decay becomes. The renovations of the recent century – Venice's last hurrah at glory – fade, little by little, into dark-wood medievalism. Doors rattle with a half-felt breeze and walls groan as the lagoon licks at their foundations. Who among us can stand still, forever, in flowing water?

I see again the widow's face, the expectation in her eyes. Not an English face, and not Italian or Oriental, either.

In the mirrored halls of the second floor, I trace the poles and contours of my face. Hazel eyes and brown hair can't hide a deeper strangeness. Will, with all his darkness, passes far more easily. He is more European than I. His skin may be sallow, but he has an English face.

By the time I reach the third floor, the passageways are twisted. I turn the door handles, one by one. A storeroom, a dust-covered bedchamber. I call his name, but softly, so softly, as though the walls themselves might be disturbed should my voice rise any further. But perhaps I do not need to worry, for they murmur quietly in their own conversation, and the water whispers up their beams and through their crevices. I follow its voice, swishing beneath my feet, and come to a sea-green door with a brass handle.

Inside, the room is dark. A sliver of aquamarine sky peers through the tapered arch window. Tapestries rock against the walls. I can hear running water.

I call his name, but no one answers. The shutters rattle in the wind and the air rushes around my ankles. It smells like age and damp wool. I open the blinds, and the room is pierced by daylight. The tapestries billow like ships' sails. There is the ivory unicorn of the mystical hunt, the three Fates spinning their web of the lives of men, Lachesis and Atropos, Clotho with her shining black eyes. She seems to smile at me. Beneath her silver thread, on a mahogany cabinet sits a box, coated with mother-of-pearl.

The lid shifts open, with resistance. Inside, there is a miniature, the white walls of Georgian marble and Palladian architecture diminished into a fairy kingdom. I remove the model, gently. In an instance, its walls expand, its roof grows. The sky brightens. I am in the gardens, surrounded by Calcutta's Town Hall.

~

He searches for her. He hears her once – he thinks. A bell-like tone, floating in the air. 'Will?' Is it his name, or some unfinished question on an uncertain future? Will? Will he? But when he walks into the corridor, there is no one there, just the darkness of an Italian house, built to keep out the sun.

He strides down to the second floor. There are footsteps in the passageway. He follows the sound into the darkness. Down the long hall, he sees her. He opens his mouth to speak, but the hall is illuminated, and his words falter into nothingness. At the end of the passage, framed in bronze and glass, stands his mother in a red dress, raising her hand toward him, clutching the other to her core.

~

I move across the second floor holding my miniature city. The hallway is lined with mirrors; the blinds are shut to keep out the glare. The looking-glasses flicker in the corner of my vision as I pass them. In each mirror, my body is reshaped and fed back to me, strange and unknown. When I reach the middle of the passage, the shutters of the final window fly open. I jump, the surface of my skin flinching across my body. A dark woman stands before me, black-haired and gowned in red, one hand held up in astonishment, the other clutching an object close to her belly. Then the light falls upon her and the hair brightens. I have been staring into the shadowed eyes of my own alarmed face.

~

'Clarissa?' His voice falters in the light.

She turns, smiling. He checks her features. Burnished hair, amber eyes. Nothing, nothing like his mother. As she opens the enamelled box in her hands, he steps back, half expecting Pandora's demons.

'Look,' she says.

The white walls of Calcutta Town Hall leer up at him.

~

There are still days ahead of them – Rome, Pompeii, Mount Vesuvius – but in hindsight it is Venice he will remember. It is in Venice that he revisits his proposal. And it is in Venice that it curdles and the air between them turns.

He asks her by the borders of Cannaregio. What they are doing there he isn't sure – she is intrigued by cats and the old Jewish quarter, where, she thinks, Napoleon did well to tear down the walls. He's thirsty and his hands shake. There's something about Italy: night sweats, blurred vision, that rasp nestled behind his sternum. It's the sound of Londonderry, of frost and blighted flowers. He wants to shake it all off, like a dog emerging from the sea.

'Marry me,' he says.

She's mid-speech, talking about the Venetian Empire. 'What?'

'Marry me. Here, in Venice. Let's do it properly and go home.'

Her eyes are stark in the sunlight – summer grass, only vaguely brown. 'I thought we said we didn't need to marry.'

'You said that.'

She drops her gaze and fiddles with her skirt while as it glides along the edge of the canal. 'Why do you want to marry me?'

'Isn't it obvious?' He sees the furrow at her brow. Not obvious. He would have planned it differently if not for the light and heat, the dryness in his throat. He says the words that need to be said – that he's said so often, so sincerely – but they emerge in tones that are cracked and broken.

She considers him. 'What would we do once we married?'

'Live in a big house in the country. Have children.' His mind spins into possibilities. Could he fund a career in politics? Or build that hot air balloon? She could afford it. The thought creeps in, unbidden.

'You know the house will go to my brother.'

'Yes, of course. But–'

'But I'll have funds to spare. Especially after my uncle goes.'

He winces. 'That's crass, Clarissa.'

'Where would you want to live?'

Ancient woodlands of wild oak take root in his mind. A sea buffets pebbled coastline. 'Suffolk.'

'Suffolk?'

'But London would also work.'

She takes a moment before responding. 'I've always wanted to live by the sea in Cornwall.'

Cornwall. Barely England at all. 'Of course.'

She walks to the edge of the canal and runs a thumb over the weathered rope on the jetty. 'Or we could go to India. Arrange passage on a boat and sail to Calcutta. I can afford it.'

His sister's wedding. Fairlie's office. His mother – no mother. 'I don't know if that's a good idea.'

'Why not?'

'What would we do there? What would I do?'

'Whatever we wanted.'

'I couldn't work, Clarissa, I don't know if you understand that.'

'You wouldn't need to. Isn't that the point?'

'The point of what?'

'Of marrying.'

Something winches around his chest. 'No. No, that is not the point.'

The air thickens around them.

'I didn't mean it like that,' she says eventually. 'It's just that, from my perspective ... for the moment my inheritance is my own. When I'm twenty-one it will be even greater. As soon as I'm married, it becomes yours.'

'It will still be your money.'

'But you won't have to work. Not like now.'

'I'll need an occupation.'

She shrugs. 'Surely you can find one in Calcutta. Painting, map-making, trading. Even soldiering. Whatever you like.'

He rubs his temples, the heat of the sun beaming onto his skull. He has not gone over this with her, not really, but still, he wonders – can she really be so naïve? No fortune or French silk dress or classical education will save her east of Constantinople, where the only currency she'll be judged on is the colour of her skin and the shape of her nose and eyes. And besides, everyone there will know who she really is.

'I have a bit of a headache coming on,' he says. 'Can we move into the shade?'

He doesn't speak of the matter again. She raises it, occasionally, in the evenings, or over breakfast, as though the green expanse of the Maidan is so completely a part of their future. He thinks of a hard stare behind half-moon eyeglasses, the light narrowed and weakened through latticework and the dust of Bow Bazaar. They joked – his brother-in-law, and others – when they heard whom he was visiting. *That mad woman.* Wasn't he afraid? Not even his own mother had raised that level of ridicule.

He catches Signora Zambon watching them during these moments, her black eyes clicking with wakeful assessment. When they return home from sightseeing and coffee in the piazza, she calls him to one side.

'There's someone here to see you,' she says.

Clarissa pauses, already part way up the staircase, removing her hat. 'Who is it?'

'Someone for the major.' Signora Zambon's eyes are blank. What did she say her first name was? Nona? None? Light waits for her to continue. 'A friend from your army days. The Peninsula Wars, he says.'

Curiosity lines Clarissa's face. 'Oh really?' She looks at him. 'How fun.' But there is a reticence that she cannot hide from him. How many people would know by now? They had run away. They were not married. Light hadn't told any army friends. The Napiers would judge him for this.

Signora Zambon holds out her hand. 'He is this way.'

He checks Clarissa's tight, anxious face. 'It's all right. You go upstairs. I'll go alone.'

He follows his landlady's gesture into her sitting room, hearing her behind him. Something tells him that she will not remain very far away.

The light from the window catches his eye. When it clears, the first thing he sees is the outline of a man and the walnut sheen of a pistol lying across the table.

Somewhere in the house, the clock strikes the hour. Light steps forward without fear and the man shifts, perturbed. The sun dips and Light sees him clearly – the pink cheeks and filmy blue eyes, the sandy hair turning to grey, sticking to his skull in the heat. The uncle.

'Sir George.'

'Light.'

Light pulls out a chair and sits down.

Sir George's fingertips rest on the butt of the pistol. 'You know why I'm here.'

Light has a better view of his face now. He looks peaky. Ill. 'I have a fair idea.' He glances down at the pistol. 'That isn't necessary.'

Sir George smiles. 'Perhaps it's the Italian heat getting into my blood.' But he doesn't remove his right hand. With his left, he reaches into his pocket. 'This is what I'm really here to show you.' He places a cheque on the table.

Light laughs. In his chest, there is buoyancy and heat. 'You don't need to pay me. I want to marry her. This doesn't have to be a scandal. We're engaged.'

The blue eyes become clear and steady. 'My dear fellow.' His voice swells strangely. 'I'm not paying you to marry her.'

The air around them is sluggish. Sweat pools within Light's collar.

'I'm paying you to go away.'

The pistol reclines on the table, its polished sheen winking up at them. Walnut wood, English make, percussion cap. New. Light would be excited in other circumstances. One of a pair. But its companion has not been presented. No challenge has been made. To go away. Light looks up. It hits suddenly, like cannon fire he should have seen coming. One asks an offending gentleman to duel, one wrangles him into marrying one's wayward daughter. One bullies a common fellow. Pays him off.

'What do you think I am?' His tone is quiet, even. The eavesdropping Signora Zambon would not be able to make out the words. He stands and the furniture flurries around him. The chair screeches, the table wobbles, alarm flashes in Sir George's piggy eyes. 'Who the hell do you think you're talking to?'

The older man waves his free hand. 'Major, I mean no disrespect. Sit down. Please. Please.'

Light feels his body complying. It won't do to be too heated. Not if this is leading where he thinks. 'If you were not so much my elder–'

'My good man, I do not mean to insult you, I don't take you for a money-grubber, but I know of your financial difficulties.'

'You don't speak to me as a gentleman.'

'Well. My boy, you are not quite one of us.'

The comment irks Light in a way that is unexpected. Not quite one of them is clear – his father, a housemaid's child in Dallinghoo, an East Indies pirate, a trader. But *boy*. Calcutta, the swish of a rattan fan, a Hindu man twice his age and an overbearing colonial master. *Boy*. That is what she cannot understand. Why they can never live there.

'I may not be a descendant of Charles the Second, but I am not your boy.' Light leans back in his chair and takes a breath. 'Your niece and I are engaged. My position is perfectly respectable. It may not be as elevated as you would wish, but I have my dignity and I am certainly not being bought off.'

Sir George opens his mouth to speak. He inhales sharply and his breath catches with a gagging sound. When he coughs into his handkerchief, it racks through him. His eyes are bright with the same sheen Light saw in Emilie. Londonderry. Snow. The pillow damp from the sweat in her hair. Despair.

'Shall I ask for some water?'

Sir George shakes his head. 'It will pass. It will be over soon.'

Light does not speak. There are two meanings to the other man's words.

'You have seen this before, I think?' he says. 'Your late wife died from consumption.'

'Yes.'

'Then you know the signs. I'm not long for this world.'

'I'm sorry.'

The older man makes a sound. 'No, you're not.' He taps the table with his left fingers. 'So, you love my niece enough to marry her.'

'More than enough.'

'Enough to do what's right for her?'

'What do you mean?'

Sir George leans back and pushes his pistol to one side, gazing at Light as he takes out a pipe. 'I care for both my brother's children, but I have an especial fondness for my niece. I worry about what will happen to her when I'm gone. She hasn't had an easy time of it. And she hasn't been lucky with her family. Her father dead, her grandfather a tyrant, her brother a fool. Not to mention her mother's actions.' His eyes flick to Light's face. 'No reaction there. So the rumours are true. You know.'

'What rumours?'

'Have you told her?'

'Of course not.'

'Good. This meeting might be productive, after all.'

Light opens his mouth to reply, but the older man continues to speak.

'She has some cousins on my mother's side – ladies, mostly – and they care for her. But it's not the same is it, as a proper head of the family. Friends, business partners, such people can't really be trusted. Look at your own father and your family's situation after he died–'

'What's your point, Sir George?'

'My point is that it's more important than ever that Clarissa makes a proper marriage. She needs someone with a position. With connections and reputation. Someone to stabilise her.'

'Isn't her own position high enough to allow her to choose?'

'I'm not talking about wealth or a title, Light. I'm talking about society. The stability of a place and a family that will keep her safe.' He looks Light in the eye. 'You can't offer that.'

'I'm not without connections.'

'Army friends. Parties with the Prince Regent. Yes, I've heard all this. They are fripperies that will fade away. We're an old family, and that's what she needs. Ancestry, foundations, roots.'

Not the son of a trader, a pirate. A landless East Indies princess.

The older man straightens his back with renewed vigour. 'If you really love her, you'll understand this.'

Light looks at the wall and the gilt-framed Canaletto. 'I can still achieve enough for her to be stable,' he begins. 'My paintings sell well. I will always have work.'

A cloud passes over Sir George's face. 'I had hoped not to go down this path,' he says, drawing on his pipe as his cough racks through him. 'Your late wife was French, yes?'

'A French Huguenot. Her family had been refugees from the Terror.'

'Yes. Yes, it makes sense. The French are less bothered by these things. My condolences for your loss. Have you considered what will happen to your children?'

'I'm sorry?'

'What their life will be like. Their opportunities.'

'We would raise them in England.' The words slip out unplanned.

'Of course.'

'And with Clarissa's – with your niece's–'

'With my niece's fortune, they'll be well provided for.'

'Yes.'

'But is that all they'll have to worry about? She is lucky, my niece, for being so fair-skinned. I am not sure the world would be so kind to her otherwise.'

He hears the bell of the half-hour and thinks, then, of his father's pepper gardens, the dappled sunlight of Penang. Yellow-lashed eyes of blue. A pressure builds inside his skull.

'And besides,' the old man is still talking. 'The world is not what it was. No one wants a corsair, an Oriental princess, a Portuguese in-law. Not in real life, outside of poetry. Everything is dour morality. Believe me, I sympathise. But even your father knew this. He wanted you to grow up in Suffolk away from prying eyes. And you – you would make a spectacle of your own children?'

Light stands, slowly this time, stepping away from the table with care. 'If you'll excuse me.' He thinks of his sisters and their pale-faced husbands, pain pricking behind his eyes.

'Are you sure you won't take the cheque?'

Light doesn't reply.

'Then perhaps you should find a white heiress – one who needs a soldier.' The old man's voice seems to roll around the room, mocking. Light glances back at him, his sweat-stained colour and pallid eyes. He looks the same as his father, his brother, his cousins. If there is madness in that family, it travels on the male line.

The door swings shut behind him. Clarissa stands on the staircase, her hair partly undone, the light shining through her and out of her. Gowned in red, she speaks as she walks toward him. 'My uncle? Is that my uncle?'

Light opens his mouth to reply, but all he can see are her alien eyes, the depth to her hair, all her strange loveliness. There is barely any English to her.

Rome, September 1822

We would linger in Naples, Sicily, the voyage back, but it is Rome I remember. The stark outline of the Colosseum inching into the past, the little crowd of English tourists and the vendors hawking their wares. Plaster busts of Caesars long since dead, a proud Minerva, Perseus holding despairing Medusa's curls. We avoided them, pleased that we knew better, laughing in secret at the rosy-cheeked English lord on his first Grand Tour who was convinced he had purchased a true antiquity. Was there something else behind your laughter, even then? I couldn't say. I was always forgetting that you sold paintings for money, that you'd once had an inheritance and it ate at you, how it had been taken away. I was always forgetting. I had that one small privilege, then, of forgetfulness.

But I laughed, and my smugness, my hubris, was only increased by the knowledge that you were no naïve young English dandy but a citizen of the world. Military veteran, Renaissance man. Hero. Half-caste.

The afternoon sun casts an egg-yolk glow over the Piazza di Spagna. The sky is different here, less blue and less familiar. The pigeons cluster by the fountains and stairs. I watch as he stops to gaze up at a small apartment at the base of the Spanish Steps. He sees me looking and gives me a half-smile.

'*Here lies one whose name was writ in water,*' he says.

I think of Keats and his rented rooms in Hampstead, south of home in Hertfordshire. I've been chasing his memory, or Byron's, or Shelley's, and I wonder now if this is its natural conclusion. Death in a faraway land. Consumption. A narrow room under a strange blue sky.

I mourned leaving Venice, looking back on the boat pulling out of the lagoon, watching the wings of the white gulls flash in the sunlight. The waterways were my last hope, my secret passage across the Mediterranean, to the East. But I was leaving them behind.

He strolls back toward me, sending the pigeons scattering. He's smiling, yes, but something has shifted in his smile. It hasn't been right since that afternoon in Venice. I want to ask him what my uncle said, but I do not. I have no speech, because to speak might be to discover the truth.

I push the thoughts away – Nona's house on the Grand Canal, my memories of the banyan tree and the hydrangeas and the gates of Jorasanko – and inhale the city's gelato colours, old splendour, remnants of an empire still stretching its shadow over the world.

'Come up the stairs.' The balls of my feet propel me along Baroque stone. Clouds streak across the golden sky – the beginnings of rain – as I pass the church and the Villa Medici. I hear his feet behind me, past the high walls and thick foliage of the Borghese gardens until we reach the promenade and the city unfolds before us, vast and enduring, the dome of St Peter's piercing the sky. He walks forward, leaning on the balustrades. He doesn't like Catholicism. The churches, the rituals. The superstition.

A blight of sadness overcomes me as I move to join him.

The clouds move across the sky, leaving alternating strands of blue and grey and gold, causing the city to glow with buttercream stone. 'Isn't it beautiful? The domes remind me of India.'

'I know.'

Silence takes its place between us.

To our left, we hear tourists chatting. A local man walks determinedly through their number, peddling red roses. He wears a tricorn hat from the previous decade and a coat worn thin at the corners. There is laughter and the sound of anglicised Italian. Other tones rise above them. 'God damn you,' the rosy-cheeked Englishman, red-faced, curses at the man as his companions gather around him, making soothing sounds. The little group moves toward the lookout point beside us.

'He tried to take my watch.' The Englishman rubs his nose. His face is familiar. A blur of parties fills my memory. His friend murmurs a reply, but it is too soft to catch. 'This wretched country,' the Englishman continues. Beside me, Will is immobile. I cannot even hear him breathe.

There are sounds of exaggerated hushing. The Englishman glances at us. 'Why do I need to be quiet?' His pale eyes flick over William, me, and back again. 'They probably don't even speak English.' He fixes us with a stare, colour blooming across his neck. 'Bloody dagoes,' he says.

I hear Will's breath now. A short inhalation. How quickly the sallow skin of his knuckles turns white.

I laugh, the sound splitting the evening air.

The group beside us moves away, the Englishman casting one backward glance of puzzlement. I tilt my face down and adjust my hat.

Will faces to me. 'How can you laugh?'

'He was ridiculous.'

He presses his temples, turns away, then back again on his heels. 'No, Clarissa. He was ridiculing us. It was humiliating. Do you understand that? Do you understand any of it? You are so naïve. You live in a world of salt air and mermaids and none of it is real.'

A cool breeze blows over the Eternal City. My cheeks burn. How can I tell him of my life lived on the shoreline, each wave passing, passing.

'None of it is real. What's real is your name, your neo-Palladian manor, hot chocolate, game for dinner. Never being hungry. Don't you understand? You're not one of them, but they protect you. I don't have that. I don't have any of it. And you're just throwing it all away, with me.'

'But you could have it, too.'

'No, I couldn't.' The harassed tone of his voice begins to calm. 'I used to think as you do, when–'

'Don't say when you were my age.'

'When I was younger. Before I went to India.'

'And what happened there that was so terrible? Why won't you speak of it?'

He shakes his head, his voice quiet now. 'Nothing. Nothing at all. There was no one thing that happened. But at the same time, it was everything. Being there for some time, seeing the way the English live, the way they treat everyone else. Seeing what happens to people like us. It gets under your skin.'

I place my fingers back over his knuckles. His hand is cool to the touch.

'What do you mean? What was it like? Tell me.'

He smiles with just one corner of his mouth, squeezing my hand. 'Nothing really. It doesn't matter. I'm sorry I mentioned it. I'm sorry I lost my temper.' he says. 'Let's go back down to the piazza.'

South Australian Coast, October 1836

He sits up slowly, rubbing grit from his elbow, his side. Fool. How had he not seen the drop in the dark? He has measured this country well. And still, it is as though the boulders reshape themselves around him.

She sits across from him, turquoise skirt bound about her legs like a tail. A ship to India would never have worked, but if they'd stayed in Venice, they might have lived out their lives in that floating city, half on earth and half on water, joyous in their hybridity, and their children would have been no different to Venetians.

As if she hears his thoughts, she places a warm hand on his knee, but when he moves to touch her, she draws away. Bile rises in his throat, and he coughs, that same racking cough of Sir George, the same rattle that tore through Emilie in Londonderry.

He tries to hide it, but as he supresses the cough it only grows, sending spikes into his chest so that it curls into itself, compressing his sternum.

'Will?' Her voice has lost its needling tone, its accusations.

He raises a hand. 'Stay back.' Twisting his face away from her, he kneels over the rocks, the band tightening slowly around his chest. A swift arrow of pain constricts his throat, and the cough tears through with a retching sound as wetness sprays over his hands and chin. When he looks up, in the moonlight, blood coats his fingertips.

'Will!' she gasps, her face drained. 'I'll fetch some water.'

He sits up slowly. 'There's some brandy in my coat. If you wouldn't mind.'

'Of course.'

He flinches as she approaches. 'Wait. Let me wash my hands.'

'But you are not contagious.'

He doesn't reply. The surf surges coldly over his fingers, the whitewater browning and washing away. 'It's a debatable point.'

Her fingers move over his coat pocket, and she takes the brandy, her hand hovering for a moment on his shoulder, before she sits back.

Although he can feel her watching him, he avoids her eyes. 'Some people believe the disease is hereditary, or a form of cancer. In England, they clung to a ludicrous custom of placing the king's hands upon the sick until a few decades ago. Country people see it as the act of a vampire. One member of a household sickens and dies, and then the dead returns to claim its family members, one by one. But that is all superstition. There is a chance the disease is catching. You should keep your distance.'

When he finishes, she passes him the brandy. In Venice, the light shone through her like glass. Now her face is hard.

'Tell me you're not dying,' she says, and immediately covers her mouth.

He wills her not to cry, but when he sees her cheeks are dry, he feels a small surge of resentment. He sips the brandy once, and again more generously.

'The air here is good, is it not? I've heard it can cure it,' she says.

'Sea air and a temperate climate, yes, that's what they say. It hasn't worked for me.'

'Not yet, perhaps, but there is still hope.'

Hope. A vision comes to him of his first sight of the country: green fringes of the white harbour under a southern sky. He felt then a buoyant sense of elation. But a squall bore down on the coast, buffeting the ship, bringing dark clouds, and he thought he would always be tormented by melancholia and gales of wind.

'I wouldn't be surprised if I were dead within a year.'

'You exaggerate.' Her voice takes on a cold quality, reminding him of his wife's former governess.

His throat rasps. 'I do not.'

'If you're dying, then you need to tell me the truth.'

The tide runs around his knees as he presses the line of his brows. Perhaps it is time, after all. He begins to speak.

India, November 1804

When he disembarks in Cochin, it is the first time he has set foot in Asia in over ten years. He arrives in the late afternoon to a sky streaked by pashmak clouds and the silhouette of coconut trees bending toward the sea. It is, and is not, familiar. Around him, the other Englishmen clasp their throats at the humidity, but he is not that sort of Englishman. For the first time, he remembers what it is to breathe properly. For the first time, he is a free agent. He has coffee and pasteis di nata with a Portuguese trader in the shadow of a Nasrani Church. The man's wife wears a sari against skin the colour of polished teak, a silver icon of the Virgin Mary gleaming at her neck.

Later, as he walks through the town, fragments of French mingled with Malayalam float over to him. He passes a shrine to Ganesha, threads of incense weaving over the street. Without thinking, without pause, he rings the sacred bell. On the shoreline, the cantilevered cheena vala hang suspended over the water, magic gifts of Kublai Khan framing the orange sun as it sinks low on the horizon. He wanders the beach as fishermen sort their catches and he sits with his toes in the water, spooning saffron curry over pearlescent rice, savouring the taste of white fish flavoured with tamarind and ginger. The dish is new and wondrous on his palate, but it calls to mind in one heated burst of scent and taste and texture the food of his childhood on that island in Malaya. It's the first real curry he's had since he was six years old, and as the spice burns and warms him in equal measure and the sunset casts its glow through the old Chinese fishing nets, he thinks his father was right to fall in love with this world. His father was right to say a man might make something of himself here. He watches as the fishermen gather by the street stall, their hands moving over their meal, neatly scooping the colourful dishes up between their fingers and placing them into their mouths. Light considers his own plate. His mother used to eat in such a way, from time to time. He balls up some rice with his fingers and begins to eat with his hands.

In that time, he would like to say he's changed, but in Calcutta, the light falls differently. The chiaroscuro sky has an egg-wash tint that speaks of England. The Portuguese architecture is replaced with the racetrack and the Maidan and the white walls of the East India Company. In the carriage, Mr Fairlie watches him with assessing eyes, blue as the colour of yesterday's sadness, as he draws the curtain across the window, blocking out the sun. When Light speaks of Penang, of his father's estate and his dreams for his son, Fairlie studies the folio in his hand.

'Your father dreamt of many things,' he says. 'He was a man of vision, you might say. That energy turned Prince of Wales Island from a backwater into what it is today.' Again, the assessing gaze. 'But then, the island is not what it could be. It is far too exposed and unprotected. In that, your father lacked foresight.' He sits back, still watching Light. 'But it is good to dream.'

'Well, it's not just an idle dream that's brought me here.' Light feels his left hand clenching. The carriage is stagnant with damp leather and the other man's heat. He has sailed here with a stomach full of tales of second sons and new riches, of poor gentlemen raised up to lords. What else could be his purpose?

'My father had plans for me to be a trader, as he was before. My guardian, Mrs Doughty, showed me his letters. She said he left me his estate and some funds, which you have cared for.' Light allows his words to hang in the air. 'You'll find I'm diligent and persevering. I don't give up easily. I believe you received the letters of recommendation from my former captain and the Reverend Doughty.'

A smile creeps over Fairlie's face. 'Yes, yes. I've heard of what a gifted boy you are. Your sister Sarah tells me you were quite the hero in France. That's good news, William, that's very good news.' The carriage shudders. Light longs to open a window, but he remains still.

'I'm sure your talents will more than make up for your natural disadvantages,' Fairlie continues.

Light holds his breath. 'I'm sorry?'

The older man's face is blank. 'I mean no disrespect.'

'I'm not sure what you mean.' Light tries to keep the strain from his voice. He has an inkling of Fairlie's intent. 'My parents were married,' he says slowly. 'According to the custom of my mother's people.' He has seen the wedding dress. Heard of a nikah performed on a still afternoon in Kedah.

Fairlie's gaze drops. 'Yes. So I have heard. Your lack of legitimacy is not ideal.'

'Sir, I have just said–'

'William, William. It is the customs of your mother's people that are the problem.' Fairlie looks back at him, smiling.

Light tells himself that the older man is trying to be kind and rests against the smooth seats. 'In what way are they a problem? I am not Catholic or Muslim.'

Fairlie sighs. 'Your mother was. And it seems your sisters really have not prepared you. You've had a fine education in Suffolk, but I always feared that might be a problem.' He clasps his hands in front of him. 'You may know that as a member of the Company, your father was forbidden from marrying a Catholic. Did you ever wonder why your mother did not change her name? She was always Rozells.'

His mother had many names. Martina Rozells. Thong Di. Mrs Francis Light. Nyonya Yeen. 'That is the way of it,' he says slowly. 'Where she was from, the ladies don't change their names when they marry. Not officially. They never have.'

Fairlie shakes his head. 'A shocking custom. A family cannot possibly be united when a mother does such a thing.' His empty eyes peer back at Light. 'But no matter. Your lack of legitimacy is not convenient, but it is hardly the main barrier.'

'Then what is?' Light speaks before he can stop himself. He needs to hear it, needs the sentiment to be given shape before him.

Fairlie rests the tapers of each finger against its opposite. 'My dear boy, you must understand that none of this is your fault. No one who knew your father would dream of holding this against you.' He presses his lips together. 'But sadly, you're not in England anymore. Our conventions are different here. They must be. I know it's fashionable back home to dress like a corsair and eat Ottoman sweets, but out in the colonies, our boundaries become important. It's like slavery, really. The Lord Chief Justice might find in a London court that to breathe English air renders a slave free, but such ideals don't function in the Caribbean. And so it is here. A half-caste can't be a trader, or an officer in the Company. I know you have your talents and your father's face. I know you've served in the Navy. They tell me you're clever. That's good. But it won't be enough out here.'

'Are you saying that I might serve in the British Navy but not for the East India Company? My mother is not Indian. And my parentage was of no concern to the Doughtys, or the Navy, or anyone in London.'

Fairlie adjusts the carriage's curtains to better control the light. 'That is interesting,' he says. 'You're rather dark, you know. But I suppose you are not Oriental about the face. Still, that makes little difference here. The lowliest street sweeper in India might have a fine European nose and still be black as pitch. I suppose it matters less back home. People aren't attuned to the difference. But it matters here. What message would it send to make you the captain over an English private? It would up-end the whole order of things. First, it will be the half-castes, and the next thing you know every native in India will have dreams of lordship and command.'

'Is that such a terrible thing?' Light's words escape him. No one has ever spoken to him thus. He imagines reaching out and slapping Fairlie across the face. But the man is old, and the act would be unbefitting of a gentleman.

Fairlie's shoulders bob up and down in a short, mannered laugh.

'I don't see what's so amusing.'

'My dear child. I mean no offence. You must understand. This is nothing personal. You seem to have inherited your father's merits. But we can hardly make an exception for you and risk the delicate balance of social order.'

'This is ridiculous.'

'I must say, I am surprised your sister Sarah didn't inform you of these matters. She has made a very good marriage, you know, all things considered.'

Pressing his closed fist against the leather, Light leans forward and opens the window in a movement so quick the older man flinches. The Calcutta air floods the narrow confines of the carriage. Stagnant water, rotting freesias, the musky scent of stray dogs and macaques.

'Damn the Company, then. Damn trade, even.' He looks back at Fairlie, whose mouth droops. 'Tell me of my inheritance. My sister Sarah claims that the estate is being withheld from us.'

'Ah. I am afraid she misunderstands the situation. You see, your father's lands were never as large or as valuable as rumour thought them. He had debts. Prince of Wales Island belongs, as I'm sure you know, to the East India Company.'

'No. That was my mother's dowry.'

'A French rumour, I'm afraid. Your mother's family never had anywhere near as much influence as dear Trapaud makes out.'

'She was the Sultan of Kedah's granddaughter. And the next sultan's niece.'

'Was she? I've never understood how these Oriental families work. Everyone's an uncle, aren't they?' Fairlie laughs.

Light shakes his head. 'She negotiated my father's settlement in Penang. The Sultan of Kedah gave it to them.' *My great-grandfather*, he thinks.

'Ah yes,' Fairlie sighs. 'And that good family is, we all know, a direct descendant from Alexander the Great.' He leans forward.

'A fairytale. Dear William, you must understand. There is nothing for you in Malaya. Rumours and mist and legal battles you will never win. Think of your dear brother. No one is ever able to take on the Company and win.'

'Are you telling me there is nothing left?'

'Very little. I myself am paying for your sisters' weddings, their dowries. I did ask Mrs Doughty to inform you of the finances, but you know how ladies can be. She had this romantic notion of your father's fortune in the Indies, of your mother gowned in silk and jewels.'

'My mother had both of those things.'

'If you say so. Once, perhaps. Not anymore.'

The carriage jolts and sways. Light feels his body lift off the seat as the cabin curves around him. Outside, the strains of rapid Bengali fill the air. There is a shriek, and the carriage swerves to a jarring halt.

Fairlie grips the cabin walls, his eyes two spots of blue against his pallid face. 'Good Lord.' He knocks against the side of the wall. 'Abdul. Abdul – what's going on?'

Light levers open the door and steps out into the brightness. His skin greets the day with relief as he leaves behind the cloying darkness of the carriage. He blinks in the sunlight. A shadow looms out of the glare. Fairlie's manservant.

'Stay back, sir.' Abdul raises his palms. Light looks past him. The horses whinny and stamp with nervous energy. A crowd gathers, murmuring. He wishes he could speak Bengali. Light steps away from the carriage and pushes through the crowd.

The carriage driver is arguing with a shopkeeper, gesticulating with his right hand while his left clutches his forehead. Somewhere in the crowd a woman wails.

Light feels himself pushed to the front of the crowd. He sees them then. There, at the base of the horses' hooves, wrapped in dirty white cotton, are the mangled legs of a man.

'Christ.' He lurches toward the prone figure. 'Somebody get a doctor.' The carriage driver seizes his shoulders, speaking rapidly, but Light shrugs him off and turns to Abdul. 'What is he saying?'

The youth's face is strained. 'He is saying you should not touch him.'

'What do you mean?' Light realises that no one is touching the injured man. Or almost no one. Down in the dirt, so still he had nearly missed her, a woman crouches, wrapped in grey. With one thin hand, she clutches the man before her.

'They're a damned superstitious bunch.' Fairlie leans out of the carriage window. 'All these rules about who can touch whom. Abdul, move the man from the road.'

Abdul blinks, not speaking or moving.

'Abdul.' Fairlie's voice is sharper.

The youth moves toward the figure in the dirt, compressing his lips.

'Here. I'll help you.' Light steps forward. Together they lift the man and carry him gently to the side of the road. The woman follows.

Light looks back at Fairlie, whose face is pink and white against the carriage's darkness. 'What now?'

Fairlie beckons to Abdul. 'Go and notify that Muslim charity you told me about.' Abdul nods and Fairlie hands him a small purse. 'Take this.'

Light reaches for his wallet and removes some coins. 'Here,' he tells Abdul. 'Take this as well.'

As he climbs back into the carriage, Light catches a smirk cross Fairlie's face.

'That was very like a gentleman of you, William. But I'm afraid you're in no position to be giving out charity. If I were you, I'd take care of those coins for yourself. We wouldn't want to see you down on the side of the road one day.'

Light doesn't reply. As the carriage draws away, he watches the crowd thin, the shopkeeper shaking his head and disappearing into his store, until all that is left are the strips of dull white fabric draped over the body of a man and a woman's grey sari blending into the road.

Calcutta, March 1805

Sunlight lances through crystal glasses of champagne and the room hums with restrained celebration. He sees the space around her first. No feet move near the hem of the vibrant sarong. Her hair, swept up, is still vividly black. How old is she? He does not know. A mother will always be timeless.

He sees Fairlie frown as he moves toward her, but he ignores him. The crowd throngs about the older man, playing court to the bride's de facto father, pinning him into a corner of adulation. It is where their mother should be, not here in this shrouded corner of civilised distance and invisibility.

She turns to him as he approaches. Smooth dark eyes, hard and shining. She is smaller than he remembers. The silk edge of her baju panjang has started to fray. Her face is blank as she looks at him. He wants, in this moment, to address her as he should, to address her as she is. Ibu. Mother. But the room is so quiet, her face so unrecognising, so fearful.

'Madam.' His voice – so restrained – splinters the air. 'I fear you do not remember me.'

Her eyes study him, hand flitting to her chest. 'Francis?'

His father. His brother was Francis, too, but they always called him Lanoon. It is not the first time in India he has been taken for his father. His mother blinks rapidly.

'Ibu.' There. He has said it. 'Nama saya William.'

'William.' The name leaves her lips in a rush of exhalation. She inhales and lets her breath out again in a swift whoosh. 'William.' Words stream from her like the tide pulling out of Penang harbour. They wash over him, a fluid mix of Malay punctuated with Portuguese. 'William. My goodness, William. My darling ... sayang ... anak lelaki ... bom Deus–' She grips his hands, his face, as her tenor changes. 'Where have you been? Why didn't you come back? Why haven't you seen me? I sent you letters.'

His sisters – years older than him, who lived in Malaya for far longer – have always claimed an untouched ignorance. They say the language has left them completely. They see no Malay, hear no Malay, understand no Malay. But he is good at languages. The polyglot meanings of another's words always stick fast in his mind. And so he is cursed to hear the fluency of her recriminations.

His mouth forms a reply, but his tongue sticks to his palate, causing the words to sound halting, with a child's vocabulary. 'I was in school when Father died. And then the navy. I had to work.'

She speaks more quickly. 'They took everything. Fairlie and the others. Our house, our investments. Your sisters. They wouldn't let me bring you home from England.'

His tongue has not been mothered well enough to keep up with her. English was never her strong suit. Light lapses into fluent Portuguese. 'What do you mean, they took everything?'

'I wanted to bring you back from England. You are my eldest son. I should have had you with me.'

'It's all right, Mother. I was well looked after. The Doughtys–'

'You should have been with me to take care of things.'

His mother blinks. Her voice has been quiet, but when she reopens her eyes, she looks around in a darting motion. Light is aware of the adhesive gazes settling on him from around the room. The guests know that something is happening here, that something is not quite right.

'Mother.' He takes her hand. It's warm and dry. 'I'm here now.' Her fingers squeeze around his own. For a moment, he thinks she is going to smile. 'What happened?' He speaks again. 'Your uncle – couldn't he help you?'

'My uncle washed his hands of me after the Company betrayed him.' Her grip tightens. 'He told me to choose. My ancestors or the Europeans. I chose you and your brother and sisters. Your father. He was my husband, my family. We built Penang together, he and I. He would never have gone to the island if not for me.' Her eyes move over his face. 'Do you remember that day when we landed on the beach, in the boat with Father Joachim? You tried to pull his beard.'

Light shakes his head. 'I was a baby, Mother.'

She looks down, alone in her memory. 'How did it come to this, William?'

A hand touches his elbow, and he glances into eyes that mirror his own. His sister Sarah.

'Will,' she says. 'Come back to the party.' She nods at the woman in the baju panjang. 'Mother,' she says, in English.

'I'll just be a moment,' Light says. He leans closer to his sister. 'And why has she been left here all alone?'

Sarah frowns. 'She hasn't been. Not really. But you know how hard it is to speak with her. All those years with Father. You'd think she could have learned English.'

A sound of frustration escapes him. 'No, Sarah, I don't know. I haven't seen her since I was six years old.'

'Keep your voice down, please.'

He pinches the bridge of his nose. 'There must be someone here who knows Portuguese.'

Sarah makes a small movement with her fan. 'I shouldn't think so. We don't have many Catholics here.'

He glances back at their mother watching them silently. Her eyes are the chiselled flint of the ancient weapons found at Hoxne.

'Come and see our sister, Will,' Sarah urges. 'You've barely spent any time with the bride.'

He is aware of their middle sister laughing in a froth of orange blossom somewhere in the centre of the room. Out of the corner of his eye, he sees William Fairlie approach them.

Sarah's face tightens. 'Please, Will, don't do this here. Think of us. You may come and go as you please, but Calcutta is our home now. We have to do things properly here.'

Light watches the refractions of crystal glass play over his sister's face. He thinks of afternoons under palm fronds when they were children. When had she become so drawn and anxious?

'All right,' he says. 'I'll do this for you. But we need to talk about it properly later. Fairlie, Suffolk House, all of it.'

Sarah nods, eyes flicking to Fairlie's approaching silhouette. 'Yes. Yes. Thank you.'

He grips his mother's hand. 'I'll come back,' he says in Portuguese. 'I'll come back, Ibu.'

His mother doesn't release his fingers.

Sarah takes his free arm. 'Come on, William.'

He lingers, taking in his mother's skin, her lineless face, the hard eyes above her scowling mouth. How warm her hands are.

'I won't be long. I'll come back.' This time, in Malay. Sarah sighs. He prises his fingers gently from his mother's grip.

'Come back,' she says. As Sarah draws him away, he again looks toward his mother, catching glimpses of red and pink and her smooth dark hair in the shining room, until the crowd presses in on him and he is forced to turn to Fairlie and his sisters, and their smiling, self-satisfied husbands.

He returns when shadows lengthen and the merriment dims. Guests begin to depart and the bride and groom retire. He returns to the same corner of the ballroom as the candles are lit, but his mother is gone, the corner empty, and no one can remember seeing the woman with the dark hair in a red baju panjang.

Penang, September 1806

Fringed fingers of palm trees droop over the shadowed garden and sourness stretches the air, taut and acidic, like lemongrass and sweat. The house is shuttered, the garden going to seed. Where there were herbs and a pepper tree, vines and shy grass cover the earth.

There are no signs of his mother. He seeks, in the green depths of the trees, a telltale flash of red or pink, auspicious colours, she called them. But for the streak of Indian rhododendron, the garden is deep with layered shades of green.

He cannot deny the movement of his heart, the way his fingers curl over his palms, clenched and damp. It has been fourteen years since he was last here. And it was fourteen years since he had seen his mother, until his sister's wedding.

Deeper in the garden stands a kumquat tree. Its orange fruit recalls a different mother in a tangerine sari, hands outstretched and grasping at a child. He sees the desperation in her eyes, the black smear of kohl across her cheek. The rumours that came to him afterwards. He feels a quiet shame.

No one told him his mother would be at the wedding. He should not be surprised. His sister was ensconced with Mrs Fairlie's relatives while Light stayed with Fairlie, went out shooting with his future brother-in-law, and tried to get some clear-headed advice about his financial standing. Meanwhile the woman who could have revealed all was right there, in the same city. But no one told him.

No. They had waited for him to settle, to become aware of the natural order that governed the fragile network of power in the East. He had left the navy and England with his father's words kept close to his heart. His guardians, the Doughtys, were to raise him, prepare him to build a life out there, like Francis before him, in governance and trade. *Send him back to the East*, his father's letter had said, *where a man may make himself.* But only a certain kind of man.

It was not his father's fault that in his independence – his resourcefulness, his own lack of bloodline or family, his kindness – he could not imagine how his dark-haired, brown-skinned son would never be allowed to be that certain kind of man.

Light walks through the gate and into the garden. In the distance, he can hear murmurs of women speaking a Malay dialect. Laughter spikes the heavy silence of the air. His pulse quickens, but the voices are young, they are not his mother.

Deeper into the garden, he can smell ixora flowers and dampness. India assaulted him with recollections of home, with impressions that conjured this island. Now that he is here, his head pounds and his veins swell. Was the boy scrambling over the ancient oaks of Suffolk, the naval hero, the same as the one whose first memories were here, coloured by the scent of pepper and combava and the sound of the Muslim call to prayer?

Whiteness flares in the corner of his vision, deep in the shade of a banana tree. A child sits in the shadows, naked from the waist up, his cropped blond hair screening his face.

Light stands still, his muscles taut with surprise and anticipation. A soft mud fort, supported by sticks, is at the child's feet. His legs are wrapped in a red batik sarong.

The garden holds its breath, the distant women falling into silence. Light steps forward slowly, half suspecting already, but he cannot be sure. The child stirs, glancing up, and the gold hair parts across his face. Eyes framed with barley-coloured lashes look back at Light. They are eyes like shards of hewn topaz, like the waters off the Athenian coast on a cloudless day.

He exhales, stepping back.

Beyond the boy's pallor he can see it. In the shape of his eyes and the length of his nose and the width of his cheeks. It is his mother's son.

The child smiles. Light wills his lips to move but they remain still. His father had ocean-coloured eyes and hair like the sand of Pulau Jerejak. Light has his father's face, but not his colouring. He has always wondered what it might mean to have that final key to Englishness, blue eyes.

The child giggles. Mud is smeared across his shining torso. Light feels his stomach twist. How early he learned, in Suffolk, the importance of neatness and cleanliness. If clothes were well cut, then all the better. No one could say then that he was one rung away from living in a tree. With his father's eyes, would that have been different?

A voice rings out through the dappled garden, but Light cannot make out the words. He hears only the strains of his mother's voice.

The child turns toward the sound. When he looks back, Light shakes his head, raises his finger to his lips and backs out of the garden.

England, November 1822

The day Light sees the grey mist parting over the rough English coastline, a fog clears in his mind. Gone is the strange magic of Venice; gone is the dour heat of Naples and the stifling history of Rome. Summer has truly ended.

When they arrive in London, he drops Clarissa at their hotel and walks to his old rooms in Brompton to pick up the bags he stored before their flight across the Channel. The walk is not short, but without Clarissa he veers back toward economy. The price of a cab could buy him tomorrow's supper. And besides, how much he has missed this. The way the streets shine with the day's rain, the lamplighters working in the gloaming, the sound of his heels on pavement. He could close his eyes and find his way around this city, his feet seeking out the contours of the streets and alleys, the elevation of the earth around the Thames. He could feel, from the way the road slopes or the scent from the market or the baker or the coffee house, the direction in which he travelled. And he could tell a stranger, a tourist, an immigrant, yes, there, down that ostentatious road, is the best mulligatawny in England, and there, by the waterways, are the lascars completing their work, and over here, in Westminster, are black men and women writing their pamphlets on freedom. He could tell them that London is the best city in the world, that London is the world. It is a world made up of so much difference that here, he is just a man. He is not strange. He is not an Italian, a Spaniard, or a Turk. He is just an old soldier returning from the Continent with a suntan. Weather-beaten.

And yet, while his heart might balloon to think of the great city's arterial streets running to the Strand, in this moment he is uneasy. The ring he bought in Venice weighs heavy in his pocket. Thick with rubies and pearls and wrought from gold, it was something he could not afford. He has held onto it, waiting for a moment like that in the Vauxhall Gardens when she floated out of the heavens, or like the one by the river in Bath. He waits for that moment, and how he fears it. They are already engaged. Precontracted, they would have called it in the old days. He has no reason to fear the significance of a ring.

As he reaches Brompton it begins to drizzle. He could not call it rain. Not after Malaya and India. He pauses and looks around him. The lights are coming on slowly in the windows of the houses and flats. He imagines their occupants. Poor gentlemen with paintbrushes and middling ancestry. The women who work as their wives and models. Artists and intellectuals. He was one of them, once. But war pays more reliably.

When he reaches his old boarding house and lets himself into the hall, the first thing he sees is a new overcoat hanging by the door. The air smells faintly of boot polish and eau de cologne. He approaches the sitting room and sees a set of friendly shoulders, the familiar curls of light-brown hair. He blinks.

'Napier?' The figure rises, a smile lifting his cheeks. 'By God, it is! Napier.' Light rushes toward him, extending his hand. 'How good it is to see you!'

Napier grasps his hand and pulls him into an unexpected embrace. 'Light, you devil. Where have you been?'

Light laughs as they separate. 'Here and there,' he says.

Napier beams at him expectantly, his eyes sliding over Light's shoulder. 'Is she here?'

'To whom are you referring?'

Napier claps him on the shoulder with a jovial force that makes Light's knee buckle. 'FitzRoy's granddaughter. We heard you got married in Italy. Congratulations, old man. I know you've had a tough time of it since the war ended. I am happy for you. I hear she's completely charming. Not to mention rich and beautiful.'

'It wasn't about that.'

'Of course not. I can imagine there are other things. I'm sure you're uniquely suited to each other.'

'Yes. Perhaps.' Napier seems different. A tall, self-assured man who has become even taller, more self-assured. What other things is he referring to?

Light thinks of the poor Eurasian women walking the streets of Bow Bazaar. 'We haven't yet had the wedding.'

'Oh?' Napier raises his eyebrows. 'Well.' A pause. 'Good. I can attend. Let me know the date and I'll bring my brothers.'

'Yes. Yes, of course.'

'Actually, I've come here because–'

'It was so good of you to come–'

Their words tumble over each other and both men stop speaking. Light laughs softly. When did speech with his old friend become so awkward?

Napier smiles without parting his lips, his eyes seeming briefly far away. 'Come and sit down, old man.'

Light's spine stiffens. 'What's wrong?' he says. 'Why are you here?'

'Come and sit down,' Napier says again. They know each other too well, over too many years, in too many crises. It was Napier who knew, from a look on Light's face, that Emilie had died. 'What is it?' Light asks again.

Napier rubs his jaw. 'I had a letter from your sister, Sarah. She had heard you were abroad, with no forwarding address–'

'Is she …?'

'She's very well, very well. Husband, children, all of them safe and happy.'

Light relaxes. 'Good. That's good.'

'But you see, it's your mother.' Napier averts his gaze, reaching into his breast pocket.

'Is she ill?'

Napier looks up. Even Light is surprised at the coldness in his own voice.

'I'm sorry, old man.' Napier's voice is quiet. 'She died some months ago. They think it was her heart. Apparently, it was very sudden. Completely painless, I hear.' His touch is warm on Light's shoulder. 'I really am very sorry. To be so far away, I am sure it's difficult. But at least you spent some time with her as a young man. It must have been so gratifying to see her again, in Calcutta and Penang.'

Light can hear the rattle of the cabs outside, the call of Estuary voices. Beyond this room, autumnal darkness settles over the city. And yet, he can see a world with no autumn, hear the traders cry on the shores of Penang. Light stares at Napier, thinking of that afternoon in the garden, the stray smile of the child, his half-brother, and his own fleeing steps at the sound of his mother's voice.

'I'm sure it made her very happy to go to your sister's wedding, and to see you there after so many years.'

The heat of the Indian afternoon. The space the other guests left around her. And the rest of it. Not yet. Not yet.

'What of her family?' Light asks the question, unsure if he wishes to know that answer. 'Her Dutch husband, her son.'

Napier looks down. 'I am not sure of the husband. Your sister doesn't mention the son. She does say that nothing was left of your father's estate. Your mother had some rented land before she died, but she was very short on money. There's no further inheritance, but then ...'

'I knew that anyway.'

'Yes.'

Light rubs his temples. 'God, Charles, what sort of man am I? A man of my age, my experience, I should be providing for my family. Not drifting around, selling paintings.'

'Come, come. Be sensible. You know what a devil the East India Company is. Without your father around, your mother had no hope of keeping his property. None of you did. And your sisters are well and safely married. Your brother would be a man by now. After your wedding you'll have more than enough means to set this right. You can seek out your brother, fund a career in politics. Take on the wretched Company and sort out the Indies, if you like.'

Light thinks again of the space around his mother as the sunlight glanced off the ballroom floor, and of the tightrope he walked in India, always somewhere between passing and humiliation, never sure which way the wind would prompt him to fall.

'All the money in the world couldn't make the British in India see me as anything more than a half-caste.' The words leave his mouth before he can regret them. They hang in the air, heavy and invidious. 'And my wife – Clarissa – would be no better, perhaps worse, than I.' He closes his eyes, remembering a woman in an orange sari, a pall of tragedy over a once great house. Napier's face is clear in his mind's eye. He paints, in neat brushstrokes, a picture of his friend's righteousness.

'But that's outrageous.' Napier's voice breathes life into the mental portrait. 'Any Englishman worth his salt knows how much value there is to the men of the East. I swear, the colonies are run by ignorant buffoons. But look, Light, this will pass. It must. There will be progress. Consider the slave trade, how far we've come in abolishing that barbarity. It will be the same in the colonies. A divide between the English and the natives cannot be maintained. It defies logic. Everything we've learned from the Enlightenment tells us that civilisation must progress. And it must be the same in India. There are nations in Europe that cannot boast such an old and distinguished history.'

'There are some, Napier, who say things in the colonies are getting worse. That the divide grows.'

'Ah, but that's defeatist, Light. You and I will make sure that such a thing doesn't happen.'

Will we? Light does not reply.

'Besides,' Napier continues, 'no one could meet you and fail to see your qualities.'

'As usual, Charles, you are too kind.'

'And your wife will be from one of our oldest families. How could any provincial colonial official say otherwise? Marry your Miss FitzRoy in happiness, and you'll have the world at your feet.'

Light smiles, for a moment allowing himself to share in the other man's buoyancy. He pictures himself, Clarissa by his side, returning in triumph to Calcutta. Isn't success the best revenge?

Napier smooths his cuff. 'But I am so sorry again, about your mother.'

When Light leaves, he refuses Napier's offer of a lift. He wants to walk, and his bags are nothing he can't carry. Packing light, to remain unattached to places, objects, people, is second nature. Without Napier, however, all buoyancy leaves him. It is easy for his friend to set himself against the established order of things, easy for Napier to say, complacent, that Light will change the world. Napier was born in the summer at Whitehall Palace, the great-great-grandson of a king, the nephew of the Duke of Richmond. He sees the world as a subservient beast that can be tamed. He could never understand Light's own struggles, how everything, from his home on Prince of Wales Island to his birthplace in Kedah, his childhood in Suffolk and his horses at the Peninsula, were only lent to him.

The wind picks up as he reaches Green Park, shaking the last of the leaves out of the branches and scattering them onto his path. He thinks again of returning to Calcutta, Clarissa by his side, the long arm of the past stretching over them. They would not respect him; they would know who she was. And how long would her fortune protect them? How long would it even remain theirs? William Fairlie and his mother, Whitworth and Colonel FitzRoy. The history of the East was filled with families that crossed the colour line, whose fortunes were chiselled away and eaten up, piece by piece, by the long white teeth of the East India Company. And their children. Their children.

He stops on the path under the murmuring plane trees. A few decades ago, the park was a place to be avoided after dark, the haunt of cutthroat mercenaries and highwaymen, and before that, a burial ground for lepers, for the poor and abject.

A cold wind blows and he shudders, pulling his coat closer around him. The threads are getting thin. The thick-wrought gold, the pearls snatched from the sea, hang heavy in his pocket. He knows what he must do.

South Australian Coast, October 1836

Stars spool across the midnight sky. I sit on the rocks with my feet in the tide, watching him speak, the threadbare gaps of our past filled in with colour and hanging between us. My uncle's voice over Venetian waters. His mother's unspoken death. Those things I had always asked about, but he never told me.

The night winds its darkness about us as his voice continues. 'I've often felt that, somewhere on the corner of Green Park and Piccadilly, I took a wrong turn in life, and I've been trying to find my way back ever since.'

I step off the rock and into the water, sinking into sand.

It has been years since I have dreamed of a life that could have been. But even I let myself wonder, just weeks ago, what our lives might have been like if he had not gone to Spain, if I had accepted him back when he first asked. 'There is no value in that line of thinking.'

'Isn't there?' he asks after a moment. 'Not even when I can choose to do things differently?'

I know his meaning and would push it away, and yet an image comes unbidden, then a sound, the rasping cough, his rattling inhalation. We have so little time.

I step out of the water and back onto the shore. Movement flickers in the corner of my eye. A figure stands on the cliff side, the bell shape of her skirt swelling in the wind. We stare at each other, her face covered by gloom. Then she steps back and vanishes over the hillside.

'What would you do differently?' I ask.

'Do you not know?' Even in the dark, I know that he smiles at me.

I pause at the water's edge and close my eyes, seeing the fireworks over Vauxhall after the rush of the hot air balloon, the scarlet bursts mirrored in Will's gaze. I taste the wine in Bath and feel the sun in Venice beating down upon the lagoon.

I hear the bells in Canterbury. They rang that day like musket shots. In the room by the waves my life grew and diminished, all at once. I think of my uncle's words in Venice, of a frightened young man in the gardens of Penang. Perhaps it is true that all things can find their forgiveness.

As I walk toward him, there is a scent in the air. Something small and resplendent brushes its feathery touch against my sternum, fluttering. Its smell is tender, familiar.

He takes my hand, and we lie on the dry sand at the base of the cave. The earth is still warm from the heat of the day's sun. There are crests of lomandra, the fuzz of a wattle, bottlebrush flowers in shades of vermillion. When I kiss him, he tastes of cigar smoke, salt air and molasses. I feel the sand of archipelagos in sunlight, the rise and fall of the intertidal zone.

He pulls away in the darkness. 'My illness.'

I shake my head, drawing him back to me. The tide is coming in, the sea's breath drawing closer. What is death but another ocean voyage, a passage, a passing?

I trace the thick fibres of his scars, following their ropes from his thigh to the join with his torso. They are new and strange to me, so different to our past, when he'd never been wounded.

His breath stills, his hands moving in hesitation. Such gentleness in his protest.

'What is it?'

'My punishment for leaving you. Meted out to me in Spain.'

'What are you talking about?'

'It's nothing. Nothing.'

His hands move into my hair, down my back to grip my hips.

I have forgotten this feeling. Skin upon skin. Salt upon the water.

I wake against the cold earth to the sight of a lightening sky and find him kneeling next to me, buttoning his shirt. When he smiles, the world expands with refracted colours. Our fingers knit together.

'I need to go back to the ship this morning.' His voice is quiet. 'I won't be long. I'll come back to you.' His words are pulled taut by promise and regret.

'I know. It's only that ... I have something to tell you.'

'Oh yes?' His voice is cautious, making me hesitate. I have nursed my truth like a jade stone, turning it over and over until its surface has become smooth and polished.

'What did you want to tell me?' He sits down again. For a moment, we could be back in Bath, by the river as the sun rises and he says those words, *We should get married.* Lightly, and in passing.

'It's about after Italy.' I watch the shadow flicker over his face.

'I'm listening.' His tone is kind but tense.

'Perhaps this is not the right moment.'

'I have time,' he says, and grips my hands.

I laugh softly. 'You're a poor liar.'

'I'm worried the men will be concerned if I'm not back by dawn. I don't want them to send out searchers.'

The implication is not lost on me, with my bare legs, my wet dress, this place.

'I understand.'

'But you could come with me. Stay with me.'

I blink. The sea pauses and the rocks listen. 'What do you mean?'

'Stay with me,' he repeats, 'here.'

'I can wait here this morning.'

He laughs and I am struck by how rare the sound is. The hairs on my neck stand up as his mirth encircles us. 'I don't mean this morning. I mean stay here properly. Forever.' His smile is white. He takes the ends of my hair between his fingers and looks at it as though he has stumbled upon a treasure trove old and precious, once lost, that he never thought to find again. 'Think about it.' He shakes his head, as if to himself. 'Perhaps it is possible, after all.'

'What is?'

'To rewrite the past.'

I don't reply.

'Never mind me. Are you sure you won't come to the ship?'

'I think I'd better not.'

'Then I'll come back for you in a few hours.'

'Yes.' The dawn quickens. I draw his coat and my tartan scarf around me, noticing my engagement ring tangled in buttons of his coat. I could do with a few hours alone. For the first time since I arrived in South Australia, something has changed. He has given me no true answers, and yet I do not feel a grasping urge to know. Instead, there is a stone ball of my own truth and all that is unsaid in my belly and my throat.

His hand snakes into my hair and he kisses me. Then I watch him leave, the silver sky turning champagne around him, a crystal glass running over in celebration. I rise and walk down to the beach. The bird call is lively now, and the beachfront draped in stardust and pearls. Would she like it here? Little Marina, always watching those waves on the Cornish coast, dreaming of pirates and wreckers. Yes, of course she would.

Clouds puff pink on the horizon, but there is darkness on the cliff face. Movement strikes my eye – the bell shape of a skirt, a stark white face, pale eyes staring at me. Time shifts, taking me back to that room in Venice, with the tapestry of three women, weaving, spinning, cutting. The symmetry strikes me. The beachfront darkens.

I step forward, but the figure darts away, scrambling over the rocks in the direction of the *Rapid.*

~

The ship is silent as he arrives. Only Hewitt is on watch, his eyes widening when he sees Light approach. The younger man opens his mouth to speak, but Light holds his fingers to his lips. He ignores the uncertainty on Hewitt's face and the doubt in his eyes. These things will be dealt with. For once, he wants to cling to this new feeling, that this unearthly adventure on the other side of the world has not been his exile or reduction, that it may yet be all he dreamed it could be.

In this briefest haze, the ship's narrow corridor takes on a gleaming turn. Like candlelight, the Assembly Rooms in Bath, the sunlight shining through auburn hair. Light pauses at his cabin door. How is it that man has not learned to distil a moment, to keep it floating in its temporal space, pure and unending?

When he pushes the door open, his feet stick to the brine left on the wooden floor. Seaweed and flotsam cling to the splinters and crevices. Maria sits on the bed in darkness, the hem of her skirt dredged in wet sand.

'Maria?' He opens the cabin window to let in the dawn. Her face glows white, her eyes blue and blank.

'I took a shortcut through the sea.' She gestures at her clothing. 'I wanted to be here before you.' She laughs. 'I thought I was going to drown.'

'God, Maria. Are you all right?' Her fingers are limp and cold. He searches her expression for answers. 'Maria. What have you been doing?'

She snatches her fingers away, moving her hands in front of her, directionless. 'What have I been doing?' Her eyes are still so blank. Everything about her is blank and colourless.

'What about you?' Her voice rises, her palm striking his chest in accusation. 'What have you been doing?'

He walks across the wet floor. 'Maria, I think you should calm yourself.'

'Calm myself?' She stands. 'I saw you. All night. All night.' Her voice continues, thick now with tears. Crying, there is always crying. He has only seen Clarissa cry once.

'You always tell me you can't, that your injury makes it too difficult. And there – out in the open – with her–'

He rests his head on the window frame. If he were another man, he would try to reason with her. Tell her she's special, that he's protecting her. That he can't marry her, so this is the way it should be. But something happens when she starts screaming, and becoming so overwrought. It was the same with his second wife. He would fix his eye on that far point where the sea meets the sky, unmoving, and yet he would begin to leave.

'Who is she?' Something thuds against the wall across from him. 'She's not your housekeeper, at any rate. Not your laundrywoman. The others say she's a witch.'

'Don't be ridiculous, Maria. There are no such things. I've taught you better than that.'

'How else would you explain it, then?' The weeping recommences as the ship creaks around them, the deck beginning to thud with movement.

'Who says such things about her? Your brothers?'

Maria turns and plays with the hem of the bedcovering. 'Tell me who she is, and I'll tell you.'

'Hewitt.' The name emerges from his lips without thought, but as soon as the word takes shape in the air he realises how much he believes it. Maria's back stiffens.

'Your men aren't fools. Not like you.' Maria's voice rings clear in the cabin. 'They know she's no good for you.'

Light thinks of Napier, all those years ago, and how different his friend's assessment had been. How much he has come down in the world since then.

'You're injudicious, Maria. This matter is beyond you.'

'I've seen the ring, William. She's engaged. Do you think she's going to break that off when you are still married, simply to become your nursemaid? She will not care for you as I do. Not when the melancholia takes you.'

Beyond the narrow wooden orifice of the window is an ocean. In its cobalt depths, there are whales and dolphins and all manner of sea creatures. Paper nautili. Seahorses. The red-gowned sea goddess Ma Cho Po, floating over the waves. Selkies, Clarissa would have him believe. Its tide and currents sweep the globe from here to Antarctica to Madagascar to Tristão da Cunha. If he focuses, just right, on the space through this window, on the curl of the ocean foam, on the seagrass spreading like mermaid's hair, he can see her shape in the water. There is no ring, no fiancé, no past or future failure. Just her, and this promise of a life well lived on the shoreline. A promise that all things are possible.

Maria shuts the window.

'Look at me, William. Why won't you look at me?'

He studies her face. Two blue spots shine on its blankness. What is whiteness but absence and loss?

Prying her fingers from his shirt, he steps away from her. She speaks but he does not hear her words. The cabin door swings shut behind him as he moves out into the belly of the ship.

South Australian Coast, October 1836

Lamprey. Squid. Golden sea dragons. I see them in the shallows of the waters. I love the dragons most. Creatures that float with the tide in the seagrass, a fairy-sized water dragon. I found one washed ashore this morning. Burnished and watchful, its fins turned slowly in the strange element of air. I picked it up with two hands and placed it back into the water. I tried to be unnoticed – what would the merchants and grocers turned would-be botanists and Linnaean scholars have done to the creature? I have lived long enough to know of the consumption that passes as scholarship. So, I drew no attention to myself, plucking shells out of seaweed, and slid the fairytale beast back into its natural home.

But the child saw me. She has been watching me all morning, ever since I left the rocks by the shore and returned to the whaler. I saw her dark hair and quick movement over the boulders as she hurried out of sight. She sits now, several metres away, scraping at a seal pelt the way the other women do, day in and day out. She wears a dress of simple cotton. Around her neck is a pendant, a scrimshaw carving of a seal. When I turn my head from her, I feel her watching, but when I glance toward her, she looks away.

Sitting on the sand, I can still see the whaler's shadow. The creaking wood of the ship, its marine stench, hold a promise of safe passage, of flight. Still, after so many years, this is what I am seeking. On the far dune, the whalers are cleaning their tools. Moses raises an arm toward me. I wave and the corners of my mouth tug up involuntarily. Behind me, the girl picks up her belongings and scrambles further along the beach, over a dune and toward the sailors. I turn my head, my body flinching. The woman from the hillside stands over me, sunlight behind her turning her bell shape dark. She clutches papers in one hand; the other is white and folded against her solar plexus.

I stand, pushing myself off the sand.

'You're the lady in his paintings. He never knew I saw them. I used to think you were a sister. Maybe even his mother.' She laughs. A skittish sound. 'Now I know otherwise.' I recognise her voice. She's articulate, but with a rural softness that speaks of tenant farming and cottages and Hampshire. The small woman in the blue dress from the settlement. Peasant stock. I take in her worn hands, the ragged look in her eyes. I have nothing to say to her. And yet. She holds out the paper. I don't take it.

He painted me. The thought creeps in unbidden, overriding all else. How long did he think of me, after my silence? I look at the woman again and speak what I already know. 'You're his housekeeper.' Maria Gandy.

She flinches. 'Is that all you know about me?'

I don't reply.

'You're not wanted here.' Her voice quavers.

'You shouldn't speak to me like that.' I hear my voice emerge with the tones of my grandfather. The woman looks down, then passes her hand over her face, shuddering like a dog shaking the water from its coat.

'No,' she says, opening her colourless eyes. 'You have no right to speak to me that way. I know who you are. *Descendant of kings.*' Her words pivot into the air as she laughs. 'Half-bred daughter of a murderess, more like.'

The horizon tilts in the corner of my eye as she holds up the paper and I trace the words. *A Memoir of Calcutta* by Sir Percy Whitworth, 1814. I catch my father's name in the subheading. My fingers graze the edge of the paper, but the woman snatches it away. How have I never seen this before?

'Does Will know you're here?' At the guilty shift in her eye, I press my point. 'You took this from him, didn't you?'

Maria looks away from me, clutches the page and reads in stilted words, '*By the morning of the seventh, my dear friend Colonel FitzRoy was found unmoving in his room. Despite my own ministrations and the attendance of his doctor, he was declared dead at twenty past ten.*'

I remember the doctor hurrying through the gate, coat trailing behind him, and the anxious eyes of our gatekeeper, Arjun.

Maria haltingly continues: '*Needless to say, the time of his death was a cause of concern, when not a day earlier I had a confrontation with his wife, the Rani Devi, and informed her that I would be forced to discuss her immorality with her husband in the morning. Furthermore, I was informed by a number of sources that the Rani Devi had been observed crushing several jequirity beans and pouring the contents into the colonel's tisane the evening before his death, leaving me no option but to lobby for her arrest on suspicion of murder.*' Maria's blue eyes stick to me as she turns the page. '*I was forced to take responsibility for my dear friend's children after this tragedy, and make provisions for their moral development, so that the boy would learn behaviour befitting of his father's son, and the girl be carefully schooled to avoid replicating her mother's mental failings and depravity.*'

The words ricochet along the beach. I think of my mother's hands, the bells on her wrist, the bright-coloured silks of her dress and the way she took me through the garden, pointing out the plants and birds.

'There was no depravity.' I see my grandfather's hard eyes gazing at me over his desk, my uncle's pallid despair at my behaviour. I have not murdered anyone, but all my life they looked on me as something flawed and deceptive.

Maria holds up the pamphlet, stabbing at the words with her finger. 'This is who you are.'

In his study, the ghost of my grandfather sits up and puts down his pen. *You are a FitzRoy*, he always said. *Behave like one.* 'I won't stand to be accused by a housekeeper.'

There is pain in the other woman's voice. 'I'm not the only one who has read this.' She holds the pamphlet up to me.

'You took this paper from him, without his permission.' I pause. 'And you've shown it to whom?'

'Everyone knows.' Her voice catches on the wind. 'I showed it to the crew, to Hewitt. The other settlers. They all know.' Her hand falls, the pamphlet fluttering. I take it gently from her. The writing curves like a sly smile. Percy. Percy.

I look back at Maria. Her pink sunburnt face. Her empty eyes.

'He won't be pleased you did that.' Already the landscape around me is strange, its unsettling brightness leaving me unanchored and bare. The *Rapid* is close by. Men's voices float in the distance. I turn from Maria and begin to walk as I feel her hot gaze follow me down the length of the beach.

Calcutta, August 1806

When the East India Company brought Tipu Sultan's sons to the city, Percy ordered the guards to shut the gates. He said there'd be trouble outside, and anger at the English and the other Europeans. But my family were neither of those.

The order did not come from my mother. She ran down the path from the main house, her ankle bells singing, telling them to open the gateway. Arjun the guard looked down, not meeting her eyes, as the English sergeant next to him shook his head, speaking in a voice too loud, too slow.

She wanted to go into the city. Did she want to see the sultan's sons? Her hair was loose, and she wore only her orange sari – she was not dressed for leaving the grounds. From my place in the corner of the garden, behind the drooping pink hydrangeas, I watched her looking over her shoulder, eyes red-rimmed and wide. I followed her gaze, but all I could see was my father's friend, Percy, standing on the verandah, smiling. He was always at the house, ever since my father became ill. His servants grew more and more numerous – eating all our food, Asha said. They were the ones I heard, speaking in the stables, of Tipu Sultan's sons and the rebellion, the green-and-gold flag raised over Vellore. They muttered about their swift defeat and the princes' exile, here, in Calcutta, the lowlier rebels blown off the ramparts by cannon fire, their heads propelled clear into the air, the vultures diving to catch the remnants.

I tried to reach my mother, clambering over the grass, but Asha caught me and carried me back toward the house, her brows drawn together. I placed my hand on her face, hard, but she didn't respond. Behind us, the voices grew louder. My mother demanded to be let out. There were murmurs.

'You mustn't touch her!' Arjun's voice, raised. Frightened.

Asha turned with me in her arms, hurrying back toward the gate. Throwing a hand up to the air, pushing Arjun against the fence, the sergeant released my mother.

Then, a face appeared at the gate. Young, barely an adult. I thought at first he was a Bengali in European dress. But the light changed, and I became certain he was an Englishman. I kept looking as the banyan tree cast light and dark across his features. Perhaps he was someone like me.

He spoke as an officer would, holding up paperwork that made the sergeant fold his body into himself, tight and obedient. The boy's eyes drifted to my mother and the veil of dark hair covering her face, and then they focused on me.

The sergeant spoke quickly, quietly. I could make out no words until he said, in tones of fear and exasperation, 'But, sir, Colonel FitzRoy is dead. He died not two hours ago.'

A deep cry left my mother at the sound of my father's name. I twisted in Asha's arms, looking back to the house where my father lay, the windows to his room shuttered and dark, Percy standing on the verandah, smiling.

On the day of my father's funeral, it rains. The drops fall slow and heavy, pooling in the furrows of the cemetery. I try to count the headstones, but there are too many. Rows and rows of crosses and urns, some gleaming white, poking out of the wet earth like baby teeth, others grey and mossy, covered with lichen and trailing vines, creepers waiting to reclaim the land that has been taken from them.

The priest speaks; the mourners are silent. The cemetery attendant watches us from the shelter of the trees, a litter of puppies snuffling about his feet. My brother stands next to me, nursing the red mark on his left cheek. He cried that morning, batting away Asha's shushes, until Percy took him aside and instructed him to behave like an Englishman. When he came back to the nursery, Asha saw his red face and took over his crying. Now, he stands quietly, eyes vacant.

I watch as they lower the casket into the open earth. I do not cry. They tell me my father is in there, that he has gone to God, but they don't meet my eyes when they speak and I know they are lying.

Percy commended my fortitude. 'Look to your sister for strength,' he told Oliver. He lifted my chin with his forefinger and inspected my face. 'Not unlike your mother.' He tugged on a curl of my hair. It hurt, but I made no sound or movement.

'Ice cold. You'll be quite the little heartbreaker one day,' he said.

A dog barks as my brother scoops a handful of dirt and tosses it into the grave. I follow him. The earth is damp and sticky. It clings to my fingers like it never wants to let go. Where is my mother? I have not cried since that afternoon when we were taken from her. My father cannot be dead. Perhaps they are together on a boat, far away, waiting for us.

The rain drums on the palm fronds and the parasols held up into the sky. The mourners begin to leave. I hear them speaking, the same voices I have heard before, at my father's parties, when he first fell ill.

'It's a sad thing. Look at those children. Orphaned, and so young.'

'They're not orphaned. Not really.'

'They might as well be, with a woman like that for their mother. I don't know what FitzRoy was thinking.'

'She was from a good family. And so beautiful. Remember her at the McKenzies?'

'Beautiful for a native, I suppose. But no good will come of it. When will these men learn? Half-caste children rarely meet with good fortune.'

'It's lucky Mr Whitworth takes such an interest.'

'Lucky! Something isn't right about that man. I can see it in his eyes. They're far too close together.'

'I heard their mother – well, it won't do to say it here. Is there a wake?'

The voices trail away. I look at Percy from the corner of my eye, studying his face. His eyes *are* close together. I file this knowledge away, convinced of its secret power.

Oliver walks before me. When I reach for his hand, he bats me aside. Percy takes my fingers. I see some of the few white women in the crowd turn and smile at him. Their eyes flick over me as though they wish I wasn't here.

We reach the gate as the crowd of mourners thin. A man and the tallest woman I have ever seen stand there, not moving. The woman steps forward when she sees me. She does not look at me like the other European ladies but fixes her eyes on mine as if for a moment I am the most important thing in the cemetery. She bends down. Her dress is rippling black bombazine and tartan lining. At her throat gleams a silver mermaid with a curled tail. 'You must be Clarissa,' she says.

Indumati, I think. But I have been trained to accept this name, the name they say my father always wanted, so I nod.

'Mrs Fiona Jensen.'

Her speech is round and soft like the Scotsman who worked for my father before Percy sent him away.

'What is this?' Percy speaks, and the fair-haired man steps forward.

'Major Edward Ramsey.' He passes Percy an envelope. 'I'm acting for Sir Charles and George FitzRoy.'

Mrs Jensen takes my hand and looks me in the eye. 'How would you like to meet your grandfather?'

She is the first grown-up person to ask me what I would like in a very long time. In the background, Percy's tone rises. 'I gave permission for the son to go to England. I knew nothing of you taking the daughter.'

Major Ramsey makes a sound like a laugh. 'Your permission is not required. Unlike his late son, Sir Charles is not a willing traveller. But you may rest assured that I have come from Sir Charles's estate in Hertfordshire with his full authority, to both bring his grandchildren home to England and resolve his late son's affairs.'

Redness surges into Percy's cheeks. It is the first time I have seen him without composure or control. My limbs lighten. I think of floating, of sailing away. Oliver walks to stand by the major.

'What about my mother?' I ask the lady. Her eyes are grey like the sea under monsoon skies; the pupils swell and rise, a black ship on rushing currents. I imagine passing, a passage over water, an endless sea voyage without a port.

'Now don't you worry about her,' the lady says. 'Don't you worry about a thing.'

South Australian Coast, October 1836

But I did worry, every day, for my entire life. I sit on the edge of the ocean, my feet buried in surf. Percy's words burn in my pocket. *Murderess. Mad.* I turn them over in my mind. We grew jequirity beans in our garden. My mother pointed out their hard red shells. They were dangerous and I was not to touch them. And then there is my father, of whom I have little memory. I spent so long thinking of her – of the woman my family robbed from me – that I have not thought enough about the man who stepped away from his country and past for a different future.

For that is what I remember: my grandfather's scorn that my father described his marriage as one of equals, gave up European clothing and stopped eating meat. And I remember, briefly, his happiness, before the long illness eclipsed his life.

I close my eyes. It cannot be as Percy writes. When I look up, Will's shadow stretches across the white sand. His feet are bare and brown, trousers rolled past his ankles. He smiles, his face aglow in hope and expectation, but it melts away when he meets my eyes.

'Why are you sitting here all alone?' he asks, hesitant.

I look for the girl who followed me along the beach, but she has gone to join the whalers. 'I wasn't alone. Besides, I needed to think.'

'I see.' His gaze is blind. I can taste his uncertainty hovering in the air.

'Are you all right?' he asks, after a pause. When I don't reply, he says, 'I've thought some more about what we could do here. Together. When you stay.'

Had he known this all along, even that night in Vauxhall, when I stumbled out of that hot air balloon and into his life?

He lays his coat on the sand and sits beside me, leaving a foot of space. I place my hand on the warm sand between us.

'Has something happened?' He watches my face.

'Your housekeeper came to see me.'

His eyebrows rise. 'I see.'

'And I do not like the eyes of the settlers. They stick to me like hard treacle.'

He frowns.

'I suppose you will say I should dress differently.' I adjust the trousers on my legs. 'Draw less attention to myself.'

I study his weathered profile, the creases that form when he smiles, the age spots highlighted by the starkness of the sun. The daylight makes us quiet, muted. We are different people in the dark.

'We both know you could never be free of attention, even if you wanted to,' he says. 'There's no blending in for us.'

I don't comment on his choice of pronoun. I am aware now – looking back across all my passings and traversings, the passage of time, the past – that I spent years seeking that unity. And now I am giving it away.

'What did Maria say to you?' he asks.

I remove the pamphlet from my pocket. His eyes flare in recognition, even before he takes it from me.

'The silly girl.' His voice is low and aching.

'This is your responsibility.' My words split in the air. 'How could you have had this and not tell me? All this time you knew so much about my past, and kept it from me at every turn.'

His fingers pinch the edge of the paper. It was there, even in Vauxhall Gardens, that flash of recognition at my family name. I thought it referred to my grandfather's fortune, my success that season, but now I see it was a flare of notoriety, a damaged reputation.

'What could I have said?' He rubs his chin. 'No one had told you. Your grandfather, your uncle, your brother–'

'What did my brother know of this?'

'He was older than you. No doubt he remembered more.'

'Remembered what, exactly? That my mother killed my father? And why? Just because every other man in my family kept things from me, what made you do the same?'

'You must understand how you were when I met you. You were so untouched by it all. Like some primordial goddess, uncorrupted by our rules, our petty fears and dreams, our cruel prejudices. I couldn't do it to you. I couldn't make the world around you a hostile place to be feared and dreaded, as it has been for me. In that I sympathised with your uncle. I know you are angry at your grandfather and uncle. But they fought hard for your inheritance and everything you have.'

'At what cost?'

Light shakes his head. 'You don't understand what your uncle sacrificed for you. He cared so much and did what was best for your welfare. I asked him, that day in Venice, why he had never married. Do you know what he told me? He didn't want his own children to challenge your inheritance, because he knew it was the only thing keeping you safe.'

'But I have not been safe. I have not been any of those things you speak of. I was not untouched. I was no goddess, I was just a child, trying to discover my family. And you kept it from me.'

'It wasn't all as you think.' He holds up the Whitworth paper. 'This isn't to be believed.'

'What do you mean?'

'Percy Whitworth was forced to retire from the East India Company after being found guilty of embezzlement and fraud about ten years ago. He seized your father's lands in 1806. After your father died, and with your mother out of the way, it was easy. I think he hoped to marry her, rather than arrest her. But he achieved the same result.'

'He was always at the house when my father was ill. Always.' That particular walk, a certain gait, seen from the height of a child. 'Always following my mother around.' Even then, sensing her discomfort, I found it strange. 'You are saying she is innocent.'

'That is what I believe.'

'How can you be certain?' The sunlight moves over his face, bringing forth a memory, unbidden: the startled face of a boy, an Englishman, a native. 'You were there.'

'Yes. The day your father died.'

'I remember.' I touch my face. 'I feel cold.' And sick. A dropping ocean in my belly.

'You're shaking.' His hand is on my arm, his fingers warm.

'Never mind that.'

'My coat is here–'

'I said never mind that.' I flick his hand away. A look spasms across his face. 'Go on,' I say more quietly.

'You must understand, she may be dead. You need to be prepared for that. But for those who told you she was certainly dead, well, they were misinformed or they were lying. Probably the latter. The last time I saw your mother, she was living in a room in Bow Bazaar, translating poetry and teaching English to local children. I've told you this.'

'Yes. In my dreams, she can't speak English. But clearly, I'm not remembering correctly.'

'I believe she always spoke to you in Bengali.'

Sunlight flickers in the walled garden of my memory. 'How would you know such a thing?'

'But she was fluent in English. Very much so. She was highly literate and that's what saved her, in the end.' Around us, the gulls cry and in the distance the sound of the settlers calling to each other echoes. 'After your father died, they said she killed him. I came to your house that day, and that's when she was arrested. He had malaria. The same as my father before him. No one thought she killed him, but your father's private secretary accused her and by that stage of your father's illness he had complete authority over his affairs.'

'Percy Whitworth.' The smiling man on the verandah. 'Go on.'

'You're still shaking.'

'Go on.'

'It should have been a brief arrest. Your mother, as you know, was related to the court of Koch Bihar. But her father had died and her grandfather disowned her. He had been against her marriage to begin with and there were rumours she had not been faithful to your father.'

A brisk wind sweeps over the ocean. 'I cannot believe it.' I close my eyes and try to remember, beyond the gardens and the smells and the haze of exoticism blown into my face every day since I left Calcutta. I remember my parents laughing, always together. She was not like me. She was safe and happy.

'Perhaps not. I don't think there was any evidence and it didn't look good. It didn't do. You understand me? It wasn't what people wanted. But her father's people didn't come for her and then she did something.'

I try to picture myself back on the whaler. I felt safe on the timber deck, the waves rising and falling beneath me. 'What did she do?'

His voice floats over to me, cool and articulate. He has always been well spoken. Better spoken than a thousand richer, nobler men. 'It appears that she may have actually killed someone.'

The smell of timber and brine. The men's voices as they work. Voices from the islands of the East and the South. 'Who?'

'A young clerk, just out from England. He was interviewing her, in a room with Whitworth. Somehow, he ended up stabbed. The blame fell on your mother.'

'Just the three of them?'

'Yes.'

I think of the ship. Its image slips away as I close my eyes, thinking harder. The wooden deck, the puff of the sails. I try to hold it in my eye. But beyond that, the slicing arc of the harpoon. The redness of the water. The smell of boiling blubber nestled in every crevice of my body, every pore. I have sailed halfway around the world on a passage paid in blood.

'I don't know if she did it. Later, she told me she didn't. She said it was Whitworth. She was charged, but there was unrest.

The Company was worried she'd become a symbol. Many of FitzRoy's friends were against Whitworth. There were rumours about his work. He mismanaged money. He was light-fingered. He wasn't from anywhere, or that's what they said. And then there were her mother's people. When I went to Penang, I met with some traders from Junk Ceylon. Your grandmother was living in Siam. She returned there, after her husband's death, to live with her family. I told the traders what had happened. I found out your grandmother was alive.'

'My grandmother was from Siam? I never knew this.'

'So many things about who we are have been lost. She was Siamese and Teochew. As was my grandfather.'

'And did you meet her?'

'No. By the time I returned to Calcutta, your mother had been released and was living in Bow Bazaar. I wanted help reclaiming my inheritance from the East India Company. I thought we could launch a case. She couldn't help me, but I gave her your grandmother's details. Last I heard, she was making her way to Siam.'

'Alone? You didn't help her?'

'She said a Major Ramsey would assist her.'

Seawater glides over the sand. I remember the major's outrage during my first voyage to England as a child, how he thought my brother and I had been hard done by, that something rotten was at the heart of it. And later, after his death, the unexpectedness of his son's help. The strange kindness in a young man, when I had done so much that they said was wrong. 'He never told me.'

'It seems we all conspired to protect you.'

'Then how great was your failure.'

The sound of his inhalation is ragged. 'That I see now.'

The gulls swoop over the skyline. English voices call and laugh across the beach. From the corner of my eye I see the little girl return, edging closer.

'But why did they accuse her in the first place? My father had malaria – is that not so?'

'Malaria is the accepted reason.'

I think of Oliver and his silences. The visitor from India. Dark patent boots protruding from beneath twisting white sheets on a Cornish cliff. 'Percy.'

Beside me, Will sighs. 'There are rumours he had an affair with your mother. But I think it's what he wanted people to believe. He benefited from your father's death. He took his job, and he tried to take his wife. But your mother escaped.'

'All these years and she might have been alive. How could you not have told me?'

He inclines his head. 'I wanted to, all through our time in Italy, but there were things I didn't know back then. I know now that Whitworth had been embezzling. You were so obsessed with returning to India, and so young. How could I break this news to you? I didn't want the thought of your mother being a murderer hanging over your head – hanging over both our heads–'

'But there was no "our" in the end, was there?'

'I did ask you to marry me.'

'And I said yes.' My voice rises, then softens. 'But then you retracted it.'

He looks away.

'Was it because of my uncle? You never told me what he said that afternoon in Venice.'

He does not reply.

'I've spent so long trying to work out where it went wrong, and I always come back to our last days in Venice. Everything changed by the time we reached Rome.'

He pinches the point between his brows. 'I don't know.'

'Shall I remind you?' Above us, the sun listens. Perhaps that is the benefit of this place: the endless coastline, the open sky, and the brightest star in our universe shining down on us, burning us up, laying everything perfect and bare. 'You said you could never have Eurasian children. You couldn't run the risk of having a child as dark as you. One who might suffer as you've suffered, who might suffer worse. Do you remember that?'

He sits immobile on the beach. Voices behind us draw closer, men from the *Rapid* completing their work.

'You didn't want a half-caste wife, pretty as she might be. You wanted a white woman.'

His lips move now. 'I would appreciate it if you lowered your voice.'

I laugh. Parallel to the shore, some distance away, the little girl has returned. She watches us.

'And how did a white wife work out for you? Was she such a better mother than a brown woman?' I stand. 'You've three pure white children now, all with your name and none of your blood or your colour.'

If he would speak now, if he would say something, I could find it in my heart to forgive him, to tell him, as I intended, of the girl in Cornwall with the brown hair and the Spanish complexion, who excels at languages and loves maps. But he is motionless, looking out over the horizon, claiming a land and a vision he can never own.

'Where did my mother go? You said you brought her my grandmother's details. That she was going to Siam. Where in Siam?'

'An address in Bangkok. I'm afraid I don't recall the exact details.'

Bangkok. A city of rivers.

I pass my hand over my eyes. 'Did she ask about me, when you met her?' I know the answer to my own question. I must know it. What mother would not ask?

Finally, he nods. I wait for more. He presses his forefinger and thumb across his eyebrows. 'I don't think I remember. You know. The usual things a mother might ask about her children.'

I laugh without meaning to. 'And what might they be, these usual things?'

'I wouldn't know. My own mother–'

'There is something you are not telling me.' I let my words overrun his. The insertion of his own mother glints, a treacherous marker, a deflection.

I place my hand on his shoulder and kneel. 'We've come so far.'

~

'No more secrets. Not now,' she says.

Her hand is warm. He breathes in and the salt air scratches and rattles through his throat and into his chest, his misshapen lungs. If he were Catholic, like his mother, then perhaps he would feel more strongly that urge to cleanse before death, to confess. But he has never liked the Church of Rome. It is his father's spirit that moves him, the spirit of Protestant endeavour to keep going, on and on, until he has left something of himself, of which he can be proud. And can he face more failure now, in his final years?

Clarissa is like and unlike that face in Bow Bazaar. He noticed the graceful curves of Siam on her mother's features, something both their mothers shared.

Calcutta, October 1806

Thin bands of sunlight stream through the slats of the closed shutters. The room is dark and stale. How quickly the wet Calcutta air turns a stone building ripe with decay. Light stares at the woman before him. Sounds from the outside pierce their solitude. The porters' call, the rattle of the ox and cart, the sound of children playing.

Even in that short space of time since he last saw her in the garden, wearing her orange sari, she looks reduced. Her hair is drawn back severely from her brow, her neck covered in stiff white muslin, European style. Her hands shake when she hands him the letters, scripted so neatly, so artistic in their calligraphy. Behind her silvery glasses, her eyes are watchful and defiant.

Why does she trust him? This is the question he will ask himself years in the future, during that first hesitation with Clarissa in Venice, the sourness of Rome, the final triumph of his cowardice somewhere on the corner of Green Park. This is the question he will ask himself on the crystalline coast of an unknown world. Perhaps she sees her children in him and trusts in his implicit similarity.

He takes the letters. He recognises the names of many of the addressees: senior gentlemen of the East India Company, the male FitzRoys in England who have taken charge of her family, and there, on scented paper, names Christian and Hindu written in English and Sanskrit. Her children.

He means to deliver them. After all, her cause is so close to his own. But this is before he will come to realise, so thoroughly, the way of the English in the East. He clings to the hope that there is a place for him here, that his mother's dowry will be preserved and his inheritance rights respected. He clings to the hope there will be justice. He sends some of the letters. Not the perfumed missives, which remain with him, tucked away in oilskin, safe and sacred with their clear instructions to give them, in person, to her children in England. She does not mind the time this takes, she tells him, when he protests and says he means to make a life in India. It is better, yes, to wait until they are older? Her eyes seek his affirmation. That way they can read the letters themselves.

He sends a few, but receives no response. The FitzRoys absorb her dowry, her property, her jewels. But not before Percy Whitworth, private secretary of limited pedigree, has mysteriously amassed a small fortune, enough to counter the FitzRoys' claims that he took the widow's remaining property for his personal use.

As the monsoon season passes, Light leaves Calcutta and makes for the fort of Palayamkottai. His sister invites him. Sarah's husband, Captain Welsh, is in command. *There might be something for you in India, after all*, she hints. Is it then that he doubts? On the journey over the waters to Pondicherry, on horseback through the mullai and the marudham, hearing tales of the death of Tipu Sultan at the close of the last century? He begins to understand.

It would be admirable, if it were not so crass. How could he not have seen it before? The machinations of the East India

Company. They wait for the death of an established ruler and the nascent fragility of their successor. It might be a man or a woman, an Indian or a European, for they are not above devouring men of their own kind. It could be a maharaja or a nawab of a princely kingdom, or simply a trader, a Company official, grown wealthy on a large estate. This man, or this woman – for many Begums and Ranis have ruled a kingdom – is in their lifetime too powerful to oppose openly or swindle. But upon their death, if their successor is a child, if there is any hint of weakness or confusion, someone will take their lands. If it's on the scale of kingdoms, the Company acts as a whole. If it's on the scale of estates, then the men of the Company do it to one another. They disinherit each other's children, abandon each other's wives.

He arrives at Palayamkottai at sunset, the walls of the ancient fort raised high above the green plains. Lights twinkle on the parapets. The tiered Hindu temple soars into the sky, towering above the flag of the East India Company fluttering against the horizon. As the sun drops behind the hills, the dusk is broken by the echoing of the Muslim call to prayer. His horse slows in this, the last moment of stillness and peace in India.

But there is no stillness, nor peace, in the fort. Not anywhere when news of Vellore breaks. His brother-in-law is new to command. Light can feel the threads of power fraying when he passes through the city walls.

Captain Welsh compensates for his tenuous hold with anger and aggression. Light sees the rippling expressions of disdain in the native soldiers' eyes. His sister Sarah is thin and drawn, her children ill and vexatious. Light plays bridge with the junior officers, talks about trade and prospects. Captain Welsh is solicitous, almost ingratiating. Why is that? Whatever tale is written in his skin, Light is still a governor's son. He is still the cleverest man in the room.

He would like to say the letters burn holes in his pockets, that he thinks of their anxious author and those children across the sea. But he does not. He puts them in a compendium at the back of his bureau in his new home (home! What hubris he has, in planning such a thing). They lie there, undelivered, like an undiagnosed illness, an ache, a sense of promise unfulfilled, like his niece's four-year-old body turning cold in the tropical heat. Vexatious no more. Her father, all Celtic fissures in an English façade, face flushed with drink, wobbling in the sitting room, his hands opening and closing against the oppressive night.

'Children are so susceptible to diseases in the tropics,' a doctor says, before they take the small body away. And Captain Welsh turns his wild blue eyes to his wife. 'What is the point of you, then? Aren't half-caste mothers supposed to stop this?'

Within a second, Welsh is regretful. But Light has seen the look in his sister's eye, the absence that colonises her face. Perhaps that is why she does it, later, that final act of proving her worth.

After their daughter's death, the Welsh family go to the coast. Taking the waters. It's too soon for a new leader to be absent and yet Light is relieved. There are no more tensions on parade, no more abuses of the native officers. A half-hearted peace hangs over the fort. He clings to the possibility of remaining in India, walking the parapets each evening, avoiding the ministrations of the Portuguese Catholic priest, rearranging the furniture in his rooms again and again, for nothing is to his liking, shifting the compendium back and forth, ignoring the scented paper letters and everything they imply.

And then there is Vellore.

It happens with turbans and beards, the forbidding of religious markers, a new hat made from the skin of the sacred cow. It happens with the wedding of a daughter of a long-dead king whose sons endure their imprisonment in Vellore.

It comes to them in rumour first: hundreds of white men slaughtered in their beds, the commanding officer's widow fleeing for her life. Wandering fakirs swirl through the fort, preaching rebellion and dissent, a call for a new world.

Light, from his rooms in Palayamkottai, smells the scent of hope and aspiration, the acrid musk of men who sense their foe is down. He sees the fear in his fellow Englishmen's eyes. But when he glances at the looking glass, his face wet from shaving, he sees neither hope nor fear, just an empty space, an interrogation point over which road to take, like he is some strange vampire from the Continent who is neither living nor truly dead.

Captain Welsh returns with his family, called back from his recuperation. Called back too soon, Light can see. The man drinks late and sleeps in. His fingers shake by mid-afternoon. He takes offence at the Indian officers, at their sidelong looks and sceptical voices. When a sepoy snaps the piece of his musket and raises the barrel, Welsh throws himself to the ground. The sepoy claims innocence – an accident. The native officers laugh.

A strange mood stalks the fort. A spectre is seen on the ramparts, the ghost of a long-dead sepoy bemoaning his grisly fate at the hands of the British. The Portuguese priest vanishes in the night. The next morning, blood is found sprinkled over the threshold of the Protestant Church.

The sepoys murmur. The junior English officers grow uneasy. Welsh shuts himself in his room. When the native officers ask to speak to him, his aide sends them away, claiming he is indisposed.

South Australian Coast, October 1836

Even now, Light cannot say the truth of the matter. He remembers his sister's eyes, glossy and dark, the way they circled her husband. So much like his mother's and his own. She was paler and more drawn than before she set out with her family, mourning her daughter's death. She was more watchful, and perhaps, more calculating.

'I can't say why she did it.'

The surf skitters over Clarissa's feet, shattering into tiny pearls as it meets her skin. 'Did what?'

'She sent her manservant to spy on the Indian officers at the mosque. She said he'd uncovered a plot to mutiny.'

'Had he?'

Light thinks of the downward glance of the man's eyes, the way he twisted the hem of his shirt in his fingers. 'I couldn't say. That was the problem. It had happened in Vellore. Because of that, we all thought it could happen anywhere. The native officers didn't like my brother-in-law, of that I have no doubt, but there is a line between dislike and mutiny.' He blinks. 'What could I say? My own sister seemed so convinced of it.'

His brother-in-law had leaped into action, abandoning all thoughts of despair. Even Light was co-opted, rounding up the junior English officers to inform them. At first, there was a thrill, a sense of action and purpose. But that changed, bit by bit, when he realised there was no evidence.

'All we had was the word of a butler, and my sister's insistence.'

'Why would she lie?'

Light thinks again of his niece's death, of Welsh's lethargy, of the blame in his eyes when he looked at Sarah. It faded in view of the new crisis. Half-castes and Europeans together.

'She may not have lied. She may have just seen what she chose to believe. But I don't think even she could have predicted what would happen. Welsh imprisoned every native officer. There was no room for innocence or guilt, just the colour of a man's skin. When they protested, he had them manacled. And as for the sepoys, he expelled them from the fort, keeping their families as hostages for good measure.' Light shakes his head. 'I was caught up with it for a while. But when Welsh's commanding officer arrived, he started asking questions. When I realised what had happened – the way the Indian officers had been treated, things that wouldn't happen to an Englishman – I was so ashamed.'

Clarissa doesn't meet his eyes. 'I suppose you couldn't have known.'

'I should have. The Portuguese priest was close to the Indian officers. He tried to be close to me, but I rebuffed him. Every opportunity I might have had to bridge a gap, or heal a divide, I kept choosing a side.' A side that meant he could have no future in India. 'I left for Europe via Ceylon and gave up on the East. My brother-in-law was court-martialled and acquitted. He was given his fair hearing, which no Indian officer received.

He wanted me to testify but thank God I was in the British Army by then, in the Peninsula, out of his reach. Out of the reach of all East India Company shadows, at least for a while.'

'And the letters?' Clarissa asks, her closed face giving nothing away.

He struggles to explain it. The hurried nature of his departure, his disgust on returning to his rooms, his borrowed house, the shakiness of his plans and dreams in Asia. He'd packed hastily. He'd like to say it was an honest mistake. That in the frenzy of the moment the letters were overlooked, lost. But in truth, he'd seized them. He could not abandon someone's correspondence to a stranger's eyes. And besides, he had thought of her thoroughly as Welsh arrested the officers. He thought of her as the East India Company soldiers arrested her for the theft of her house, the desire of her body, the ragged motivation of their self-interest. So he took the letters, and felt their weight in his satchel on that smooth passage to Ceylon. And he thought of his mother, and his sisters, and his own clear failure, and looking back at the Coromandel Coast for the last time, he turned the letters over in his hands.

'Will?' Her face is clear, but already he can hear the flint creeping into her voice. 'What happened to the letters?'

'I let them go. Somewhere over the Palk Strait.' Already damp from the sea spray, they left scent and smears of ink on his fingers. Last he saw, they were floating on the surface, refusing to sink, then the ship passed on and took them from sight.

She stands in one swift movement, the wind pushing her hair across her face.

He struggles to stand as she strides down the beach.

'Wait. Wait!'

His fingers graze her shoulder as she leaves. She moves in a blur of white fabric and writhing hair, arms flapping like a trapped bird. Something strikes his temple and he steps back, surprised.

'Don't touch me.' She hits him, her fist against his chest. 'Don't touch me. Everything you've ever done to me has been a lie.'

He opens his mouth but cannot speak. The tighter you squeeze hope, the more quickly it runs through your fingers. Like water, like love.

Cornwall, June 1815

Sea mist rises from the shelf of the ocean, wind nipping at my nose and ears. My fingers chill, probing the rough sand until I feel the hard edge of a shell. The tide helps me as I dig, each ebb pulling the sand further away. My fingers numb and blunted, I tug at the sand to release my prize, lifting the rainbow shell up to the sky. When I hold it to my ear the sea repeats itself, over and over. I raise it to my lips and pretend to be an old war goddess, riding over the ocean.

Behind me, my brother kicks the rocks, beating at the boulders with old driftwood that crumbles in his hands. We tolerate each other but do not speak. He does not want to hear my failing Bengali, my attempts to speak of our mother, of Asha, of all those people we left behind when we were taken. Nor will he listen to other tales. On that long voyage from India, crying into Mrs Jensen's skirts, she told me of the selkies and their changing skin, creatures of the sea who also walked the earth. Here, they speak of mermaids, of the lady in the church who lured a man away with her singing, of the midnight washerwomen with their sea-green dresses and webbed feet.

My brother laughs hearing these stories. He's grown tall and strong and quick this last year, and his face lights up at the way his body takes him through the world. We are not playmates anymore, and I miss the only friend I have in that big house in Hertfordshire. Soon, he will go to university, and it will just be me in the white walls of the white house.

But try as I might, I cannot resent him. His long limbs bring him such comfort now; they delight him. His arms haul him up trees, reach further in the boxing ring, hold his shotgun steady on a hunt. To the men in my family, my brother finally exists. He might be a man, and a man of England, too.

Gripping my skirt in one hand, I step into the tide. The current drags as if it would tug me out into the ocean. Above us, over the hill, the women work on the house's laundry and the white sheets flap on the line like puffed sails. I close my eyes. The sea bites my ankles with cold. The *tug, tug, tug* of the waves and the *puff, puff, puff* of the sheets conjure a boat that would sail away, that would take me to a further place, a world of islands and coastlines, a winding archipelago of sand and ocean.

A shock of cold water hits my face and I gasp, blinking. My brother runs away laughing, drying his hands.

But I cannot resent him. He doesn't have my natural advantages, my uncle says. By which he means the pallor of my skin, that strange red tint to my hair. My brother is my mother's son, and no one here will forget it. Nor will they forget his tears, his sensitivity, his Eastern lack of character.

I saw the disdain in my grandfather's eyes when he first met my brother. My uncle tried to be sympathetic. But what did they know, these hard Englishmen, of my mother and Asha, the warm air and the banyan tree, and all that we left behind?

'They expect less of you because you're a girl,' my brother tells me. 'It doesn't matter if you're weak.'

I taste salt in the cold water on my face as I kneel into the chilly depths. My brother cannot stand the cold.

'Oliver, be kind to your sister.' My brother's tutor stands on the soft dry sand of the beach. I do not hear my brother's reply. Walter Fraser's voice takes on a sharper turn. 'It's unmanly to bully little girls.'

I rise, clutching the hem of my skirt as I drag my legs from the tide. I feel Walter's gaze from my cheeks to my chest to my spine and down my thighs. He looks away, blinking. I drop the rest of my skirt, leaving it to drag against my feet.

'Come, Oliver.' He places his hand on my brother's back. 'There's a visitor at the house. Someone you might remember.'

'Who is it?' I call. But the two young men, heads bent in conversation, ignore me as they stride up the slope toward the house.

The midnight washerwomen have webbed feet. In France, they are called Les Lavandières. Some say they wash the shrouds of men, and to cross their paths is to be cursed. Others say they might grant you three wishes, but to win this favour you must help with their washing. Twist the sheets one way, and they will grant you your wishes. Twist the sheets the other way, and they will twist off your arms.

Wind tears off the Atlantic. I leave the water and sit down. The skin of the sand is already starting to warm. Placing my seashells around me, I wiggle my toes in the sunlight and close my eyes. How much can I remember? A name. Indumati. My name. And words? No sound forms in my ear. I can see my mother's smooth face, but when she speaks, her words are just the swell of the wave before it crashes to shore, the wind in the sand over the dunes.

A shadow falls across me and my eyes snap open.

One of the scullery maids from the laundry stands on the beach, holding the hem of her sea-green dress out of the water. 'You'll catch a cold, Miss.'

They are more forward here in Cornwall. But she's right. I stand up. I am not tall, but the woman comes barely up to my chin. Her skin is the colour of warm earth, and her hair is rich and black. They aren't really English in Cornwall. My grandfather's voice. She sees me staring, and I look away, a hot, ugly feeling coursing through me.

'Master Oliver is up on the hill.' Her voice is quiet. 'He's been looking for you. He says it's important.'

I want to ask her who the visitor was, but the words don't come. She watches me silently, then curtsies when I nod and begins to walk away. I try to catch a glimpse of her feet as she goes, but they are hidden from view.

The white sheets on the hill beckon to me as I walk. They billow out and then in, like the lungs of an unseen giant. I take the shortcut, gripping the heath as I scramble up the steep side of the hill. As the washing lines draw closer, I see my brother pacing by the large laundry tub. Steam rises against the cold from the frothing vat, and I can feel the warmth of the fire and the water from here.

The white sheets obscure all but his two dark legs and the shape of his feet, then I see him, his hand on his chin in thought. As the white sheet flits back with the breeze, there are two more legs, the black patent shine of shoes for town. There are also voices. I look around, but I cannot see the washerwoman, nor the scullery maid from the house.

The sheets half tug out again, and there is a shape, a bearing, the figure of a man from deep in my memory. His back is turned to me as he speaks to my brother. There are bright red spots on my brother's cheeks. The wind steals his words as he gesticulates at the man. I have never seen my brother so angry.

'Oliver?' My voice echoes in my ears, blown back to me. My memory surges deep in time and water. Warm air, rain. A crimson handprint on my brother's face. Fear.

I quicken my pace as the fabric blows back and obscures my view. My brother should not be alone with this person. 'Oliver?'

I smell it before I hear it. It's sweet and acrid and unnatural, and makes my belly flip over. There is a crack, a shout that gurgles into a shriek that sets my hair on end, the sound of feet pounding across the heath.

By the time I reach the laundry, my brother is slumped over the rim of the tub, one arm dangling into the angry water. I pull him back. The sheets beat the world around us. The scullery maid appears, white-faced. Her feet are bare. Wet, fleshy, green. They grip the earth in folds of flesh between her toes. I scream for water. She stares at me, her mouth opening and closing like a fish, pointing to the laundry tub.

My brother lies motionless in my lap, his eyes staring at the sky. Two ink drops on a blank canvas. His arm is a slash of white, broiled skin riveted by blood and protruding bone. The smell colonises my nostrils, the steam heating the air around us.

Small jerks rock my brother's torso. I lean toward him. He is laughing, each *ha*, *ha*, *ha* vibrating against my knees in uncanny merriment. 'I'm white,' he says. 'I'm white, I'm white.'

I look at his arm again. The olive skin has been stripped away into a shiny whiteness crowned by pulpy broken flesh. I hold my breath and will away the sight, the smell, but all I can see is the thin, unrelenting line of bone.

My brother lies in his bed. The doctor emerges, russet smears edging over his hairy forearms. He speaks to my grandfather. When I approach him, my uncle waves me back. 'Not now, Clary, please.' I hear the word *amputation*. My uncle gestures. 'Walter.'

My brother's tutor touches my elbow. 'Come along, Clarissa. Let's go into the other room.'

'Who was there?' I say. 'This morning, at the laundry?'

But Walter only frowns and shakes his head.

'Who was there?' I say again. 'I saw Oliver at the laundry. Before the accident. He was with somebody.'

'The laundry girl didn't see anyone. But maybe you saw one of the washerwomen.'

'It was a gentleman. Dressed for town.'

Walter puts a hand on my arm. 'You're in shock, confused. Come into the drawing room.'

'I'm not confused. Don't you understand? Someone did this to him.' I study his face. His lips are pressed into a thin straight line. 'I know there was a man here earlier.'

He fiddles with his cuff and strokes his ear. 'That man left hours ago. Well before the accident.'

'You said Oliver might remember him.'

'Clarissa, you know I'm not permitted to talk to you about India.'

'So, he was from India.' I watch the lines of Walter's face. 'Someone who knew my parents?'

He shakes his head. 'Come and sit down.'

Behind us, my brother's screams pierce the hardwood door.

I see the boots again under the flapping sheets. Boots change, feet change. Did I recognise the gait? Percy?

South Australian Coast, October 1836

I stumble on the sandy hillside. The land is eerie away from the sea. Inland, amid the drooping eucalypts, the banksia and the scattered rolling spinifex and saltbush, I feel a stranger, a guest for whom the land has not yet extended welcome. But in this moment, as I grip the wattle to gain my balance, I am grounded. The weaving eucalyptus branches rub together in the breeze, whispering of a world where my past might not always be my future.

I walk on, further inland, away from the man on the beach, away from betrayal, from my own doted-on guilt, a stone of sea-green jade trailing behind me.

'Are you all right, Miss?'

I start. At the base of the dune, under the shade of blue gums and a drooping she-oak, the girl from the beach sits, packing dried skins into bundles. She pauses as I approach, watching me. Moses Widlow sits next to her, his shirtsleeves rolled up to the elbow. Between his fingers are the slim shapes of eucalyptus leaves. He rubs them together as the girl watches. They smell like pine, but sweeter. I see again the gleam of the shells around his neck and think of Moses's words, of his grandmother's hands harvesting the rainbow kelp, of loss. I watch him pass the leaves to the child.

He turns back to me. 'Are you all right?' he says, again.

I try to smile, but my face is unsteady. 'I will be. It is all bearable.'

Moses blinks, then looks at the land around me, as though searching for something. 'This is Judith,' Moses says. 'My daughter.'

'Hello, Judith. A strong name. I'm Clarissa.'

Judith studies my face. 'Like in the book.' She fiddles with the rope in her hands. 'And the paintings. Have you seen them?'

I think again of Italy, the striking painting of the woman with the sword, the hot sun on the sampietrini, the Neapolitan sea. 'I have indeed,' I reply.

The eeriness of the previous moments begins to evaporate. The earth is firm beneath my knees; my skin ceases to prickle. I'm warm. Judith smiles for the first time.

'Are you sure you're all right?' Moses speaks again as I press my palms onto the soil. He holds out a flagon of water for me to drink. It's warm and clear, and tinged with brine.

'Perhaps I'm not entirely sure.' The leaves of the eucalypts murmur above us. 'Does everyone lie?'

My question sits between us. Judith looks at me. Moses is quiet.

'That's not quite what I meant,' I say.

'You meant,' Moses begins, 'does everyone here lie? Do *they* always lie?' He places his carving down on the earth, stilling his hands. 'Of course they do, Clarissa.'

It's the first time he's used my given name, despite my requests he do so.

I shake my head. 'But he was supposed to be different. He is different. There's no supposing about it.'

'He's made choices, hasn't he? He must have done, or why else would he be here?' Moses picks up his carving again. 'I could have gone to live in America,' he says slowly. 'Lived on some other people's stolen land. Had slaves, even. Escaped all this. But I didn't.'

'Had you done so, at any moment you might have been mistaken for a slave. You would never have been one of them.'

'But you and I both know that there are men like me – like you, like him – who spit on their past. Who want nothing more than to mimic the men they permit to pose as their betters. Even if they spend their lives hating themselves for it. And yes, they always lie.'

I take another sip of water. It tastes like dust and dry clay. 'I don't suppose you have anything stronger?'

'I do at the tent. Shall I fetch it for you?'

I shake my head. 'No. It's not important.'

'Have you got what you wanted?' he asks. 'Out of your stay here?'

'No. But perhaps enough.'

'Maybe it's time, then.'

'So soon.' Already I can feel the drag of the surf, the wind in white sails. 'Is that what you want?'

I follow his gaze into the boughs of the she-oak, then down into Judith's face.

'Leaving is never what I want,' he says. 'But for now, it's the way it must be. It's rare for me to stay for more than a few weeks. I am always sorry to go, but I will return.'

'That is something I will not do.'

'No.'

I lean back, thinking of Will on the shore, his feet sinking into the sand. If there is more that he knows, I do not have the stomach to ask him. 'Then perhaps it is time.'

Moses nods and stands. His eyes slide to the child beneath the tree. 'I'll let the captain know.' He ruffles Judith's hair. 'I'll be back soon, sweetheart.'

As he walks over the sandy hillside, Judith continues packing the skins. The sun is at its zenith. The air hums with the soft drone of bees. I sit down, leaning against the trunk of the she-oak, my mind crowding with a rewritten past, the sweetness of the night spoiled and bitter with the hot gold noon. There is a rhythm to the girl's work, a type of percussion that lulls. I listen as I lean against the tree and close my eyes.

~

I wake to laughter and a child's hand on my arm. It reminds me of Marina, the form of the girl as a child, the rushing sea of Cornwall, a dog's bark. But it's Judith's anxious face looming over me, and behind her, the shape of unfamiliar boots.

I spring to my feet, my body pulled taut.

The men from the *Rapid* stand further along the hill, silent and open-mouthed. They hold their spades, their running chain, their rope. They drop their gaze when I stare at them, but I feel a shiver of exposure, the chilled air of danger and dislike.

Before this moment, they were always different from the other settlers. Their eyes didn't linger on the shape of my legs in trousers, they didn't gape at my face or hair or the sight of my skin. A crew reflects its captain, Moses says, and I supposed these men exemplary. But something has changed in them today.

Everyone knows, Maria Gandy told me. *Half-caste daughter of a murderess. Mad. Depraved.*

I watch as the men move slowly up the hill. Judith crouches

behind me. One man dawdles until the others are almost out of sight. He has dark-blond hair and a soft jaw. I know his face.

The man with the crew of the *Cygnet*, confronting the whalers. The man with the musket and the free tongue. Hewitt, Will called him.

I wait warily. There is a studied slackness to his limbs; he swings his arms and they take up too much space, greedy for attention.

When he passes the stacks of sealskins the girl has built, he pauses. Turning his pale eyes to me, he runs them up and down the length of my body, and for the first time I feel the joy and freedom I have found in my whaler's outfit falter. Eyeing the child now, then the sealskins, he swings back his booted foot and kicks.

The skins scatter. My breath hisses in my ears as he raises his foot again and again.

'Stop that.' My words whip out with my grandfather's tones. 'Stop that at once.'

The man looks at me and for a moment, I think I have won. Who is this little man, after all? But he again kicks Judith's handiwork into the dust. And then he takes a step toward me, smiling.

My hand finds Judith's shoulder. 'You should go,' I say. 'Go find your father.' My voice is decided, but the child doesn't move. She seems strangely accustomed to this display of violent entitlement. There is something in her eyes that I understand. I can imagine what would happen to a native whaler should he become enraged at an Englishman of a British company. There would be no good outcome. My mind swirls with Will's stories of Palayamkottai and Vellore.

What world is this? I think of the day of my father's death, the gates closing on my mother, and step forward. I will manage this.

'You there. Tell me your name.' Out of the corner of my eye, I am aware of movement along the hillside, but I dare not break my gaze.

The younger man laughs. He is young, I can see that now, at least a decade younger than me, with smooth cheeks and a sunburnt neck, a musket slung over his back. A boy.

I will not be afraid of a child. I cannot be.

'Your name,' I repeat. 'I will be informing the governor about this.'

The man smirks. 'The governor's not here.'

'The colonel, then.' I had not wanted to use this, to invoke his name.

The man laughs softly. 'The colonel. Yes, I'm sure he'll hear all about it.' He steps forward, and in a move that is frighteningly familiar, he takes a lock of my hair between his forefinger and his thumb and studies it.

Was he there, at dawn on the beach? Did he see us?

At his touch I freeze, seeing Percy's boots haunting my mother's steps, his hands always upon her back and arm, seeing the strained creasing of her face.

I knock the man's arm away with my hand. His pupils dilate in surprise. For a second time, I think I have it, that he is chastened. We stare at each other, and I wonder how much he knows of who I am. In my lifetime, I have known my grandfather to have had common men whipped for less than this. This must be how it starts. Those same men flee to the colonies, to recreate fresh violence abroad in the pattern of the old country's tyrannies.

The young man steps back, dragging his foot. As he turns away from me, he kicks the sand, flinging grit into Judith's eyes.

I open my mouth to cry out as Judith raises her arm up in defence, rolling her body across the sandy earth, out of Hewitt's reach. Without warning, Moses darts past me and reaches Hewitt in a cloud of sand. The men collide, sending Hewitt sprawling across the earth under the whaler's weight.

Moses stands, shouting, but I do not hear the words. Beneath us, Hewitt fumbles with his musket. I step forward, in front of Moses, as the barrel rises.

'Hewitt!' Will's voice slices the air as he strides toward us from the surveyors' group.

Hewitt crouches; for a moment, fear stalks across his face.

Will strides past me. I can feel his eyes searching for me but I avoid his gaze. His feet are booted now, his clothes pressed with military precision. He takes the musket from his subordinate with a sound of exasperation and turns to Moses, who stands, fingers curled into his palms. I hear Will's clipped words of apology, of charm. Moses's hands begin to loosen their empty grasp.

Hewitt stands. 'He attacked me,' he says.

Will shakes his head. 'Go and wait with the others. I'll deal with you shortly.' As Hewitt passes him, Will grabs his arm. 'What were you thinking, man?' Hewitt flinches as Will releases him and begins to walk away.

'He won't be around forever, you know,' Hewitt hisses as he nears me.

I look back at Will in his clean, white shirt and at Moses holding Judith's palm in his own. When I turn back to Hewitt, he is now out of earshot, standing on the rise with the other surveyors, staring back at me. It makes my skin prickle, and I rub my arms in response. Deep within me, my heart knocks an unsteady rhythm.

'Are you all right?' Will's voice pulls me back. He's holding out his hand, but I step away. I don't need him here. I don't need this.

'Clarissa, wait.' His tone is measured, but I feel the undercurrent of his desperation pulling me under. I turn and walk across the hill, toward the whaler, calling to Judith, the sun lancing off the waves and into my eyes.

~

Light watches her go, feeling her pull like the tide feels the moon. But all the water he has to offer is his blood, straining toward her out of old wounds ripped open. He applies his sutures carefully. He would not be any good to her, to anyone, bleeding out here over the dunes.

He strides across the rise, toward Hewitt. 'Clear this up.' His tones are clipped. 'Now, Hewitt.' His rebuke hangs over the beach, and Hewitt flushes. The boy's apology is muted. 'Sorry means making amends,' Light tells him. 'Rebuild it for her.'

Hewitt opens his mouth in protest, then kneels as he begins gathering the skins. When he stands, the pile is rough and misshapen.

'Do it properly.' The edge in his own voice surprises Light. On the voyage from England, the crew were harmonious. Hewitt was almost a favourite. But the land has changed things. Hewitt kneels again, smoothing the pile. When he finishes his eyes shine, with tears or anger, Light cannot say.

The girl gazes at them, crouched on the hillside. Light cannot see Moses, but the whaler will not be far away. As Hewitt leaves, Light adjusts the edges of the skins and reties the bundles, then holds out his hand to the girl.

'It's all right. I've fixed it.' He moves forward on his knees, but the girl recoils, folding in elbows and knees and scrambling sideways up the beach. Light sits back. She gazes at him from her vantage point on the dune, queen-like, her eyes unblinking, her face closed. She's like the other sealing children that he's seen. At least she knows who her father is. Are the others' fathers alive or dead? And do they know of their children, do they care?

He stands slowly as the child vanishes over the sandbank, not stirring the long grass or the silver banksia.

It's best not to think too hard on it. It mattered less once, being someone's natural child. He once saw his mother's wedding gown, lined with gold embroidery. That didn't carry, in England.

He dusts off his knees. How much he would like to tell the child that the provenance of her birth won't matter, that in this colony, his colony, a free and fair future awaits her. But he has seen how the settlers have changed. Each passing day brings them both more surety over the land and more disdain for its first occupants. Bolstered by their increasing numbers, by their growing familiarity with the new land, they have become instilled with judgement and bravado. No longer reliant on their goodwill, there are subtle shifts in how they treat the natives. There are shifts in how the bourgeois women treat Maria. And there is fear when they see Clarissa.

His eyes follow her tracks. He can still see the place where her feet have left furrows in the dust. If he looks at them from a certain angle, they glisten like scales of an old snakeskin. But it is just a trick of the light.

~

I walk across the beach, among the sea's relentless roll, lifting my chin to the wind. The whaling ship swings on its anchor in the distance, the backdrop of clouds crowding the horizon.

Hewitt's fingers in my hair. Percy's grip on Oliver's arm. There are things I remember now. The fine angles of my mother's face. The way they crinkled in Percy's presence. I press my temples. There was no affair. It was all one more act, one more tightening of the fist. The sultan's men blasted over the fort of Vellore. A booted foot in the work of a child's labour. Englishmen in the East and their quest for dominion.

I reach the place where the shadow of the whaler drapes over swelling water. The tide reaches for my toes. It smells like death.

~

In the years he has left, he will remember her movement on the coastline, the way she pummelled into him and swallowed him like riptide, the way she charted her path out of his life, evaporating.

He sees her on the side of the hill, swathed in sea-green silk and pearls, descending, like her balloon descent that first night, so many years ago. He sees her swing the musket, bringing its long line to rest in her arms, the butt nestled deep into her shoulder.

'Clary.'

Her face still, she swoops past him as though he is not there, gliding across the sand like an albatross, toward the surveyors on the beach.

He smells the cordite before he hears the shot. The crack sends birds spinning into the sky and men scattering.

'Clary.' He runs now, toward her.

She reloads and raises the barrel. The surveyors have taken cover in the rocks, but one kneels in the sand, fumbling with his own weapon. Hewitt.

'Clary!' He is close enough to see her flinch from the kickback as the shot cracks the air. Hewitt falls, the sand crimson beneath his arm.

Light takes the musket and tilts it into the sky, grabbing her arm with his other hand, blocking the view of her from the men on the beach.

'Christ, Clarissa, this is not the way.'

She looks at him for the first time, hair swept off her face, leaving the lines of her cheek thin and fine. 'I have stood here, Will, and I have listened to you, as I did fourteen years ago, and you have filled my head with lies and fantasies as you did then. Look at him.' She gestures to Hewitt, lying in the sand as the others attend to his arm. 'Look at the world you are making here. You say it will be better, but you are lying to yourself and you are lying to them. People live here already. You know this. You know what happened to our people in Malaya and India. You know what will happen here, what will happen next.'

He shakes his head. 'It isn't like that.' He sees Moses in his peripheral vision, the girl clutching his knees. Behind him, the surveyors move closer.

She tugs at the musket and he grips it tighter.

'And still you protect them. Like you did in Calcutta, against your own mother. Like you did in Vellore.'

'I'm protecting you. Don't you know what they will do to you if you keep firing?'

'You have never protected me.'

'Don't be like this, Clary. I am trying to make things better here.'

She releases the musket, and he casts it onto the sand. 'You will die trying to be an Englishman.'

Her body loosens in his arms. He wishes for a different dissolving, for their time back in the caverns of the rocks, the way she slid across him like water. But now he senses only the anger flowing from her, her muscles slackening, wrung dry of the fight.

When she stumbles, it's to Moses Widlow she turns. Shells wink around the whaler's neck as Light watches her reach out, her hand amber against Moses's wiry arm, inked with the signs of his mother's people.

~

I make my way down to the hewn rockface of the cliff, where the narrow ledges lead to pools of seawater nestled in the stone. Sitting with my toes in the warming tide, I unpin my hair and lean back, allowing it to loosen in the wind. The sun beats down, unyielding, making me yearn for rain, but this is a dry country.

The scene replays in my mind. The boy buckling on the beach, the shock of blood spreading over the sand. A throbbing bruise purples my collarbone. Is this how a soldier feels, the first time he shoots a man? A pain, a triumph, a disarticulation? The prints of Will's fingertips still dance over the skin of my arm, evoking the same touch on a different night, what has already become a different world, where betrayal had not riven so long, so deep. As deep as the Palk Strait of the Laccadive Sea, where your perfumed letters were caught and waterlogged, dragged down to dissolve in the cold.

For what would you tell me, if those letters had taken their path? Would you speak of the days leading up to my birth, the nights of expectation, the fear (for there is always fear), the dusk-blooming flowers, my brother's face? Were they letters of entreaty, of hope, of resignation? Was I a difficult child, were you glad of my birth? Did the temple bells ring, did you love my father, was I born with a caul?

And what words would you have for me, in English, in Sanskrit, in Bengali? What language is there that takes shape in your lips, your throat, that has been taken from me? All my life I have lived on the shoreline, in the space between words, where the tide creeps up to engulf me, only to ebb and leave me discarded. What speech is there for this? What language for this dissolution?

~

He finds her as the sunlight grows long on the hinterland, sitting with her knees pulled up to her chest, hair rippling down her back like a flag of fire. He picks over the still-warm rocks to reach her, his fingers brushing her arm, but she does not turn.

'Here, it's all written down.' He places the paper into her hands. 'Your mother's old address, your grandmother's name, her last known residence in Siam. Everything I learned.' The sun dips further into the skyline, the world around them turning to gold. 'I'm sorry. I should have told you. I can't describe how much I hoped we could have a future that wasn't ruled by our parents' misfortunes, or our pasts. But it seems the past is never past enough.'

He takes her in his arms and rests his head against the curve of her skull, his chin against the tender region of her neck. Still, she does not turn, her back and shoulders angling into him like the hard cartilage of sea flotsam. He closes his eyes. The narrowing horizon of his future has made him patient about the things that matter. He can wait out her anger, her silence.

~

With the greying of dusk, I know what I must do. My move has been made, my crime, with its fevered print on my collarbone, and now I cannot stay. No weakness or persuasion can change this terrible reality; this replication of my mother's sin on a beach in the new world has taken the decision from me, as I knew it would.

With this new certainty, I look at the man beside me with different eyes. As one might look on a thing of beauty that will not be here tomorrow, a flower that blooms for a single day.

~

In the dark, she kisses him with red lips as swollen as seaberries and just as bitter. Her dress is samphire in his hands; her nails caress his back like kangaroo thorn. As he rocks into her, he thinks of shipwrecks and castaways, of men condemned to eternal thirst.

He knows then that he cannot hold her, though he will try. But still, he is unprepared for the striations of dawn, for her burning desire to leave.

'I have something to tell you,' she says. 'There was more to my anger at you, after you went to Spain. More to my reasons.'

His eyes droop but his limbs still thrum with the day's tension. Despite their exertions, he cannot sleep.

He waits.

Hertfordshire, November 1822

I run my nail along the window's edge of my bedroom. Outside, the November moon spills her light through the last leaves of the oak trees. I did not think to see another winter in this house. I imagined a small wedding, perhaps in Marylebone, and then our own house away from this place with its empty rooms, white walls, the shadows that speak of my dead brother and grandfather, my dying uncle. His cough pierces every wall in the house and every cough seems to resound with the greatness of his disappointment in me.

I rest my head on the window frame. In the best fairytales, dead mothers leave charms. A fairy godmother, a speaking doll, a magic name, white as snow. At the moment of true crisis, this glittering charm appears to aid the heroine and avert some great and terrible misfortune. When I was a child, not long after we were brought here from India, I was determined to find such a charm. We were in a crisis, my brother and I. But no fairy godmother appeared, and I had no speaking doll. As for names, I was renamed a long time ago, and while I have spent the past few nights sitting in my window seat, staring at the moon and mouthing my old name to myself – *Indumati, Indumati, Indumati* – I feel no freer of my predicament.

My uncle doesn't know that I have ended things with Walter. I have kept out of his way these past few weeks, and now that he has gone to London the space around me has exhaled.

Turning in my seat, I open my jar of rahat-lokum and begin to eat. The servants, I think, know. I've seen the housekeeper watching me with sad eyes and the maids bring extra food to my room and take away the pots after I've vomited.

The sweets stick to my teeth. It will only be a matter of time before my uncle finds out about Walter, before he understands I have a deeper problem. It's warm and swelling. A marine secret. A serpent's tail. An expanding fish in a Venice lagoon.

The moon rolls over the clouds. *Indumati, Indumati.* I close my eyes, wondering what my mother hoped for me, in giving me this name. It cannot have been this cold imprisonment, the slow death of hope, a scandal without words.

Indumati. Grey seas, a crescent moon, the sway of a keel over a swell. Whispered words. Rough wool between my fingers. Strange stories from the Faroe Isles. Women living between the land and sea, shedding their skin. The tallest woman I had ever seen.

I open my eyes. Where is Mrs Jensen now?

~

I arrive in Torquay as the town emerges from the rain, swelling around its sandy harbour, crowned with auburn leaves rising over the rocks. The torrent followed us from London, casting cold rain over my fleeing steps. Now, the clouds part high over the Devon cliffs.

Meadfoot Abbey is not like my grandfather's house. Ancient and in disrepair, it overspills its boundaries, bleeding ritual, heresy and Catholicism. There are no neat borders here, no narrow white walls or Classical aspiration. It is pure Gothic excess, built on a site that was pagan before the Romans ever knew of such a place as England. The gargoyles speak of woodland gods; there are mermaids hewn into the banisters.

The Ramseys are not such a family, my uncle has always emphasised. An old name, but not ancient, they are more recently wealthy and fond of mercantile comforts. They bought the Abbey some fifty years ago. I have heard they are refurbishing the rooms, piece by piece. When I leave the entrance hall of dark wood and Italianate pillars, the drawing room opens into a plush peach room lit by large, silk-framed windows that startles me with its currency.

The figure standing by the fire looms straight out of my past. The governess in stiff black silk – she is shorter than I remember. Yet still, to see her with her sea-storm eyes is to be back at the docks of Portsmouth, the open Indian Ocean, the graveside of Calcutta.

She comes forward now and kisses me. Heat spreads out of my chest, tight and thick, hooking into my cheeks. We look at each other. This woman I have not seen since I was four years old, and I, the strange child she took halfway around the world.

A young man steps toward me from the far side of the room. In the glow of the fire, his face shines like the flash of hope I felt in the Calcutta cemetery when Major Ramsey waited by the gate.

'I was so sorry to hear about your father.' I speak as he bends over my hand. When he looks up, I see that he is both like and unlike the major. There is a brightness to his face like sunlight through new spring shoots.

~

I spend December at Meadfoot Abbey, watching winter roll over the sea. My uncle arrives before Christmas, his travelling clothes slick with mud and rain, blue eyes filmy with disappointment, and something else. Our host blunts our sharpness to one another. Hot tea, cake, a suggestion that we walk in the garden. Dainty, civil things that I would sooner cast aside even when I can see my uncle cracking. But when the winter sun peers from behind the endless gloom, I take his arm and we leave our companions, stepping into the pointed air.

'I thought I'd lost you all over again.' His voice is muted over the wind, which beats a steady rhythm through the tapering branches.

'But even if you had, you would have found me easily, as you did in Venice.'

His breath beside me is ragged. 'Why did you come here, Clarissa?'

'Isn't it obvious?' I hold up my left hand, smooth and bare of all adornment.

'I heard you ended things with Fraser. And what of it? I never liked the wretch. Your grandfather was the one who hired him. I don't know what you were thinking, accepting his proposal. But it doesn't matter. You can always come home.'

I stop walking. Before us, the garden's pond sits, stagnant and grey. A robin flutters on the magnolia tree's branches, releasing a shudder of raindrops. I let go of my uncle's arm and turn to face him. 'Do you really not know?'

He doesn't meet my eyes. 'Know what, my dear?'

'Why I agreed to marry Walter. I didn't love him. I never loved him.'

'I never thought you did.' He hesitates. 'I thought perhaps, after what happened in Italy, you were lonely.'

'No. I wasn't lonely.' My hands drift to my belly. 'I am never alone now. Do you understand?'

'I see.' My uncle frowns. 'Fraser's?'

'Of course not.' I step back. 'I only accepted his proposal because I thought it would give me safety. Give us safety.'

'Major Light's, then.'

It is not a question. I do not reply.

'Does he know?'

I shake my head.

'Then, in the circumstances, I will tell him. And he'll marry you. Surely, that is what you want.'

Leaves crisping to gold over St James' Park. And those words – he could never have Eurasian children. A curdled scent of betrayal.

'No. No,' I say again. 'It's not what I want. And he can't know.'

My uncle looks up at the strength in my voice.

'You need to promise me.' I seize his arm, my fingers fashioning furrows into his coat sleeve. 'You can't tell him.'

He nods slowly. 'If it's so important to you I won't say a word. But why not? You were willing to marry Fraser, of all men.'

'Because I thought it would keep us safe. But I was wrong about him.' Bruised wrists and insistent questions and no time that I was ever alone. I had been very wrong about him.

My uncle's eyes roam across my face as though he can see every memory. 'But Major Light was different,' he says quietly.

I release his arm. 'I don't see why it should matter to you. You went all the way to Venice just to warn him off. What did you say to him, anyway?' I study the loose pouches under his eyes, the redness of his nose, his flaccid cheeks. In Will's rejection of me,

I heard words that I had not believed could ever be his own.

My uncle paces, shoulders hunched against the pallid air. 'I wish I hadn't said anything at all.'

There is no home, now. No life with my uncle in Hertfordshire. 'I'm not coming back.'

'I don't have long, you know.' His blue eyes gleam against the winter sky. I have always found them overprized, blue eyes.

I shake my head, and, setting my gaze in front of me, walk back toward the house.

~

Later, my uncle is finally content to leave me, persuaded by Mrs Jensen's ministrations and James's words. We'll see each other again soon, my uncle says. You always have a home with me. I know then, in his filmy eyes and raspy breath, how deeply he regrets his Venetian intervention. But when he looks at me, he finds no forgiveness.

James Ramsey softens things between us. When my uncle leaves, there is relief in his eyes when he looks at Major Ramsey's son. I am no longer solely my uncle's problem.

The days pass slowly. I sleep and dream and draw up plans with Mrs Jensen. Eventually, James joins us. His father's death has made him, despite his youth, the master of the house. It is he who, with Mrs Jensen, makes the arrangements. And when Walter Fraser comes to the Abbey, rattling the doors and demanding to see me, it is James who turns him away.

I watch Walter leave from my sitting-room window, with his familiar stride, the shadow of his cane. The last time I hid from him crawls into my mind. Springtime, in Vauxhall, with Will. I cared for Walter once, but that didn't stop me using him. The engagement should have benefited us both. I was in need of a husband, and I was a match that was far beyond his usual reach. But I didn't account for his anger, his finely tuned attempts at control. I simply could not have traded what I had – freedom in Bath, a flight over the Channel, the lagoons of Venice – for a life of servitude.

'He seems to think you owe him something,' James tells me. 'Or that you have something that might be his.'

I shake my head. 'I have nothing of Walter's, at all.'

I dream, that night, of Walter, of the days after our engagement, his shock at my forwardness, yet how easily he was persuaded. The nausea in my belly, the crawling feeling of his touch, the way my body shrieked for another. I wake, sweating, to the sound of rain on the windowpanes, the cold ash of an old fire long dead in the grate. I rise and dress, lighting a candle against the cold. The very early morning wears the guise of night; not even the servants will be up yet. But I can't sleep.

The hallways in the guest wing rustle with draughts. Unrenovated, they bear the marks of their historic purpose. Walls with icons hewn from their pedestals, scarred plasterwork, vaulted ceilings that speak of old censers filled with frankincense. I run my fingers over the pitted walls as I walk. Where comes this urge for dissolution, for violence, to always destroy? As I walk, the world around me changes. The Ramseys' restoration becomes apparent. Thick carpet appears beneath my feet, and the scarred walls are replaced by wainscotting. At the end of the hall, warm light peers out from beneath the library door.

When I enter, James looks up. He sits at the desk, surrounded by paperwork, his young face creased in the candlelight. He's trying to get ahead on the books, he tells me, to get everything sorted before the army, and in case he's called away. He shares his pot of chocolate, and I sit in the armchair by the fire, resting my feet on the ottoman. The frown migrates over James's face as he works. I do not think he has a knack for books, for a deskbound life, but I admire his persistence. I try to read – I have found a copy of Keats's poems and my eyes wander over 'The Eve of St Agnes' – but I have no appetite for husbands, or for dreaming. The rain drums its rhythm on the roof. James stands up and stokes the fire, and when the room grows warm, he returns to his desk. Outside, past the window's glass, the first slivers of a grey dawn take shape beyond the rain. I rest my head against the armchair and close my eyes. The fire swells in the grate. I fall asleep.

Canterbury, March 1823

There is a house in Canterbury within the sound of cathedral bells, where an oval window looks out over the grey coast. The sea rolls in under the milky sky and lonely gulls circle.

We made the voyage in reverse, a strange replication of that first journey. Mrs Jensen, a male Ramsey and I. But instead of travelling inland we made haste for the coast, a flight under cover of darkness, with my determination charting the path before us and the younger Mr Ramsey bringing up the rear. Our talisman of respectability.

On the day of your birth, it rains. The drops strike the windowpane like cannon fire, each liquid missile shattering against the glass, leaving our view swirling into a world of water. Outside, the earth turns grey and silver, the stony beach glistening and running with brim, the waves reflecting the watercolour sky.

In the morning, the gulls flocked across the horizon and scattered over the pebbly shore, searching for food. Their insistent cries became my consolation. Now only a single bird hangs suspended in the firmament, wings spread out, a dark stroke buffeted by wind. When the pain starts, rhythmic and twisting, I watch how it floats in the blankness, riding the oncoming deluge, navigating swathes of rolling clouds creeping in from the Channel.

You push yourself out relentlessly. In my haze of pain, I can feel you, deep in your underwater cavern, slippery, turning, all muscle and fin, pushing toward the light. An old drowned city like Ys straining for its resurgence. A bird strikes the window. A crack rends the air. I think of a musket shot over Spain, a horse's scream and arterial blood, the sound of being split wide open.

The midwife murmurs. I can hear you already, a creaking, kittenish sound, crying in tempo to the rain drumming on the window. The midwife moves to take you across the room, but I hold out my hand and she pauses, passing you over. 'She's been blessed,' I hear Mrs Jensen say. You are sleek and slippery, a wet pup crowned with tufted dark fur, a sleeping face behind a watery film, an oceanic cocoon. The midwife breaks the sac and removes the caul. 'You must keep it.'

A gift from your grandmother, a second skin, eternal protection from drowning.

As the veil of skin is drawn from your face, your nose crinkles. Your eyes open, dark and questioning. Disdainful of the world around you, the soft pink of your lips splits and you release an outraged cry. I laugh, holding you, and I understand now that I will never be unmoored again. My port, my anchor. My Marina.

South Australian Coast, October 1836

'Why did you never tell me?' As he speaks, he already knows the answer. Those words he said, the decision he made. *I can never have Eurasian children.*

He rolls onto his back, the rocks pressing into him. Leaving one hand buried in the tangle of her hair as she lies beside him, he looks up. The sky returns his gaze, its dark face punctuated with still-strange stars, smeared with the vivid cream of the Milky Way. How wide it is here, how open. How filled with possibility. *I have a child*, he thinks. *I have a child, I have a child, I have a child.*

'How could I tell you?' Her voice is quiet. Behind it, he can hear the waves. 'I could not expose myself to more pain, more humiliation. I couldn't expose my daughter to your prejudice.'

'Our daughter.'

'Our daughter.'

'But yes. I understand.'

'You are not angry?'

'Angry? No. No, I am many things, but I am not angry.' The cavern in his chest swells, buoyant and light, freed for a moment from that grating rasp, from his own mortality. *I have a child.*

'I'm glad. I could not come all the way here and find you and leave it unsaid.'

'It's why you came, is it not?' He speaks before he thinks. Her eyes drill into him.

'No, Will. I came about my mother.'

'I cannot believe that is true.'

She rolls away from him. 'Marina has a good life. She lives in Cornwall as my ward and has my old Scottish governess. She knows how much I love her.'

'And what of me? What does she know of me?' He turns to face her, propping himself on his arms.

'She knows you were a soldier in Spain.'

'You told her I'm dead.'

'I told her I don't know. And I didn't really, not for certain. She knows not to ask me any further.'

He looks at her face in the night. 'How well you have mimicked your grandfather.'

'That is unfair.' She pivots onto her elbows. 'I have always planned to tell her when she is older.'

'And did you ever plan to tell me?'

'I never thought I'd see you again. Not after you married and went to Egypt. I wanted nothing to do with you for years. And then I heard your name that afternoon in Calcutta. I was already halfway to Australia and I thought you could help me. That I would see what sort of man you've become. That I could see you one last time before I marry.'

He laughs. 'It's what – your third engagement?'

'Fourth, if you include ours. The engagement that never really was.'

'You don't need to worry about that now.'

'What do you mean?'

He pauses. What does he mean? He has made amorphous plans for her residence in Australia, for a future that contains her. But this is another step.

'I'll get my affairs in order. I'll finally settle my divorce. We'll finish what we started. You don't need to marry this ... whoever he is.'

She sits up slowly. 'James Ramsey. His name is James Ramsey.'

He is already not listening. 'Whoever he is, you don't need this wedding anymore.'

'Will, it's not that simple.'

'Of course it is. What do you mean?'

She looks inland, toward the greying east. 'I have never needed to marry James. That was never what the engagement was about. And besides, I can't stay here.' Her hand moves to her collarbone. 'I shot someone.'

'I've spoken to Dr Woodforde. Hewitt should be all right. You grazed his arm. There was a great amount of blood, but that's under control now. We can't be certain, and it will take time, but the doctor thinks he'll make a full recovery.'

She runs her hand over her face. 'It doesn't mean I can stay here. I still took the shot.'

'I'm sure we can work it out.'

'Somehow, I doubt your man will feel this way. Or the settlers. I will not allow myself to be arrested.'

'It won't come to that.'

'I am not so sure. Not out here, so far from England. Thank goodness the whaling ship is American. They will not be easily bullied.'

'You don't need to concern yourself with that. We can resolve this. Once they realise who you are, all you will need to do is apologise. Make amends somehow, a gesture, and all will be forgotten.'

'Are you suggesting I pay him off?' She shakes her head. 'I can't do that. I am not even sure I am sorry. I am not sure he deserves it. I am not sure any of them do.'

'What are you saying?'

'This place, the things that have happened here. You say that it will get better, that things will change–'

'This is a colony, not an enclave of escaped thugs.'

'Is it really so different? What about the people here? Can you think of anywhere–'

'Of course it's different.'

She presses her temples. 'I don't know, Will. I need to think.'

'What is there to think about?'

'You would have me stay here. What about our daughter? You would leave her in England? Or have her travel here alone?'

'Your Scottish governess could take her. Like she did you.'

'She's too old for that now.'

'She could find someone else to do it. I have so little time, Clarissa. I cannot just up and leave for England now. It will take me months to arrange such a passage, to get my work in order. I am only part way through my surveying and I still need to plan the location of the city. But Marina could join us here. We could all have a life together.'

'I need to dress.'

He watches as her body is swathed in layers of cloth, her fingers efficiently tying knots and pulling laces. The fresh bruise on her collarbone disappears into buttons and silk. He thinks of the shots on the beach. Her figure in the hot air balloon. Their flight in darkness across the English Channel. She has always been impulsive, and he has loved her for it. But now he feels a prickling unease, a sense of fear. What madness will she follow next?

~

I stand and let the pebbles and shale fall from my skirt.

'Where are you going?'

I don't answer him. Behind us, the morning pierces the skin of the eastern sky. The dark face over the ocean recedes, slick forms shining black against the mirrored surface, rising and falling like piano keys.

'Seals.' His voice cuts the air behind me.

I watch their ebony heads, their circling fins rippling in the tide.

'Come on,' he says. 'Let's talk about this some more. Let's go back to the ship.'

I don't reply. I have seen them before, floating in the shallows, foraging with their vibrissae as they stalk redbait and molluscs. I have seen them dive deep into the darkness of the Southern Ocean, spinning against the cold. And I have seen them, row after row, skinned and dismembered, pelts staked over the white sand to dry.

'Come with me,' I tell him.

He raises his eyebrows. 'Where?'

'To see Marina. And then to Bangkok, Calcutta. Or Penang. Singapore, even. Away from here.'

In the half-light his coat gleams red. I think of all he's done and been, the scent of old cordite, the Union Jack over Spain, a light-brown boy hustled onto a ship in George Town, bound for Suffolk.

Dark skin, English face. And now he is here, with compass and surveying chain, map and allotment plan, and men in the North awaiting their profits. He shakes his head. 'I have responsibilities here. I can't leave. The settlement would collapse. And besides, can't you see the opportunity? For you, for our daughter. Europe, Asia – there's no space for people like us there. This is a new world.'

People like us.

I look around. I can hear the rustle of dancing eucalyptus leaves, the breeze in salt-brushed bushes. There are no clouds in the sky, and the morning holds the promise of an adamantine noon.

'This is not a new world. There are people here already.'

'I know that. This will be better for them. As it will be for us.'

'How can you say that?'

'Think of everything we have to offer. We are building a new society here, this land, the best of English civilisation–'

'You have seen the women on the beaches.'

'All that was unregulated. Ex-convicts from Van Diemen's Land – the worst of human society. Now that we're here – I'm here – it will change.'

'And what of your mother, and mine? What did this civilisation do for them?'

His jaw clenches and his brows furrowing and shifting. He would like to counter me, to parry, but the truth is there is no defence.

As the daylight lengthens, the seals disperse, trained to avoid this coast at certain times, to sniff out the scent of tar and burning blubber. In the north, seal pups are born white. Their pelts thicken with darkness over time, the whiteness of their fur serving to protect them; they lie very still against the snow to escape predators, yet still some are taken.

He stands next to me, watching the seals leave. His coat has dulled to burgundy. Silver threads shine against the blackness of his hair. He will never wear a uniform again. 'Remember that story you told me, about the selkies? I'd heard the stories might have been based on truth. That women from the north used to sail their canoes wrapped in sealskins to Scotland. If a man caught one and hid her canoe, she had no way of going home. So, he could take her as a wife, have children with her.'

'Until the day she found her canoe.'

'Yes.'

'Why are you telling me this?'

'Because she always left. No matter how many years had passed, or how many children she'd had, she always left, and she left the children behind. In Scotland, in Europe. That was where they remained.'

'Our mothers didn't leave us. We left them.'

'But they moved on, into their own worlds. And we, we were left behind to make sense of this one. And that's what I'm doing here.'

To make sense of this world.

'It's not going to work.'

He makes a sound and turns from me, his boots crunching and thudding upon the rock. Then I feel his hands on my back, my hair, my waist, his head against my shoulder.

'Come back to the ship with me.'

I move out of his grasp and turn to face him. 'No, I can't go back. And I can't stay. And I will not have my daughter brought here to live this frontier life of violence, to see the way women are treated when they are almost the same colour as she is. You cannot ask that of her, of us. You need to make a choice, Will. Take a month if you need to. Wrap up your work here.'

'It will take longer than that. And there are no ships scheduled–'

'I'll pay for your passage, if that's what it takes.'

'I don't want your money, Clary. I have never wanted your money. There are things I need to do here. I need to see it through. To achieve something for once in my life.'

'Then that is your choice.'

'Is it? All I ask is that you wait here with me until it's complete, and then, maybe then we can move elsewhere.'

'I can't do that. You know I can't. How can I live in this world? Or raise my daughter in this place? Your men have been here but a few months, and already they treat the natives with disgust. I don't understand what you're doing here or what you hope to achieve. How long do you think your ideals will last? You are just one man.'

'Do you think so little of me? I have a chance to make a difference here, Clarissa. I may be just one man, but the settlers listen to me. What sort of man would I be if I left now? My ideals mean something. You're right – some of the men are being corrupted, but I can change that.'

'I can't stay and sacrifice myself in some frontier life, for men who wouldn't do the same for me.'

'Then let it be on your head that your daughter is without a father, as you were without a mother all those years.'

'Don't try to place the blame with me when what really keeps you here is your own bloody cowardice, your own fear that you are a failure.'

'A failure? Is that what you think of me?'

'Will, I–'

'A failure I may be. But at least I'm a sane one. At least I am not mad.'

~

He sees the closed look settle upon her face, an oyster shell turning inwards, sealing off its pearls. The beach front dims despite the growing dawn. He steps forward.

'That was uncalled for.' He takes her hands. 'I'm sorry.'

Her fingers are cold. She looks up at him, blinking, but does not speak.

'Clarissa, don't be upset about this.' His words are quicker than he intends, and his grip tightens on her fingers.

She pulls her hands from his grasp. 'So that is what you think of me.' She holds up a palm to stop him speaking. 'After all this time. You are just like the others. Or you try to be. You do not understand me at all. You think because I am different and female and untrammelled, because I will not live in the walls someone else has built for me, that somehow, I must be mad. But don't you see there can always be another way? There is always another way of being in this world. Of seeing it.'

'Do you think I have not tried?'

She flinches at the volume of his voice.

'What would you have me do? Where would you have me go? There is no escape. Not in India, not in Malaya, not in England. The sun doesn't set on these injustices. The sun doesn't set. There is no freedom, no blank slate, no Eden without consequences. There is no place for us to build a moral life, no country. There is only survival in the ruins of what we have.

'Do you think I have not tried to be this other way, to see the world as you do and thrive in it? It is not possible to succeed or survive in such a manner. And yes, I do think that if you persist in living as you do, if you continue to reject the hands that help you and flout all social convention and continue this foolhardy quest to live beyond all strictures, despite all your advantages, then yes, I think you are mad.'

'And was my mother mad, for rejecting Whitworth? Are the women here mad for drowning in their attempts to escape Kangaroo Island? Was your sister mad for all her fears of what would happen to her, after Vellore?'

'It is not the same.'

'I see now where this will lead us. A small room in a cold house. A constant seeking of permission. The narrowing of my daughter's world. My name will not be worth the paper it is written on, because everything I own will become yours. Including my own body. My self.'

The fight is running out of him and something creeps into his bones in its place. Dread. 'Clarissa, let's talk about this properly.'

When she turns, he sees the sparks grow hot beneath her feet, the surge of electricity in water, the silk of her dress caught in the shimmering rage of fire.

He tries to stop her, but his voice is just a whisper in a squall. When he reaches for her arm, she slips through his fingers, saline, marine, with a flick of her tail.

~

His voice echoes down the coast as I walk, my wrist burning with his invisible prints. The sun rises higher, making me thirsty.

I shed my layers like an old skin – my shawl, the netted muslin at my throat, my underskirt – until all that remains is the shell of my dress, as sea green as the gown of Loro Kidu.

I am bleeding water. I can't breathe.

In the haze of the light dancing off the sand, I see the rows of seal pelts darkening the shore with fur and purple blood. The black-haired women work rhythmically on the skins, scraping and drying. Judith brings them fresh pelts.

I pause by the sandbank, waiting. The women ignore me, all but Judith, who watches me out of the corner of her eye. As I sit on the sand, sunlight lengthens over the expanse of sea, and my lips are brittle and bleeding. I can think only of water, its sound, its taste. The feeling of silver fish between my teeth.

The women begin to leave. I would call to them, but my body is limp. I am thinning, deflating, absorbed into the sand. Above me, gulls circle, like birds over the Hooghly lined with marigolds.

Fingers touch my arm, cool and wet. By the time I open my eyes, Judith has already stepped away, watchful. I move to follow her and then I see it. Fresh, moist, lined with blackening blood like treacle. The fur smells of seal pups and the open ocean. It smells like the way home.

I unlace my dress and the fabric floats free – the Queen of the Southern Sea calls back her colours. Judith is gone, the beach is empty. The wind rips the silk from my fingers. I lie on the sand and wrap the pelt about me. The blood and blubber are cool, the skin is softly fibrous. I shudder as I feel it upon my skin, the pelt seeping into my muscle and bone. The world curves around me; the sea sings. I roll into the waves, into sound and silence.

As the sun dips red at the horizon, Judith approaches the dune.

She touches the dress, studies its oceanic green, its fine-spun silk. She sees a crown of silver stars, a rush of aquamarine. There are murmurs in the water.

She tosses the dress into the sea.

Bangkok, April 1837

We travel by river, leaving the island port of Ko Sichang with its mountain shrines and marine air, the seafarers from Hainan and Fujian, the ships of the Dutch East India Company. In the late-afternoon sun, we step from our ship onto a barge laden with trade goods from the West: wool and steel, coral and lead, English silver. Other ships take woven cotton to India. They resell fabric grown in Indian soil and harvested by Indian hands, made into cloth in heaving Pennine mills.

I wear such cotton now. A high-necked white dress, designed to be breathable. A white cotton corset, white gloves. A stiff silk parasol to keep out the sun. White like a Hindu widow. I do not know who I have dressed for, or from where springs this urge for memsahib conventionality. Perhaps Will was right all along; for one such as I, the strictures of colonial life in India are not to my liking. I have been more aware of it since my time in Australia. The fine rules of Calcutta's society, the question in everyone's eyes, the growing hardness of the line in the city. White town, and black. Every day the port of Calcutta swells with men, women, children, their bodies indentured into labour, bound for plantations across the ocean. I was naïve not to see its emergence, this fruit of abolition.

I know that British Calcutta is not for me now; I do not intend to make a life there. But in my dress, for this moment, I have conceded to its rigidity. On this day, of all days, I do not wish to be seen and thought too wild, too disreputable.

The barge progresses through the estuary and onto the river. The green foliage curves around the shape of the banks, the smooth surface of the water punctuated by floating houses rising from the depths. I imagine what it would be like to live in such a structure, to wake each morning to the endless motion of the current, the surface beneath me rushing into the sea.

Neither of us has been here before. From his friends in Calcutta, James has a neat list of sights and palaces. All the beautiful things to do in this unceded kingdom, a place that survives by hedging its bets against its neighbours, against the world. He tells me of a glorious ancient Buddha, wrought from gold, of the temple's roofs tapering into the sky, of the value of Siamese poetry. I think of other things, too. The Burney agreement and the Siamese–American Treaty, the value of spices and land. What happens when people own things desired by others.

News has reached me, about South Australia, in the months since I have left. I hear the colony struggles, that they regret their choice of governor. I hear they dispute the tract of land Will has chosen for them, the site of their new city. I hear he sickens and longs for England.

I do not hear from Will. How would I? He has no address for me beyond my nephew's estate in Hertfordshire, or my house in Cornwall. If letters were sent, they would not find me here, on the other side of the world. But despite this, I know there have been no letters. He is a man too accustomed to loss, to letting go of meaningful things.

After arriving at dusk, we leave the barge at the river port and change transport to a canal boat with our guide. We float through the city, past Chinese settlements and market traders, the vendors navigating canoes laden with fruit. In the distance, the city opens to us. There are neat gardens and clean walls, the golden spires of the palace reaching toward the light. Our guide takes us around the bend of the canal toward a green expanse of acreage and a wide, low-lying building.

When the guide tethers the boat, James helps me onto land, but it is not long before I overtake him. My steps set their own tempo, my heels sinking into damp earth, my balance wobbling with my speed. I ignore the grass stains and the river mud flicking onto my dress. The building draws closer.

Above me, the last of the season's swallows chart their arc in the afternoon sky. I think, just briefly, of a long past Italian summer.

And then I see it. The open verandah of a schoolroom. A woman's silhouette. Plain European clothing in place of a tangerine sari. The last thing I ever saw her wear. Shining half-moon eyeglasses. Hands and wrists that I see every morning as part of my own body. I watch as her profile turns, as her eyes fall upon me.

I collapse my parasol, ignoring the sun. I would show my face. As her eyes move over me, papers fall from her hands. When she steps from beneath the verandah, her glasses gleam in the light.

Adelaide, January 1839

It starts at his neighbour's cottage. They had just finished lunch. A thin, plain meal that he fought to swallow. These daily tasks are harder now. Eating, drinking, waking, sleeping. Breathing. But he had breath enough to notice this, the scent that strikes such fear into the heart of a sleeping sailor. Fire.

Outside, under that violent January sun, Light sees there is no hope. His household has escaped alive and that is all that providence allows him. Bright, marigold, the flames surge skywards from roof to roof. The wood of their cottage is aged and brittle, split with dehydration, the water leached out of it by the relentless, infernal heat of the Plains. As fire blossoms around its structure, the cottage sizzles and spits, its last remaining moisture burning up under the cerulean sky.

Behind him, Maria sobs. As the air fills with black smoke, sulphur-crested cockatoos shriek, laughing.

He does not speak. Within this small and temporary structure lie thirty years' worth of journals, letters and reflections. They were days from being moved to the house he has been building. He thought to publish them soon – before the slow flooding of his lungs drowns him.

Not just papers. Sketches too. Paintings of France and Switzerland and Italy. His work on the South Australian coast. A portrait, permanently unfinished, of a woman doubled, gown in sea green and red. He thinks of that portrait now, as he runs with the others, fruitlessly carrying buckets of river water. He sees the painting rupture and split, blistering and dissolving into fractured memory and inferno.

He pauses for breath after hurling the water. The liquid does not even bubble against the root of the fire but sighs and vanishes into steam and air. He is aware of his coughing, of the others drawing him back. He had been close, too close, to that licking, hypnotic fire.

He clutches his bucket, doubled over, and gulps torrid air. These summers will be the end of him. How can he go on living here, in a country that burns and burns? At this time in Suffolk there would be chestnuts, cold starlight, sleet and rain, the promise of snowdrops slowly waking. And elsewhere, the tropical rains, the irrepressible greenness of Penang.

Light straightens his back, slowly. The cottages, the offices, they cannot be saved. But the fire can be stopped from spreading.

He turns to fetch more water, but something catches his eye at the site of the fire. Someone moves in the distance, behind the collapsed roofs, barely visible through the leaping flames. A figure, gazing back at him.

Light blinks. He knows the outline of this person, knows the set of her expression, her queenly eyes and jaw. The whaler's daughter. But it's been years, and he last saw her far from here. Can it be? He steps forward, searching for her name. Julia? Judith?

Who is there? he asks, but his voice is weak, and it does not travel over the rush of burning. *Who is there?*

He steps closer again, but the figure is gone. When he tries to call, no sound emerges. There is only the roar of the fire, the crackling of wood, the collapsing buildings. Conflagration.

Bangkok, October 1845

In the growing humidity, Clarissa moves with precision. The windows of the schoolroom are open, but there is no breeze. Outside, the evening sky is thick with cloud. It is the end of the wet season, but they have not seen the last of the rain.

She packs away the day's chalk and wipes the dust from the desk. There are students who could do this, her mother tells her, but she likes the moment of quiet and solitude in the evening, this chance to settle her day, to make it right.

By the river, on the edge of her grandmother's land, her husband and children are lighting the lanterns. For the locals it is Loy Krathong, the festival of lights, a time of gratitude to the goddess of water, a thanksgiving for her abundance in flooding the fields of rice. As Clarissa stacks the encyclopaedias on their shelves, she pictures her family: Marina's deft fingers threading flowers into banana leaves and trimming the lantern's wick; the humour of her middle-born as he lopes before a colony of macaques and magics frangipanis from behind her youngest's ears. He inherits that from her husband. This exuberance, this joy in life. In their family, faces range from cream to brown. They glow together as the wick ignites and lanterns float on the river's surface. The offering wobbles, its edges curved into the goblet shape of a sacred lotus flower, the thick stamen replaced by guttering candle flame and a glowing pool of molten wax.

Elsewhere in this country, they release the lights into the sky, a fleet of flaming lanterns like balloons launched into the swift sunset to welcome the new year. But here, the river shapes the city, and on this evening it snakes beneath the stilts of the houses and the flower-laden canoes, its streams transformed into rivers of light.

Clarissa pauses by the window, catching a glimpse of this glow. It was during this festival, five years ago, that Moses told her the news. His letter arrived salt-rimmed, still scented with the tang of brine and eucalypts and blubber. She could feel her feet back on the slick and swaying deck, face turned to the wind, straining for the shore.

Will's death was not unexpected. She sensed it coming in the years after she left Australia. When she thought of him, knowing the disease would spread its colonies further into his lungs, inch by inch, she would breathe twice as deeply, as though by doing so she could send him the air she was inhaling. But there are some people she cannot save.

She sits on her tidied desk and looks out at the schoolroom. The compass, the globe, the abacus. What would he think of her now, his mad woman? Teaching local girls logic and geometry, tracing the trade routes of sailors over English maps. One should always know the mind of one's enemy.

But despite her time here, there are days when she misses the bright wind beating at their house on the Cornish coast, the rhythm of the seasons, the first sign of daffodils at the breaking of spring. It makes her smile to realise, after all this time, that she is British, too.

Thick raindrops beat across the roof, slowly at first, then with an increasing tempo. A flash of blue light illuminates the city. There is a pause and then, right on time, the crack of thunder.

Beyond the schoolroom, laughter shrieks above the weather. Clarissa steps onto the verandah and holds her palms out to the pulsing water.

Familiar footsteps pound into the garden and scatter up the drive. Her children run toward her with delighted cries, wet hair slick like the fur of marine seals. Clarissa laughs.

She walks out beneath the humming rain, and into her children's arms.

Author's Note

Salt Upon the Water is a work of fiction. The character of William Light is inspired by the historical person, but the character of Clarissa FitzRoy, and their relationship, is entirely fictional. I have taken pains to remain true to the spirit of Light's voice and outer personality, as I have understood it from his letters and journals; his inner life, however, and the opinions, fears, and desires that accompany it, are products of my invention and speculation. I say speculation here because, while I do not know how Light felt about his mother or his ancestry, based on the history of the time I can speculate that it had an effect, and a complex one at that.

For those who are interested in the historical facts of Light's life, Geoffrey Dutton's biography, *Colonel William Light: Founder of a City,* remains a detailed source of information, and it has been highly useful to me in piecing together the chronology of Light's travels and life. I recommend the text with some hesitation, however. While comprehensive – in no small part due to David Elder's dedicated research – the biography is inflected with Dutton's personal opinions and the inclusion of racist terms with regard to William Light's Asian mother, Martina Rozells. It is unfortunate as the use of such terminology and the derogatory assumptions about Martina Rozells are both unnecessary and, from what I can tell, historically unfounded. Sources contemporary to Rozells' life appear to indicate that she was a figure of some importance. In Western scholarship, discussions of her over time have appeared to both diminish and disparage her. The President of the Penang Heritage Trust, Khoo Salma Nasution says it best when she writes, diplomatically, in relation to Rozells that '[t]he inability of British administrator-historians to deal with cultural complexities in this part of the world has contributed to the muddle, resulting in disrespectful asides against this pioneering woman who most likely played a key role in bridging many cultures and power relationships'.

While Dutton's biography is certainly worth reading by anyone with an interest in the historic figure of Light, I would counsel a contemporary reader to conduct this reading with a critical eye. In light not only of the racist terminology in Dutton's work, but also changing understandings of settler colonialism and the experiences of First Nations peoples, I suggest that it is time for other historians to re-assess Light's history and legacy.

In terms of historicity, while Clarissa is a fictional character, she has also been inspired by historical figures. William Dalrymple's *White Mughals*, particularly his research on Kitty Kirkpatrick, has been invaluable in helping to shape Clarissa's backstory and understanding the social context of mixed marriages in India during the late eighteenth and early nineteenth centuries. Similar figures who have inspired the character of Clarissa and her family include Elizabeth Sharaf un-Nisa Ducarel, Helene Bennett, Katherine Scott Forbes, and Sarah Redfield, the mixed race half-sister of the novelist William Makepeace Thackeray. David Ochterlony Dyce Sombre is another notable historical figure of mixed heritage whose life illustrates the complex interplay of racial discrimination, tenuous class status, and the ways in which possessing wealth as a person of colour in the nineteenth century could render one vulnerable as well as privileged.

In an Australian context, elements of this novel have also been inspired by the agency demonstrated by First Nations people during colonisation as discussed by the scholars Lynette Russell and Rob Amery.

From an international perspective, this novel also owes a debt to Jean Rhys' seminal work, *Wide Sargasso Sea*, and the broader writings of Michael Ondaatje, particularly *The English Patient*, as well as Helen Oyeyemi's *Boy, Snow, Bird*, Zoe Gilbert's *Folk*, Arundhati Roy's *The God of Small Things*, Jeanette Winterson's *The Passion*, and the work of Toni Morrison.

Within Australia, *Salt Upon the Water* sits in a field of increasingly thriving multiracial Asian Australian fiction. I'd like to acknowledge the pioneering work of Brian Castro, whose novels have transformed the field of Asian Australian literature, particularly *Shanghai Dancing*, *The Garden Book*, and *Street to Street*, which explore multiracial Asian Australian identity through fictional and historical characters. Mirandi Riwoe's work such as *Stone Sky Gold Mountain* and *The Fish Girl*, which also explores Southeast Asian water-based mythology, has also been significantly influential in diversifying historical fiction. I acknowledge the foundational work of Michelle Cahill's novel *Daisy & Woolf*, which excavates a post-colonial and metafictional space for the Anglo-Indian historical narrative in Australian and world literature. Similarly, I acknowledge the complexity of Michelle de Kretser's writings, particularly *The Hamilton Case* and *The Lost Dog*, and the nuance with which they engage with multiplicity and subjectivity. Simone Lazaroo's *The World Waiting to be Made* and *The Australian Fiancé* and Christopher Cyrill's *The Ganges and its Tributaries* are also early examples of multiracial Asian Australian literature. There are increasing writers in this field each year, all of whom have important and valuable stories.

For further novels on South Australian history, readers might be interested in Molly Murn's *Heart of the Grass Tree*, Hannah Kent's *Devotion*, and Lucy Treloar's *Salt Creek,* among others.

Selected Sources

Archival Sources

Letters from Malcolm, as Private Secretary to Lord Wellesley, with related letters from Wellesley and James Achilles Kirkpatrick, concerning the latter's affair with an Indian woman (Khair un Nissa), India Office Records and Private Papers, the British Library, Mss Eur F228/18.

Light, W., *William Light Collection*, State Library of South Australia, PRG 1.

Light, W., *Autograph Letter Signed to George Jones*, Western Manuscripts, the British Library, RP 8802/1.

Light, W., *Light Papers*, Barr Smith Library, University of Adelaide.

Raffles Papers, Western Manuscripts, the British Library, Add MS 45271.

Sir C.J. Napier Papers: Correspondence and papers of Lieutenant-General Sir Charles James Napier, the conqueror of Sind (b.1782, d.1853) 1801–1853. Western Manuscripts, the British Library, Add MS 54510-54563.

Non-Archival Sources

Amery, R., (2016), *Warraparna Kaurna!: Reclaiming an Australian Language*, Adelaide: University of Adelaide Press.

Anonymous, 'The Ruin,' translated by S. Echard (2015), original Old English first composed in the 8th or 9th century.

Chatterji, J. and Washbrook, D. (eds.) (2014), *Routledge Handbook of the South Asian*

Diaspora, London: Routledge.

Coke, D. and Borg, A. (2011), *Vauxhall Gardens: A history*, Newhaven: Yale University Press.

Coleridge, S.T. (1816), 'Kubla Khan: Or, a vision in a dream. A Fragment,' *Poetry Foundation.*

Dalrymple, W. (2002), *White Mughals: Love and Betrayal in Eighteenth-Century India*, London: HarperCollins.

Dutton, G. and Elder, D. (1991), *Colonel William Light: Founder of a City*, Melbourne: Melbourne University Press.

Fisher, M.H. (2010), *The Inordinately Strange Life of Dyce Sombre: Victorian Anglo-Indian MP and a "Chancery Lunatic"*. New York: Columbia University Press.

Fossett, R. (2001), *In order to live untroubled: Inuit of the Central Arctic 1550 to 1940*, Winnipeg: University of Manitoba Press.

Keats, J. (2009), *Bright Star*, London: Vintage.

Keats, J. (2017 edition; first published 1820), *Lamia, Isabella, The Eve of St Agnes and other poems*, London: Penguin Random House.

Khoo, S.N. 2012, 'Exploring shared history, preserving shared heritage: Penang's links to a Siamese past', *Journal of the Siam Society*, 100, pp. 295–322.

Light, W. (1984), *William Light's brief journal and Australian diaries*, Adelaide: Wakefield Press.

Light, W. (1991), *The diary of William Light in Switzerland 1826*, Lyndoch: Pump.

McEntire, N.C. (2010), 'Supernatural beings in the Far North: Folklore, folk belief, and the Selkie', *Scottish Studies*, vol. 35, pp. 120–143.

Miller, L. (2020), *L.E.L: The lost life and mysterious death of the 'female Byron'*, London: Penguin Random House.

Ray, S. (2011), 'Thackeray and India: re-examining England's narrative of its Indian empire', *Victorians: A Journal of Culture and Literature*, (120), pp. 36–50.

Reynolds, I. (2021), "'Writ in water": The gravestone of John Keats,' *Wordsworth Grasmere.*

Russell, L. (2012), *Roving Mariners: Australian Aboriginal Whalers and Sealers in the Southern Oceans, 1790–1870*, Albany, NY: State University of New York Press.

Scott, W. (2011 edition; first published 1814), *Waverley*, London: Penguin Random House.

The Spectator (1712), Tuesday May 20, Vol. V, No. 383, J. and R. Tonson and S. Draper, London.

Shelley, M.W. (2018 edition; first published 1818), *Frankenstein*, London: Penguin Random House.

Shelley, P.B. (2011), *The Poems of Shelley, Volume 1*, London: Routledge.

Trapaud, E. (1788), *A short account of the Prince of Wales's Island, or Pulo Peenang, in the East Indies: Given to Capt. Light by the King of Quedah*, J. Stockdale, London.

Vauxhall Society 2020, 'Who was the mystery "lady of colour" who sang and gave a pianoforte recital at Vauxhall Gardens in 1822?', *Vauxhall History*, 16 September.

Victoria and Albert Museum 2025, 'The Wedgwood anti-slavery medallion,'.

Welsh, J. (1830), *A memorial, addressed to the Court of Directors of the Honourable the East India Company*, London: Smith, Elder & Company.

Wollstonecraft, M. (2004 edition; first published 1792), *A vindication of the rights of women*, London: Penguin Random House.

Quotations

Page 36 contains a quote from the 20th May 1712 edition of *The Spectator*.

Page 39 contains a quote from the 1812 poem 'Sonnet: To A Balloon Laden With Knowledge' by Percy Bysshe Shelley.

Page 119 contains a paraphrased quote from the 1816 poem 'Kubla Khan' by Samuel Taylor Coleridge.

Page 134 contains a quote from the tombstone of John Keats.

Reading Guide for
Salt Upon the Water

---

1. Throughout the novel, seemingly magical occurrences take place at unexpected moments, often relating to seals, mermaids, and selkies. How do these events contribute to our understanding of the characters, their experiences, and concerns?
2. Discuss the relationship between Clarissa and Light. What draws them together? Are they right to travel to France and Italy without informing Clarissa's family? What does the conflict between them reveal about race, gender, and power?
3. Clarissa and Light both demonstrate a keen awareness of the presence of First Nations people in South Australia. What do the characters' respective attitudes towards the settlement of South Australia reveal about them?
4. Discuss the characters of Moses and Judith. What is their significance to the story, and to the lives of Clarissa and Light? What do you think it means when Judith tosses Clarissa's dress into the sea, and seemingly appears to Light at the very end of the novel?
5. Family, heritage, and identity are large elements of both Clarissa and Light's desires and fears. What do their different responses to these drivers tell you about how multiracial heritage might have been experienced in the past?

6. Water, islands, and coastal zones are significant physical locations in the novel. What role does the natural world play in *Salt Upon the Water*? How does water and coastal-based imagery shape our understanding of the novel's themes?
7. While *Salt Upon the Water* is a work of fiction, William Light is a real historical person. What does it mean for Australia's national identity that one of Australia's capital cities was designed by a man of Asian heritage? In what ways was William Light a perpetrator of colonisation? Was he also a victim? What does his complex legacy mean for discussions about the future of Australian identity?
8. Over the course of the novel, Clarissa and Light discuss the ways that society is changing, moving from a more liberal and tolerant world in the Regency period to an increasingly rigid and discriminatory one in the Victoria era. Does this cultural change surprise you? What relevance does it have for our own time period?
9. *Salt Upon the Water* is described as an 'alternate history'. As a work of historical fiction, in what ways does the novel speak to the past as well as our present?
10. Despite her connection to Light, Clarissa ultimately leaves him and Australia to marry her English fiancé and travel to Siam (now Thailand). What is the significance of Clarissa's choice? Was this outcome inevitable? Do you see it as a romantic or political decision?
11. At various points in the novel, both central characters experience adversity and discrimination, yet they also each develop a strong sense of hope. How do feelings of hope influence them? Do you think the end of the novel is a hopeful one? Why/why not?

Acknowledgements

This novel was written on the unceded land of the Kaurna, Ramindjeri, and Ngarrendjeri peoples. I acknowledge the Traditional Owners of Country throughout Australia and their connections to land, sea, and community, and pay my respects to Elders past and present.

My deepest thanks to my editor Maddy Sexton, Michael Bollen, and the wonderful team at Wakefield Press, for bringing this novel to life, and to my agents, Clare Forster and Alexandra Christie, for championing my work. I would never have written this novel without the support of the University of Adelaide and a Research Training Program Stipend, and I am incredibly grateful to mentors, friends, and colleagues in the Department of English, Creative Writing, and Film, and the J.M. Coetzee Centre for Creative Practice. Particularly thanks must go to my supervisors, Brian Castro, Patrick Flanery, Anna Goldsworthy, Matthew Hooton, and Jennifer Rutherford. Thanks must also go to Alexandra Nahlous for her editing, and the many readers of my manuscript over the years, in particular my writing group at the University of Adelaide. Thank you to the Barr Smith Library, the State Library of South Australia, and the British Library, for their assistance with my research. Thank you to Stephen Beaumont, for very generously showing me William Light's Suffolk home. I am also incredibly grateful to the judges and the South Australian Literary Awards for recognising the novel as the winner of the 2024 Unpublished Manuscript Award.

The earliest ideas for this novel began to take shape as a result of an Asialink Arts Fellowship at the Centre for Australian and New Zealand Studies at Himachal Pradesh University in India. Thank you to Asialink Arts and Arts SA for their support. Deepest thanks are also due to the wonderful La Muse Writers and Artists Retreat in France. Early extracts of the novel were published as short stories in *StylusLit* and *Litbreak*.

I would also like to thank Penguin Random House for awarding me a Write It Fellowship, and Amanda Martin for her editorial insights. Thank you, too, to Catherine Hill. My heartfelt thanks to Kooma/Kamilaroi/European writer and editor Angie Faye Martin for her keen cultural sensitivity reading and advice on the representation of First Nations characters. Thank you to Ngiyampaa researcher and editor Mark Lock for his initial advice on cultural safety and for introducing me to Angie. All errors are my own.

Thank you to my parents, Ron and Patricia, for encouraging my love of books and learning, and thank you to both my parents and parents-in-law Clinton and Pippa for support with childcare while I worked.

Thank you to my family, Matt, Hamish, and Josephine, for taking this journey with me.

Wakefield Press is an independent publishing and distribution company based in Adelaide, South Australia.
We love good stories and publish beautiful books.
To see our full range of books, please visit our website at
www.wakefieldpress.com.au
where all titles are available for purchase.
To keep up with our latest releases and news,
subscribe to the *Wakefield Weekly* at
https://mailchi.mp/wakefieldpress/subscribe

Find us!

Facebook: www.facebook.com/wakefield.press
Instagram: www.instagram.com/wakefieldpress

www.ingramcontent.com/pod-product-compliance
Lightning Source LLC
LaVergne TN
LVHW091119080826
845145LV00008B/1983